About the author

Susan Parry began writing when her twin daughters were small, and she was working full time as a university professor at Imperial College. She now devotes her time to consultancy work, including forensic studies and archaeological investigations that form the basis for her writing. Her husband, Mark, is retired so they are now able to spend more time together in the family home in Swaledale, where the views from her farmhouse provide inspiration. Together they have walked many of the areas described in the books, accompanied by their Airedale terrier. Her grown up daughters, Elspeth and Alice both have careers in crime – on the right side of the law. Visit her website at www.SusanParry.co.uk.

By Susan Parry

GRAVE HAND

SUSAN PARRY

Viridian Publishing

First published in the United Kingdom in 2009 by
Viridian Publishing

This edition published in 2011 by Viridian Publishing

Viridian Publishing
PO Box 746
Woking
Surrey
GU24 0AZ

www.viridian-publishing.co.uk
e-mail: viridian.tc@virgin.net

ISBN 978-0-9544891-7-5

For Mark

Chapter 1

As winter dusk turned to darkness, the tractor headlights formed a beam that wavered across the moorland as the digger cut into the icy peat. The cab was freezing and the farmer's breath formed white wisps as he lurched and cursed to manoeuvre the machine. Finally, admitting defeat loudly although there was no-one to hear, he switched off the engine and stumbled out into a sightless and silent world. Setting off in the direction of the house, he struggled against the freezing wind until his eyes became accustomed to the dark. It was a clear, frosty evening and marvelling at the thousands of stars caused him to slip and slide down into the old drainage channel. His back and legs were wet and painfully cold and he swore as he struggled upright, bracing himself against the side of the ditch while he regained his breath. As he clambered out onto the track he almost put his hand on an old glove, leather or maybe even rubber. He barely paused, hardly gave it a thought but carried on quickly to the house, keen to get into a less hostile environment.

'What *have* you been up to?'

'Don't ask.' His tone caused Sheila to hesitate for a second.

'You look as if you've been bathing in the ditch not filling it in, Brian!' she said, forcing a laugh.

'I'm going for a shower. What time's tea?'

'Not till six-thirty,' she called.

But he was already on his way upstairs and she continued preparing the meal until he re-appeared looking more relaxed. He separated the children who were competing for his attention, seating young Richard on his knee while his daughter told him about her day.

'…and next week we're going to do a project on how we can reduce our carbon footprint,' she announced.

'That will be nice Kate. You can tell your teacher that your father has been working very hard to cut carbon emissions all day today.'

Sheila lowered the steaming dish onto the table and began ladling pieces of chicken onto their plates. Brian strapped the boy into his high-chair while Kate sat down next to her mother.

'How's Dad stopping carbon emissions?'

'I'm filling in them damn ditches that my great-grandfather dug afore you were born.'

'Why?'

'Ask your teacher, 'appen she'll be able to explain it best. It's to do with the peat. It can store more carbon when it's wet, so if the ditch is filled in it will stop the carbon escaping. Summat like that.'

'We've got a booklet about it somewhere,' offered Sheila. 'If I can find it you can take it in to show.'

'Wasn't your great-grandad environmentally friendly then, Dad?' asked Kate with a grin.

'No, it wasn't that. In them days it was a good thing to do.' He looked across at his wife for support.

'It was supposed to improve the grazing. There were probably even grants to pay for it. That's why he did it, dear.'

'Can I come and see it tomorrow?'

'If you like. There's nowt much to see, mind you. Just a ditch.'

*

The pasture was white with frost as they walked hand in hand up to the gate onto the moor. The girl had to run in between to keep up, hanging onto her father's hand. When they reached the open ditch she stared into it in silence.

'I said there was nowt to see. Do you want to go back now?'

'Can we go up to where you've filled it in?'

'If you like.'

They carried on up the open moorland, Brian, deep in thought, was calculating how much longer it would take to completely block off the ditch.

'Dad! Dad!'

His daughter was tugging at his arm.

'What's that?' She was pointing into the ditch.

'Just a glove.'

'It looks like a hand. Isn't it a hand Dad?'

'No.'

'Please stop and look. It looks just like a hand, Dad.'

Lying in the mud at the bottom of the ditch was the dark brown glove, half hidden in the peat. His daughter had already jumped down and was poking at it with the toe of her Wellington boot. She looked up at him and he was struck how like Sheila she was growing.

'Dad, I think we should call the police.'

'Don't be daft.'

'No, honestly. Come and look.'

Brian was still confused, even as he ran back to the house with Kate. If it was a human hand it was empty, just the skin, like a leather glove. He'd seen dead sheep and rabbits but they always had bones. They weren't hollow. He didn't want to appear a complete idiot by contacting the police over a leather glove that had become too much like a real hand. By the time he reached the farmhouse his daughter had found her mother and was describing the hand to her.

Sheila looked over Kate's head at Brian and raised her eyebrows.

'I know what it looks like but it could be a weathered glove or summat.'

'We should ring the police. There might be a body on the farm somewhere,' the girl was making for the phone.

'Calm down, Kate,' her mother insisted. 'We need to think about this.'

'You never listen to me!' She stamped out and slammed the door.

'I'll make some coffee.' Sheila picked up the kettle and Brian sank onto a chair still panting from his run down the hill.

'What are you going to do with your "hand" then?' His wife had turned and was grinning at him.

He shrugged. 'I need a second opinion. Come and have a look.'

'No thank you, I'm sure you can tell the difference between a hand and a glove.'

'Well I'm not going to ring the police, that's for sure.'

As they sat quietly drinking their coffee, the door opened slowly and Kate came in waving a piece of paper.

'It says on the internet that you have to report any human remains that you find to the police. It says so here.'

'May I suggest that we ask for a medical opinion first?' said Sheila. 'I can ring Linda and ask if Martin would pop and have a look. It might save your father a lot of embarrassment.'

Kate brightened up, 'Yeah, that would be cool.'

Sheila glanced at Brian. 'I'll give her a call then.'

He shook his head slowly, 'I'm telling you it's a glove.' He picked up the paper and went towards the door, 'Let me know when he's coming.'

Just an hour later Sheila announced that Martin was on his way.

'You mean he's coming all the way over here to look at it?'

'He is. Linda said he was quite excited by it.'

'Takes all sorts. But I'm not going up there again on a wild goose chase.'

'Kate can show us where it is.' She sighed and went back to the kitchen where her daughter was sitting on the window seat watching for the doctor's car. She was as stubborn as her father when she wanted to be, Sheila thought.

'He's here, Mum. Shall I let him in?'

Without waiting for an answer she was through the door and out in the yard. Sheila followed, pulling on her boots and grabbing a coat.

'I'll get you some Wellingtons, Martin. It's very wet up on the moor.'

'Not to worry Sheila, my love. I've got them in the car. When Lindy told me what my mission was, I came prepared.'

The ground was still covered in frost and they followed the tracks that Kate and her father had made earlier. She showed them the section of ditch where she had examined the hand and stepped back to allow the doctor to take a closer look. He bent over it and gently probed it with his fingers. When he looked up his lips were curled in distaste.

'You can just make out nails on some of the fingers.'

'Oh my God. You mean it's a real hand? Dad will never believe you. He is going to be so freaked out by this.'

'Kate, calm down. So, what do we do now Martin?'

'I think we have to call the police.' He was wiping his hands on a handkerchief as he climbed out the ditch.

'Just wait till I tell Kirsty.' Kate ran down to the gate into the pasture and disappeared towards the house.

'But surely it can't be real? What's it doing there? Has it been there long?'

They stood staring down into the ditch.

'I'm sorry Sheila, I really don't know. It looks quite recent but there are no bones, not even in the fingers, so it's a strange find. I am wondering if it is actually very old and just has been preserved well.'

'What d'you mean by "old"?'

'Possibly hundreds of years.'

'Oh I do hope so.' She pulled her coat round her. 'There's something rather horrible about finding that so near the house.' She turned away and then back again. 'Can we leave it here?'

'I think we should, at least until the police have been.'

They walked slowly down to the farm where Brian met them in the yard.

'Kate told me. What happens now?'

'Sorry mate, we have to call the police.'

Sheila asked Martin to stay for a coffee, knowing that her husband would want to know all about the hand. By the time he left, Brian was convinced that it was simply an ancient piece of human remains that had been unearthed by his great-grandfather when the ditch was dug. Kate had been on to several of her friends to tell them about it before Brian insisted he made his call. She asked if she could cycle down to the village and her parents agreed for a bit of peace. Brian was laughing over her excitement when he went into his study to ring the station in Ingleton but came back a few minutes later looking serious.

'They're coming straightway,' he said. 'Told me to touch nowt. I hope they don't think it's owt to do with us. Asked a lot of questions mind you.'

'What did they ask?'

'Name and address and such.'

'Anything else?'

'Wanted to know why I was digging up on t'moor.'

'Oh dear.'

'Why, what's up?'

'Nothing, I suppose. It'll be all right, I'm sure.' She went over to where Richard was lying on floor playing with his toys. 'Now then, I expect you want your nappy changing, young man.' She picked him up gently and carried him out of the room without looking at her husband.

Brian sat in his study for over an hour until he heard a car on the gravel in the yard.

'Brian! I think it's the police!'

A slim man was climbing out of a black Vauxhall.

'Mr Ryman? My name is DC Rodriguez.' He lowered his voice. 'I've come about the hand.'

Brian had been expecting someone in uniform. 'Thank God for that. I'm sure we can sort this out pretty quick. D'you want to see it?'

'If I may.'

The man was wearing sturdy boots so Brian led him straight round behind the house, up the pasture, through the gate and onto the moor. They struggled against the wind that continued to buffet them once they were standing at the spot where the hand lay. It had begun to take on a sinister quality now that its presence had been acknowledged by an official body.

'Well that's it.'

The policeman moved agilely into the ditch and spent several minutes examining the hand without actually touching it. Eventually he climbed back out, ignoring Brian's offer of assistance.

'I would appreciate it, sir, if you could leave it *in situ*, so to speak. I will report back to my superiors and they will decide on the procedure.'

'Will it take long?'

'I don't know, sir. It's not often we get such a bizarre object to deal with.'

'The doctor thought it might be old.'

'To be honest with you sir, I haven't a clue. We just tell the Coroner's Office. I expect they'll send an expert over … a pathologist or an archaeologist.'

'Will it take long?' Brian asked again as they started back down the hill. 'I'm trying to get yon ditch filled in.'

There was a long pause. 'May I ask why you want do that, sir?'

'It's environmental, supposed to stop global warming or summat.'

The detective made a note in his book then climbed into his car. Brian stood watching him leave and then turned back to the house.

Sheila was standing with Richard asleep across her shoulder. 'All sorted?'

'Not really. They're sending some pathologist over next week.'

'Is it still up there?'

'Aye.'

'I wish they'd just take the horrible thing away. I was thinking that it must have got ploughed up when your great-grandfather dug the ditch. It's horrible. The sooner it goes the better!'

Brian settled himself at the table and opened the paper.

'Well, it saves me flogging myself to death filling it in for now. Every cloud has a silver lining.'

And so Brian refused to go up to the ditch until the Coroner had been. He ordered his daughter to stay away: it was no plaything for young girls to be around. And his wife agreed. But no-one appeared on the Monday and it was not until after lunch on Tuesday that Sheila rushed into the barn to tell him that the Coroner's Officer was coming in the afternoon.

'Well, he'd better hurry up or it'll be too dark to see it.'

'She actually, darling. She is a woman. She's bringing someone from the National Park with her, an archaeologist. It had a special name, a forensic osteoarcheaologist she called him.'

Brian shrugged and carried on working. 'I'll just be glad to see the back of it, that's all.'

An hour later Sheila was lending the Coroner's Officer a pair of wellingtons and a warm jacket before she called her husband to lead the party up to the ditch. The sun was shining but the wind was still bitter. The archaeologist was dressed more appropriately, his woolly hat bobbing as he marched along talking animatedly to Brian. The two women hung back as Brian pointed down at the shrivelled object that had brought them all up to the moor.

'Wow!'

With one bound the young man was down beside the hand and was examining it thoroughly, without actually touching it. He searched his pockets, producing a magnifying glass which he placed close to the ground, almost lying in the damp peat.

'This is truly amazing!' he called up to the three faces peering down at him.

They watched him for some time as he recorded dimensions using a smaller ruler. Then he produced a camera and took a number of photographs. Sheila could see that his trousers were getting damp at the knees and wondered if he felt as cold as she did. Suddenly after he had made copious notes in a battered red exercise book he leapt up and stretched.

'Well, it is fascinating but I'm not sure I can help you. My area is bones but this thing, well it don't have any.' He grinned at the official who was peering anxiously down at him.

'I was told to find out how old it is. The critical thing is the age.' She sounded anxious.

'It's got to be pretty old. All the bones have gone, as I said.'

'Over a hundred years?'

'I should think so.'

Sheila nudged her husband and smiled. Now he too looked relieved.

'So what happens now?' Brian asked.

'Anything that old is out of our jurisdiction, Mrs Ryman,' replied the woman. 'It's an archaeological artefact now.'

'So will you be taking it away?' He addressed the young archaeologist.

'Oh no, I'm not going to touch it – except to cover it with the peat to avoid deterioration. We need to get an expert in. I'll contact the university.'

'I'll have to ask you to complete some paperwork,' the woman told Brian as they returned to the farmhouse.

He didn't reply and Sheila took her inside with the document. Brian went straight through to the study and stayed there until their visitors had left.

'Nice boy,' said Sheila. 'So enthusiastic about his job.'

'Not so keen that he'd take that bloody thing away though.'

'Oh no, he mustn't move it. He thinks it's probably hundreds of years old. Quite an unusual find, he said.'

'Maybe we can sell tickets to the visitors then.' He pulled a face and went out into the yard.

Dr Terence Lang was leaning back in his chair half-listening to the students as they stumbled through their first presentation of the term. He knew it didn't really matter because it wasn't assessed, and so did they. Some of them had obviously spent time on their work but the majority were rambling and unfocussed, constantly referring to their notes and some even reading their entire talk. Eventually the last student had returned to their seat.

'Listen up, guys. Next time your presentations will be assessed, so I expect you to do a much better job than this.'

There was a general drone as the class muttered to one other and groaned. Dr Lang swung his rucksack over his shoulder and fought his way past the crowds of students into the corridor. He took the stairs and was down in the front hall before the lift. Outside he threw his scarf round his neck and buttoned up his coat, plunging his hands into his pockets. The walk to the car park only took five minutes but by the time he reached his van he was frozen by the bitter wind that whipped round the tall buildings of the university campus.

The Yorkshire Dales looked at its best this time of year in his view, when the trees were bare and dramatic and the fells were tipped with snow. The stone cottages huddle together in the tiny hamlets and the smell of wood smoke hanging in the air. The pubs were quiet and welcoming in the winter with an occasional group of visitors huddled round the open fires. In his experience only serious walkers or cavers ventured into the Dales in January. He preferred caving when it was quieter on the roads and he could get a pint without queuing at the bar in a pub full of kids. The idea of a pint sounded good and he decided to carry on to his favourite drinking hole after he'd been to Long Witton Farm. He wasn't expecting it to take long. In his experience the public were eternally full of hope that they would find something exciting on their property: Roman coins, treasure trove, ancient bones, buckles, rings and axe heads had all turned out to be a variety of bits of rusty metal and animal remains. He would keep a polite and friendly exterior while he explained the error to the incumbent but he would really want to tell them how they had wasted his afternoon.

He was roused from his reverie as the car rumbled across a cattle grid and he was forced to slow to avoid a sheep wandering across the road. It turned to stare insolently at him, munching slowly and deliberately. The sun, sinking behind the hill was so low that it was almost blinding. He put his foot down but the sun had disappeared by the time he reached the farm.

Then farmer appeared immediately in the yard.

'Professor Lang?'

Terry offered his hand. 'Better show me what you've found straightaway, it'll be dark soon.'

'Right you are.' He led the way round the back of the farm and up the hill. There'd been snow on the tops and it was still wild up there. The noise of the wind made talking difficult so they strode along in silence until they reached the ditch.

'Here it is. I'll just uncover it again.' He was soon back, pointing down at the hand lying on the surface of the peat in a grotesque arrangement. 'There it is.'

Terry stepped gingerly and half fell down beside the bizarre object. He had watched the farmer jump into the ditch and pull at the earth. The ground was hard and he knew what damage might have been done if the artefact was real. He crouched down and surveyed it. Although it looked like an old glove he could see that aspects of it were definitely those of a human hand. The fingers had ends that were shaped like nails. He touched it gingerly and turned it over to reveal the wrinkled palm. Despite its shrivelled appearance it was fairly certain that it was indeed human.

'What d'you think?' The farmer was leaning over the edge of the ditch.

'I guess we'd better give the National Park Office a call.'

They walked back to the farmhouse and rang the National Park archaeologist He was obviously expecting some answers.

'How old do you think the hand is, Professor?'

'Difficult to say…'

'What about the age and sex?'

'I really can't say without a thorough investigation. I would need to consult my colleagues.'

He hadn't any idea and would have to find someone who did, but he wasn't going to admit that.

'Thank you, professor. I'll report back to the Coroner. I expect they'll want you to carry out a proper examination, sir. Is that all right with you?'

'Oh yes, of course.' He could feel his heart beating faster. Here was an opportunity he could not resist.

The farmer's wife found him a plastic ice-cream carton which he carried back up to the ditch. Watched by the farmer he half-filled it with peat and placed the hand carefully in the box, sprinkling some loose peat on the top before replacing the lid.

The lanes were dark and winding until he emerged onto the road towards Ingleton where he was able to press his foot to the floor. The engine roared and the old van rattled as the equipment rolled about in the back. He didn't bother to take out his caving gear so it remained a damp and muddy heap in the back.

'Hi there Hunter!'

A few of his caving mates were in the pub as he expected: where else would they be on a Friday night? Once he had sunk a few pints he couldn't resist telling them about how he had spent the afternoon and was rewarded by their fascination and admiration.

'Are you coming down with us tomorrow, Hunter?' The man who asked was Chas, the natural leader of the group, tall with thick dark hair and a full beard, which he rubbed as he spoke. Terry considered him more mature than the rest, speaking little and only when necessary. His black hair and deep brown eyes added to his serious demeanour.

'Yeah, why not? That's if I can crash down somewhere.'

'We've got space but you'll have to put up with Ewa's snoring!' offered Steve, the comedian of the group.

Terry looked at Ewa and she held his stare. She clearly didn't want him to stay but she was silent and the pause became embarrassing.

'Great, thanks.'

He leaned back in his chair and soon someone was putting another pint of "Old Peculier" in front of him. The evening went quickly in the cavers' company and work was forgotten in the warm glow of the fire and the dark ale.

Back at Steve's flat, he collapsed on the sofa and fell into a dreamless sleep... until he was woken by a piercing scream. Ewa had discovered his plastic ice-cream box in the 'fridge.

Chapter 2

'Mills Sanderson speaking.'

'Is that you, Millie?'

'Yes.' She would recognise the Welsh lilt anywhere. 'Nige?'

'How are you?' they said together.

'Oh I'm all right. How are things down in the big city?'

She moved out into the corridor where they wouldn't be overheard.

'It's OK actually but I do miss everyone,' she said.

'Everyone? There's no-one left; everyone's gone off to exciting places.'

'Really?'

He fell silent and she knew he was thinking of Jake. She missed him more than anyone but it had been her decision to come to Manchester and they had agreed not to continue their relationship – it was just too complicated and expensive to keep it going long distance.

'Anyway,' she said brightly, 'what can I do for you?' She knew Nige well enough to recognise that it wasn't a social call.

'Actually I wanted to pick your brains. There's a new guy in the department, a visiting lecturer from the States who specialises in osteoarchaeology.'

'Really?'

'Yes and he's got a hand, a preserved hand. He doesn't know what he's doing and asked me to find anyone with expertise in the area.'

Her research supervisor was the expert, which was why Mills had come to study with her. But Maria was in Tennessee to work at the body farm until June. She went through the people in her department and decided that she probably knew as much as they did about tissue preservation.

'There's no-one here at the moment except me.'

'That's a pity. He wants to try and date it but he doesn't know how.'

'Is it old?'

'He thinks so but I don't believe he has a clue. Bit of an arrogant bastard to be honest.'

'It may be possible to tell by measuring sections through the skin to look at the gradient of the tanning chemistry.'

'Sounds like you know all about it.'

'Not really but it's very interesting. And the hand - I'd like to see it some time.'

'Look, why don't you come up. The department will pay your fare and Nina would love to see you. She hasn't had the excuse to cook properly for weeks.'

'How can I refuse?'

She was smiling when she put down the phone and she was soon typing a polite e-mail to Dr Lang offering to come up on Thursday to see the hand, asking if it was possible to visit the site on the following day. That would mean she would be able to stay up in Yorkshire at the weekend, if Nina and Nige would put up with her that long.

She spent the rest of the day on the web, collecting any papers she could find with reference to tanning of human remains. She missed lunch and almost forgot her afternoon commitment to demonstrate for the undergraduate practical class. By the time she turned off her laptop that evening, she had over twenty references on the subject of preserved bodies.

She picked up a sandwich on the way to the bus stop and ate it while she waited for her laptop to spring into life again. The flat was empty but she knew that soon her housemate would be back with her boyfriend in tow. They would spend hours preparing their supper, leave the washing-up and disappear for the rest of the evening. Mills was used to the routine and had given up trying to be sociable.

She brushed the crumbs from the table and settled down to review the papers she had stored on her computer. Most of what she knew was because of the Lindow man. He had been found preserved in peat over two thousand years after his death. But Mills wanted to find out more about how the peat acted to prevent the tissue breaking down. It was something to do with the acidity of the soil and she had seen reference to the chemicals in the moss reacting to act as a natural preservative. She read and re-read the paper she had found that afternoon but the chemistry was difficult to understand. It seemed that it was the sphagnum moss that acted on the skin to cause an effect like the tanning of leather but the body had to be buried in the peat, without access to air, for the reaction to be effective.

A message came up on her computer to signify that she had an e-mail. It was from Dr Lang. *Cool,* it said. *Great to see you. Come to my office at noon on thursday, we can grab some lunch.* Smiling, she replied politely that it would suit her fine. She found his personal webpage. Apart from his room number and telephone extension there was nothing; not even a photograph. Finally she checked the train times and sent a text to Nige to let him know that she was arriving on Thursday.

*

There had been a light covering of snow overnight. It was beginning to thaw but the pavement was slippery as Mills made her way to Picadilly station. She was catching the nine fifty-seven to Northallerton. She hadn't checked with Nige but she assumed that the Archaeology Department would pay her travel since she was acting as the 'expert' for them. She was anxious about assuming that role but she had the museum to give her advice and she had done her research thoroughly. She had absorbed all there was to know about preservation of bodies in peat since Monday and felt confident she could present a coherent seminar on the subject if asked, since it had occurred to her that she might be.

The snow thickened as they travelled north and by the time she arrived in Northallerton it was getting heavy. The taxi driver told her he would keep to the main roads because the smaller ones had not been cleared yet, so the journey would take a bit longer than normal. She didn't mind; she enjoyed seeing the familiar places again. As they drove through the gates, past the red brick buildings and the modern eighties blocks, she felt a nervous anticipation at the prospect of visiting her old department; even though she knew that Jake was working abroad.

'You a student here then?' asked the driver.

'Yes... well actually no. I used to be but I'm somewhere else now.'

She paid him, took her receipt and entered the Archaeology Department for the first time in six months. As she walked past reception the girl called to her. Mills explained that she knew her way around but she had to sign in before she was allowed to take the lift up to the floor where Dr Lang had his office.

'I don't think he's in yet!' the girl called after her.

'Oh he's expecting me!' Mills replied.

There was a note pinned to his door. *Dr Lang has been held up by the snow*, it read. *He expects to be in by lunch time.*

Mills knocked gently and opened the door. It was a small office but somehow he had managed to fit a small sofa along one wall opposite his desk and chair. She perched on the sofa and waited, determining that she would wait for a little while before going off to get something to eat. Occasionally there were voices outside in the corridor but they would pass by and disappear. She became restless and examined the many books stacked on the shelves behind her head. They were mainly undergraduate textbooks and the sort of thing she read at school. It was impossible to tell from the titles what Dr Lang's area of expertise was. Except there, next to the books, was his PhD thesis dated just two years previously, with an impressive sounding title that suggested he was working on the provenance of human bones. She reached for the thesis and sat down to study it. Half an hour later she replaced it on the shelf, impressed by the sophisticated nature of the work and the clarity of its presentation.

She was preparing to leave, having given up waiting, when the phone rang. She could hardly answer it but paused, waiting for it to stop ringing before she opened the door into the corridor.

'Terry? Why don't you ring me? I wait last night but I give up after one hour. I can't get away until Friday now. He's got meeting until ten and then they'll be in pub.'

The answer machine clicked and a red light on the phone flashed. The door opened and Dr Lang burst in.

'Was that the phone?' he asked, reaching his desk in one stride without looking at her and throwing down a pile of mail.

'Yes. There's a message.'

He swung round glaring at her and then reformed his face into a charming smile.

'You must be Mills Sanderson,' he said, offering his hand.

'Yes. Hi.'

'Gee I'm sorry I'm late; I got delayed. One of the down sides with living in remote parts I'm afraid.'

'Was the snow bad?' Mills asked.

'Not too bad – I left the hand at home and had to go back for it. I live in Richmond, so it's a bit of trip.'

'Left it at home?'

'Yes. I had it in my 'fridge.'

Mills kept silent, unable to think of a suitable reply. Had he really had it in his own fridge alongside his groceries?

He was placing a plastic box on his desk.

'Is that it?'

'Yes, I thought you'd want to see it.'

Mills was horrified. He had in his possession an artefact that could be thousands of years old and he was carting it around as if it was his packed lunch.

'I don't think we should open it here,' she said haughtily. 'It could be affected by bacteria in the environment.' She was aware that she sounded bossy. 'Have you got a 'fridge in the lab?'

'Probably.' He sounded disinterested as he looked idly through his mail.

'Shall I go and put it in the research lab?' she suggested.

He looked up in surprise. 'Sure… and then we'll go for lunch. There's a really good gastro pub near here

– the "Partridge and Pear Tree". It does an excellent lunchtime menu.'

'Right.' She ran up to the laboratory clutching the box and searched for a felt tip pen. *Important material – do not touch! Dr T Lang,* she wrote. Before she placed it in the fridge she opened a corner of the box and peered in. She could see parts of the hand exposed above the peat and quickly replaced the lid. She would contact someone for advice on storage procedure as soon as they were back from lunch. Despite the fact she was feeling hungry she considered it would be quicker to go to the college cafeteria but when she reached Dr Lang's office he was already in his coat, rattling his car keys.

'It's not far but we'll take the old bus as it's so cold.'

They had to walk to the staff car park, where a battered Dormobile van stood with a layer of snow on its roof. Mills clambered in and settled herself on the dirty fabric cover. The van smelt like a wet dog and she noticed that the back was full of old ropes, blankets, boots and clothing. Dr Lang was rotating the ignition key but nothing was happening. After several attempts accompanied by swearing there was a faint whirring and finally the engine turned weakly. After another expletive and several more turns the engine burst into life and they shuddered towards the college gates.

The gastropub was only round the corner, an old student pub known to Mills that had gone up-market. The publican greeted them with a smile, drawing Lang a pint of bitter while he asked her what she would like.

'Just an orange juice please.'

He led her over to a table in the corner by the fire and pointed out the menu, written on a chalk board above the bar, saying that he liked the steak but the sea bass was good. She said she preferred a sandwich and asked for cheese and tomato on granary. Mills wanted to know how Dr Lang came to have the hand in his possession and he took just a few minutes to tell her what he knew about its discovery. After that he diverted the conversation to his trip in the previous summer. It was not a sabbatical at all but a sort of gap year after his PhD studies finished. Mills deduced that he had some difficulty finding a job and was filling in with something to put on his CV until he did.

She was relieved when the food arrived and for a brief interlude he stopped talking about himself. He took no interest in her background but seemed to assume that she was some kind of expert in human preservation. She wondered what Nige had told him.

'We'll take a look at the site tomorrow,' he announced, placing his knife and fork together with a flourish and pushing the empty plate away from him. 'There's nothing to see but it will help you build up a picture, eh? Now what about a coffee or another drink?'

Mills declined and suggested that she should be getting back, reaching for her purse. He waved her offer aside, remarking that he had an account because he was in so frequently with visitors. Mills asked him to drop her by the entrance gates and they arranged to meet next day to take the trip to the Dales to see where the hand was found.

Mills examined her street map to find the location of the house which Nige and Nina bought after they were married. She estimated it would take her about forty minutes to reach the edge of town; a pleasant stroll now that the snow was almost gone. The pavements were drying in the winter sunshine but there was still a chilling wind. Her hands got colder, her rucksack heavier and she was relieved when she turned into a narrow street of neat terraced houses and found number twelve, Priory Road.

Nige welcomed her into the tiny sitting room, taking her coat and indicating a chair by the open fire. She could hear sounds from the next room and assumed Nina was in the kitchen.

'How's Nina?' she asked.

'Oh not bad, considering.'

Mills was about to ask what he meant when the door swung open and Nina appeared, in a wheelchair. She was as beautiful as ever, her glossy black hair falling around her face, her slender figure upright as she wheeled herself into the room.

'Nina!' She couldn't stop herself from calling out.

'Millie! How are you? I like your hair; it suits you with it really short like that.' She smiled as she surveyed her.

Mills was thinking back to when she had last seen her friends. It was at the wedding last July and since then they had only exchanged Christmas cards. Unsure how to ask she could only say, 'What happened to you?'

It was Nige that answered. 'Being the courageous copper, that's what happened.' His voice was level, not angry but not sympathetic, almost proud.

'I was doing my job, Nige.' She wheeled herself closer to the fire and turned to face Mills. 'I was jumping some garden fences; we were after a drug dealer who ran out the back door when we went in the front. I was doing fine until I landed on a cold frame.'

'She lacerated her back real bad like.'

'But you're getting better?'

'Yes, but it's not clear how much better it will get.'

'Oh Nina.' Mills didn't know what to say.

'We're just pleased that the baby's all right.' Nina smiled at Nige.

'Baby?'

'Yes I was three months gone when it happened but it's fine.'

'When is it due?'

'June, a summer baby.'

'Congratulations, both of you. That's brilliant.'

'Nina's going to stay off work until the baby is born,' said Nige, putting his hands on his wife's shoulders. 'We want to be sure everything goes OK up until then, don't we?'

She smiled up at him. 'Yes, you old worrier. Now what about some tea for Millie?'

She watched him go and then turned back to Mills. 'He's been so anxious all the time, it drives me crazy. What with him and my parents I feel like a china doll.'

'But you must look after yourself. It was an awful thing to happen.'

'I suppose so but I don't want it to affect us too much. I want to get back to work after the baby is born.' She lowered her voice. 'But at the moment Nige won't hear of it.'

'I'm sure you'll change his mind for him, although you might not want to go back to work afterwards.'

'Of course I will. By the time the baby is six months old I plan to be out of this thing and back to normal. Now, what about you? You must tell me all about Manchester.'

Mills was happy to describe her new life and her studies in forensic archaeology. Nina was naturally interested in a professional capacity and by the time Nige returned with a tray they were deep in conversation about experiments at the body farm in Tennessee.

'You two have a morbid turn of conversation. Can't you discuss handbags like normal ladies?'

'No,' they replied in unison.

'Well have you met our new mister smooth now?'

'Who's that?' asked Nina.

'D'you mean Dr Terry Lang?' asked Mills. 'I saw him this morning. He took me out to lunch at the "Partridge and Pear Tree". Seems a bit of a poser.'

'He certainly is. He only arrived in October and he's already making his presence felt. Personally I'm not convinced that he knows his stuff although it's probably more down your street, so to speak.'

'I was looking at his thesis when I was waiting in his office. It's very impressive.'

'He told me that he'd worked with the world expert in bones, whatever that's called, but when I looked the man up on the internet he'd been dead for five years.'

'He only got his doctorate two years ago,' added Mills.

'Perhaps it took him a long time to write it up. You can hardly talk Nigel Featherstone! It took you a long time too didn't it?' Nina was laughing.

'I suppose. Still I don't go round being arrogant, do I?'

'Oh I don't know. But seriously, is he really that bad?' Nina asked.

'I didn't like him very much but I have only met him for a few hours. Perhaps he grows on you.' Mills said.

'He's got this van that he drives about in. Falling apart it is. Thinks he's some sort of surfing dude I reckon.'

'He insisted on driving me to the pub in it. It smelt like an old dog.'

'Well, you better be nice to the man, if you want to get paid.'

'What d'you mean, Nige?'

'Didn't he tell you?'

'What?'

'There's some departmental money for investigating this mysterious hand. Since I've said that you are the expert, it should be used to cover your expenses.'

'Are you serious?'

'Deadly.'

'What is this hand?' Nina asked.

Mills recounted what she knew about the discovery of the hand in the peat bog and told them what she had found out about the preservation process. Nina wanted to know how the police had been involved while Nige was interested in the place where it had been found. He put more coal on the fire and they chatted until it was time to prepare dinner. Nina insisted that she and Mills would cook, telling Nige to go round to the supermarket for some ice-cream. Mills watched Nina struggle upright and pull herself around on the kitchen surfaces preparing vegetables until she finally collapsed back into the wheelchair.

'You look exhausted, Nina.'

'I've got to do it. I'll go mad otherwise. I really miss work. Just as it was getting really interesting I have to go and do this,' she said angrily.

'Can I do the potatoes for you?'

'No. I can do them sitting down,' she said sharply and then looked up. 'I'm sorry Millie, I mean I can manage thank you.'

They laughed and peeled them together. Mills put the saucepans on to boil and helped with the serving dishes when the vegetables were ready. She lifted the dinner out of the oven and carried it to the table just as Nige returned.

Only once during the evening did Mills think of their days in the flat together with a small pang of regret that Jake wasn't there with her. Neither of her friends mentioned him and Mills assumed that Nina had given Nige strict instructions to avoid any reference to their days together. The mother-to-be excused herself early after she had ensured Mills had everything she needed. After Nige had carried his wife upstairs he told Mills how concerned he had been when Nina had been injured. For days they were unsure if she would be able to move at all and even now it was uncertain that she would ever be able to walk unaided.

'And all she's worried about is getting back to work. I tell her it's always going to be dangerous.'

'But it's what she wants to do. She was doing it before she met you, Nige.'

'But I care about her.'

'I know.'

Nige coughed. 'Anyway,' he continued, 'what have you planned with Terry Lang? Is he going to show you the ditch where the hand was found?'

'Yes, we're supposed to be going tomorrow, if the weather's OK.'

'Well be careful. He's a smooth character and I wouldn't trust him as far as I can throw him.' He picked up the poker and rattled the fire violently.

'What makes you say that?'

'Nothing really. Just a hunch. I've seen his CV and it looks very impressive but it just doesn't add up. I looked up a few of his papers and they just seem a bit, well, too good to be true.'

'Really?'

'Don't say anything, will you? He's on an exchange with this university in the States – well you know that.' He looked embarrassed.

'Yes, I know.' Of course she knew; it was Jake that went over to the States in exchange.

'Well, I had a look on the web and his list of publications is enormous.'

'So?'

'Does he strike you as dynamic?'

'No but he must have good references to have got the post here.'

'Not necessarily. There are ways and means, aren't there? Anyway, that's not all. I asked, well…'

'Jake?' suggested Mills.

'Yes, him, to make some enquiries over in the US. He says that over there Lang has a reputation as a really smart guy.'

'He is - I saw his thesis in his office.' She hesitated. 'And how is Jake getting on over there?' she asked casually.

'Oh fine.' Nige reddened. 'Anyway… all I'm saying about our Dr Lang is that there's something funny about him and you should be careful.'

Chapter 3

'So how come you have such an unusual name?'

They had been travelling in silence for some time, mainly because Mills had been concentrating on the road ahead, clutching the seat as they swung out to overtake and shutting her eyes occasionally when they were travelling too close to the car in front. Her responses had been limited to yes and no as she wished he would concentrate on the road ahead.

'Mills,' he continued. 'It's a strange name.'

'Not really. My name is Millicent.'

'Nige told me you were called Millie.'

'I was. I am. It's just at Manchester they thought it was Mills. It was the registration form they have for the e-mail. It can only cope with thirteen letters so I put down MILLSANDERSON and they thought my name was Mills Anderson and it kind of stuck, as a joke really.'

'Well I think Mills sounds cool.'

As if I care, thought Mills, staring out across the snow covered fells.

'You can't beat the Yorkshire Dales,' Terry announced. 'Have you been here before?'

'Yes.'

'I've climbed most of these hills and gone down most of the potholes in the area.'

'You're a caver?'

'Yep. I try to get down here at weekends. Hang out with the guys. Explore a few caves and sink a few pints. Ever done any caving?'

'No.'

'You should come one weekend. It would be a blast.'

Yeah right, thought Mills but just smiled.

'Like some music?' Terry asked after another few minute's silence. Without waiting for an answer he pressed a button and the van was vibrating to an unfamiliar sound.

'Authentic music from Afghanistan. Really cool.'

The music was not easy listening and Mills was relieved when they turned down the road signposted to Ribblehead.

'That hill there is Whernside, one of the three peaks. Ever walked the Three Peaks? No? I've done them several times. Last time it took me just eight hours.'

The diesel fumes were making Mills nauseous and she tried to shut out the music and Terry's droning voice as he described his marathon walk, step by step. She was woken by a rocking sensation as they moved onto a rough track and pulled up outside a traditional stone farmhouse at the foot of the hillside. Terry was already at the front door before Mills had managed to struggle out of the van. She was doing up her jacket and knotting her scarf when he returned, the door still firmly shut.

'No-one around,' he said. 'Never mind, I know where to go.'

She followed him through the gate and up the fell at the back of the farm. They took a rough track just discernible through the light layer of snow that persisted. The white covering was thicker higher up and soon their prints were covering a set already leading the way. Mills could make out two figures ahead of them.

'That's the farmer,' shouted Terry, who was several metres in front of her.

She finally caught him up as they reached the two men, who were standing beside a deep ditch running the length of the field.

'Hi it's me again,' said Terry, extending his hand to Brian. 'Turning up like a bad penny again, eh?'

The farmer looked at Mills and turned to his companion. 'This is the professor I was telling you about, Jack.'

Terry didn't make any effort to introduce her so she held out her hand. 'Hello, I'm Mills Sanderson from the University of Manchester.'

'Another professor… we are honoured.'

'No not a professor, not even a *doctor* like Terry, Dr Lang.'

Terry frowned at her. 'We've come to have a look at the spot where you found the hand, if it's not inconvenient?' He looked from one to the other.

'No, no. He's just come over to give me a figure for using the ditch-filler-in. It's a quick way of filling the ditches, much easier than using a digger on the tractor.'

'You're not going to fill it in yet I hope?' asked Mills.

'I'd like to get it done this side of Christmas.'

'Surely the ground will be too hard at the moment?' she said.

'Aye, but it won't be long afore it's warm enough,' Brian's companion offered.

Mills looked at Terry for support but he was looking at his watch.

'I'd like to examine the place where you found the hand, please. It may be a very significant find. Did Dr

Lang explain to you that it could be extremely old…
maybe thousands of years?'

'To be honest, love, I'm just glad to be shot of it
but if you want to have a look it were over here.'

He led her further up the field and pointed down
into the ditch. The bottom was covered in snow.

'It were down there. Not that there's owt to see
now.'

'There may be other parts of the body hidden under
the peat. We may want to do a thorough survey.'

'Do you have to?'

'What d'you mean? Don't you want to know the
history of what happened to the rest of the body?'

'I just want to get on with me work, young lady.
It's nowt to do wi' me.'

Mills sighed. 'I wondered if I might ask you about
the history of the farm. Has it been in your family
long?'

'My father and his father 'afore him. It goes back a
long way. My Sheila takes more interest in that side.'

'Would she mind if I ask her about it?'

'I'm sure she'll be pleased for the chance to tell
you all about it, if she's back.'

He turned and started walking back down to join
the others. Mills quickly took some photographs of
the ditch and followed him to where Terry was
consulting his watch again.

'Will you be much longer?' he asked. 'I've got to
make a call and there's no signal up here.'

As they walked back to the farm, Mills suggested
they see if the farmer's wife had returned home.
Terry shrugged and said he could pop into Ingleton if
she was going to be long. To her relief the door was
opened by a pleasant looking woman who
enthusiastically invited her in to talk about the history

of the farm. Half an hour later she was surrounded by photograph albums, newspaper cuttings and e-mail messages.

'And this is a copy of Brian's great-grandfather's marriage registration that I downloaded from the internet,' said Sheila, offering her a page from a file she had on her lap.

'So the farm has been in the family for at least four, or is it five generations?'

'Probably longer. His dad was so proud of the farm. He was really pleased when Brian took it over. He was their only son so there was no-one else.'

'And would his dad have dug the ditch?'

'I've been trying to think. In fact I was looking at the photographs and I think there is one that could have been taken at the time. Let me see…'

She picked up one of the albums and began leafing through it.

'Yes, here it is.'

She passed it to Mills with the page open at a small black and white snapshot of a group of two men and a boy. They were laughing as they leant on their spades, an old tractor in the background.

'When was this?'

'Well, this man is great Uncle George - he went to Australia as a young man.'

'And who is this older man?'

'That's Great-Grandad. The boy is Grandad. He looks about nine or ten there.'

'Is Grandad still…?'

'Oh yes he's alive and kicking. That's one of the reasons my in-laws are in Ingleton now. He lives with them in a nice bungalow on the outskirts of the village.' She stood up. 'Would you like a cup of tea?'

Mills turned over the pages of the album, looking idly at the pictures of an ordinary family growing up: the weddings, the christenings, Christmas and birthdays.

'Do you know why the ditch was dug in the first place?' she asked when Sheila returned with the tea.

'To improve the drainage I suppose, help improve the pasture. I'm not sure it made any difference; it's poor grazing up there.'

'Presumably the ground was untouched until the ditch was put in?'

'I would think so. I don't know of any reason why that horrible thing should have appeared up there.'

The door opened and Brian appeared alone.

'I asked Jack to come in for a bit but he was in a hurry,' he said. 'You still here?' he added when he noticed Mills.

'We've been having a very interesting conversation, Brian,' said Sheila. 'This young lady is very intrigued with the farm.'

'I don't suppose she knows where that hand came from?'

'Well that's what I'd like to find out,' said Mills. 'Would either of you mind if we wanted to do any excavation work up there?'

'No,' said Sheila, putting her hand on her husband's arm as he went to open his mouth. 'I would like to have the matter settled.'

Brian left the room without a word and Sheila smiled apologetically at Mills.

'I think it unnerved him, finding it like that. It's just his way.'

'I ought to be going anyway. I've taken up a lot of your time.'

'I would be happy for you to stay but I've got to pick Kate up from school soon.'

'Don't worry, I'll wander down to the road and wait for Dr Lang there. He should be back soon.'

'If you want to come back just let me know,' offered Sheila. Mills made a note of her phone number before setting off back to the road.

The track, which ran parallel to the road for some distance, took her back towards the Ribblehead viaduct. Terry Lang would have to come this way and she would easily spot the orange van. She counted the twenty-four arches of the huge Victorian construction and stopped to watch a train travel slowly across it. As it disappear into the moorland, she continued unhurriedly, stopping to admire the wintery view but it still took her only twenty minutes to reach the Station Inn at the foot of the viaduct. She sat at the edge of the road, her hands and feet getting colder, until half an hour later the van appeared.

'Hi. What are you doing here? I would have picked you up from the farm.'

'They were going out,' Mills replied, slamming the door. 'I've been waiting for ages.'

'You should have sat in the pub. Have you had lunch?'

'No.' Mills didn't trust herself to say more.

'I had a pie and pint or two in Ingleton.'

'Oh good.' She did not do sarcasm well and she knew it was lost on him.

'So what do you think?' she asked after a short silence. 'What happens now?'

He paused while they overtook a tractor. 'What do *you* think?'

Mills considered. 'I think we should have some proper scientific examination of the hand to begin with.'

'Good.'

'Once we know the age we can decide whether there is a case for further excavation.'

'What's the point of that?'

His response surprised her. 'To look for the rest of the body?'

'Ah yes, quite right.'

They swerved as he took a corner too fast and Mills clutched the seat.

'So will you deal with that?' he asked.

'If you want me to.' She wondered why he was so detached. 'Is there money to pay for an investigation?'

'Oh yes, there's a fund in the department for just this sort of thing.' He grinned at her. 'You get it done and I'll write the cheques.'

'But obviously you'll want to be involved in the work?'

'I'm very busy at the moment. You know… lectures, papers, research.'

'Papers? What are you writing about?'

'Oh this and that. Things I did in the States.'

'What were you working on over there?' Mills persisted.

'Oh a number of things in osteoarchaeology.'

'And what exactly is osteoarchaeology?' asked Mills, determined to pin him down.

'You know… bones and stuff.' He reached forward and soon music from Afghanistan was filling the van again.

It seemed rude to interrogate the man. He was after all her boss, albeit temporarily, but she was surprised that his replies were so vague, almost evasive. Possibly he was embarrassed by his high-flying academic career although his behaviour so far did not seem that of a shy man.

She went straight to the university library on their return and began searching on the web for the relevant scientific tests that she would need to use. If she had a complete body there were numerous investigations that could be done. Information could be accumulated from the size of the skeleton, the shape of the head, diameter of certain bones, information from the jaw and teeth; they could even reconstruct the face as it would have looked in life. But there weren't even any bones that could be used to define the age of the hand. She compiled an e-mail message to her supervisor in Tennessee to ask her advice, knowing that it was still early morning in the USA. Then she searched the e-journals for inspiration. She had assumed that the hand was hundreds if not over a thousand years old because of the absence of bones. It was clear from what she read that their decay would be accelerated in the acid soil of a peat bog. Articles on radiocarbon dating to estimate time since death generally referred to the skeleton, which was usually all that was left but Mills wasn't sure how it worked on skin. She found the website of a group in Oxford who were the experts in the subject who referred to forensic work on human skin using just a tiny sample of material.

She knew from her lectures that it was possible to date a burial by the effect of soil on the body. But she assumed that skin preserved in peat would behave in a different way and began searching for papers on bog bodies. She reached for her pen and notebook as she found what she was looking for. A number of scientists had examined the bodies found in Cheshire but carbon-14 dating had not been able to differentiate between the Iron Age and the Roman period, leaving palaeobotanists to confirm that they were from the Iron Age. Chemical analyses had been made on the skin which indicated that the composition of the peat bog did have an influence on the elements found in the skin. This was the interesting bit... pigmentation due to decoration applied to the body before or after death, could contain metals such as copper and these were detected on the skin. She scribbled down the details, downloaded copies of the relevant publications on her laptop and packed her bag.

A plan was beginning to form and she needed to discuss it with someone. It was nearly four. She rang Terry Lang's office but there was no reply so she left the building and began walking back to Priory Road.

'I wasn't sure if you'd be in,' she said, when Nina opened the door.

'Not actually going out very much at the moment,' she said with a smile, as she manoeuvred the wheelchair back down the narrow hall.

'Oh, I'm sorry; it was a silly thing to say.' Mills reddened.

'Don't mind me. I get a bit fed up sometimes that's all. Actually I'm glad you're back... you can help me with these.'

Nina pulled sheets out of the tumble dryer and Mills folded them neatly.

They sat in front of the fire as darkness fell, drinking tea and discussing the methods the police might employ to determine the origin of a mysterious hand.

'I guess the procedure is much the same as one an archaeologist might employ,' Nina said. 'If you know where it was found then the question is who does it belong to? That means you need DNA, although that might not necessarily help, and you need to know when the victim died.'

'It's going to be difficult to pinpoint the exact period. Anyway, it's important to understand the area where it was found, so I'm going to get samples of peat from the ditch and see if there was any mining in the area. That's what the experts did for the Lindow bodies.'

'I've heard that name... it's a place in Cheshire isn't it?'

'Yes.'

'Well I've read about that because the police were investigating a man who they thought had murdered his wife. And when a body was found almost next door to his garden they assumed it was her.'

'But it was thousands of years old!'

'Well apparently it was first identified by forensics as the skull of a woman. The man actually admitted killing her and chopping her up twenty years before.'

'But it wasn't her? It was the Lindow man, thousands of years old?'

'Exactly. They used some scientific dating...'

'Carbon-14. I was reading about it today. It's not perfect for really old bodies but it could certainly differentiate between two thousand and twenty years! So what happened to the man, did they let him go?'

'No. He'd admitted killing his wife so he was imprisoned.'

The front door slammed and Mills looked across the darkened room at Nina, her face lit by the flickering fire.

The door opened and the room was flooded with light.

'Telling each other ghost stories?' asked Nige.

'Hi, darling. Yes, we were… sort of. You tell him, Millie, while I start the tea.'

She was pleased to discuss her plans with another archaeologist even though his area of expertise was neither radiocarbon dating nor chemical analysis.

'So I need to go back to the site, at least to get some samples of the peat and soil, even if I can't do an extensive search of the area for other parts.'

'When will you do that?'

'I thought tomorrow,' Mills replied, thinking it would leave the couple alone for at least part of the weekend.

'How are you going to get there?' Nige asked.

Mills hesitated. Nige was right, it wasn't exactly well-served by public transport.

'Why don't you borrow our car? We don't need it tomorrow, I want to get on with the decorating and we can get the shopping on Sunday.'

'But…'

'But what?'

Mills hesitated. 'Are you sure?'

Nige called through to Nina, who agreed it was the obvious solution.

'Well, thanks. That would be brilliant.'

Next morning Mills departed for the Yorkshire Dales armed with a packed lunch that Nina had prepared. She remembered her camera, notebook and there was equipment that Nige kept in the boot for site visits, planned or unexpected, including, she noted, a trowel and plastic bags for collecting samples. The first few miles were a little unsteady as she became accustomed to the clutch on the Polo but she soon settled back comfortably, enjoying the feeling of independence that it gave her. She knew the way to Hawes and it was not too far from there. Once through Leyburn she recognised the familiar landmarks in Wensleydale: Pen Hill with a light covering of snow, the Fox and Hounds at West Witton, Bolton Castle off to the right of the road. She wound slowly round the village of Bainbridge and was soon entering the narrow one way system that led to the busy main street in Hawes.

Sheila watched from the kitchen window as a VW Polo made its way slowly along the farm track. She didn't recognise the car and called her husband, thinking it must be a visitor for him. His face screwed up as he leaned across the sink and peered through the window.

'It's that young lass from the university,' he said, as the car drew to a halt in the yard. 'You can deal with her.'

Sheila sighed and went to the back door, picking up Richard as she went. She watched the young woman carefully checking all the doors before she turned towards the farmhouse.

'Hello again,' Sheila greeted her in as friendly manner as she could muster.

'I am so sorry to bother you again.'

'That's all right.'

'I want to collect some material from the ditch if I may. It would be very helpful in dating the... artefact.'

Sheila invited her into the kitchen for coffee. Her daughter had come down from her bedroom and was standing in the corner listening intently. While she played with Richard, Mills explained that just a small sample of skin could be used to date the age of a body with carbon dating.

'But how does carbon in the body tell you the age of it?' Kate asked.

'There are several different isotopes of carbon. Carbon-14 is radioactive and decays while carbon-12 is stable so as the carbon-14 disintegrates the ratio of the two isotopes will change. You can work out how long the body's been decaying by measuring the two isotopes using mass spectrometry.'

Sheila nodded, she was interested but she was distracted by her son who was pulling at her hair. Mills stood up saying that she should get on.

'I can walk up with you - I'll just ask Brian to keep an eye on Richard.'

'No, please don't worry. I can see you're busy.'

'Can I go Mum? Please?'

'I don't see why not, Kate.' Sheila smiled. 'But wrap up warm.'

Brian appeared in the kitchen as soon as the outside door closed.

'What's she want now?' he asked gruffly.

'Just some samples of peat,' Sheila kept her tone light. 'A nice girl. I hope Kate grows up to be as polite as her.'

'Don't matter if she is polite, it's the inconvenience of not being able to finish the job.'

'It's not really a problem, is it Brian?' She turned to load the washing machine, moving him aside gently.

'Well I'm off out.'

'Oh yes?'

'Aye, I'm going down to see Dad.'

'What's that for then?'

'Nothing in particular. I said I'd drop in some time this week.'

Sheila shrugged and moved quickly to stop their son playing with the knobs on the tumble dryer. 'Why don't you take Richard? Your Mum would like to see him for a bit. Don't you want something to eat first?'

'No, I best get off.'

Sighing, she found Richard's shoes and sorted out a bag of toys to keep him quiet in the car. It was not like her husband to be disturbed by unexpected events, she thought, as she watched him strapping Richard into his car seat. There was a bitter wind and she thought how cold it would be working up on the fell. As soon as she was back inside she made a flask of coffee and, putting on her thick coat, she carried it up the track behind the house.

Mills preferred to work uninterrupted but had spent some time explaining to the girl what she was doing and why. To be fair, Kate had been quiet and was hardly a distraction.

'Here's Mum,' she announced after they had been on the moor for about half-an-hour.

Mills, grateful for the hot drink, put down her trowel. She had been thinking about the background information she needed to build up a picture of the origin of the hand.

'I wondered if you knew whether there were any settlements round here in the past?' she asked, sipping the scalding coffee.

'There's a Viking settlement at the quarry by the viaduct,' Kate announced. 'I went to look with the school. There wasn't a lot to see, just the foundations. And there's the settlement where the railway workers lived while they built the viaduct and the tunnel. I did a project on that too. I've got some pamphlets on it if you're interested.'

'So when was that there?'

'In the eighteen-seventies.'

'I'll go and look them out,' offered Sheila. 'Remind me when you've finished. Don't go without them!'

When Mills had finished her coffee, Kate took the empty flask and left her to continue her work. She systematically collected peat from where the discovery had been made and further away, measuring the distance each time she took a sample. It took over an hour and her stomach was rumbling as she staggered back down the hill with her samples. Refusing the offer of tea, she took the booklets that Sheila had looked out about the building of the Settle-Carlisle railway and left, having decided to eat her lunch at the site of the railway settlement.

She stopped the car before the farm lane met the main road, almost in the shadow of the giant stone viaduct. She peered up at it as she ate the sandwiches and washed them down with tea from a flask. First she consulted the map and identified the large fell in front of her as Whernside, one of the "Three Peaks". The information Sheila had provided described a miserable existence on the moor for the hundreds of navvies who had built the line in the eighteen-seventies. It was almost impossible to believe that the empty moorland stretching ahead of her had been the site of a shanty town, complete with schools, shops and even a hospital. Smallpox and cholera had been rife and over two hundred bodies had been buried in the local churchyard. She peered into the rear view mirror to wipe the crumbs from her face, then zipping up her jacket and pulling on a woollen hat, she stepped out into the cold wind.

She joined a track that followed the railway in the direction of the fells. There was no-one about and the silence was broken only occasionally by the sound of a car speeding past on the main road. Mills felt instantly at home as she walked along, barely disturbing the hardy sheep browsing on the tough moor grass. She admitted to herself that she really was not happy working in Manchester; the city life was fun for a short – very short – time but the novelty soon wore off. Here she felt truly at ease with herself, she decided, as she took deep breaths of the cold air. Soon she drew level with a signal box and, although she was aware that diesel trains travelled from Settle to Carlisle, she was surprised to see that the box was occupied. She couldn't restrain a smile when she realised how excited she was by the prospect of seeing a train cross the viaduct. However, the railway track was empty and she saw nothing as she carried on towards Whernside.

At first she thought it was raining but soon she could detect small white flakes settling on her sleeve. The sky was quite grey and it felt late although it was only early afternoon. Mills wanted to see the entrance to Blea Moor tunnel where the railway line cut through the hills for over a mile. She would walk on for another ten minutes and see how far she got; after all, the way back was easy enough to find. It was snowing harder now and Whernside was disappearing in the grey haze. Mills carried on until she was able to make out what she had been looking for, a bend in the path as it crossed the line and continued up Whernside. If she looked down on the right she could see the entrance to the tunnel and perhaps she would see a train emerge, if she was lucky. To the left was a stream that crossed the track on a stone aqueduct. The snowflakes were beating on her face now and despite her hat and gloves she was beginning to feel quite cold. It was tempting to run back down the snow-covered path to the car and turn on the heater but the child in her insisted on waiting for a just a few more minutes. She continued to lean over the dry stone wall and stare at the entrance to the tunnel.

'You'll have a long wait.'

Chapter 4

She looked round quickly. A striped scarf and woollen hat covered most of the man's face and she backed away from him quite unconsciously, reaching out to the wall for support.

'The train,' he continued, 'there's not another one now for at least an hour.'

'Oh, right,' she said politely and, when he didn't move, she added, 'thanks.'

'They might cancel it, with the bad weather.'

'Right.'

She waited for him to walk away but he remained, as if it was natural to stand discussing train timetables in a snowstorm.

'Which way are you going?' he asked. 'Only it's getting quite bad and it wouldn't be advisable to go up there.' He pointed up the route to Whernside. 'It's getting quite nasty.'

'I've got my car down by the viaduct,' Mills replied. She knew it was unwise to get engaged in conversations with strange men in the middle of nowhere but she couldn't avoid him and actually he seemed quite nice.

'That's cool. I'm going down that way myself.'

There was nothing to do but walk along beside him. The snow was falling fast now. It was a real snowstorm, Mills admitted. She agreed that it was important to get down off the fells for her own safety. She acknowledged that she wasn't prepared for bad weather and no, she didn't know the terrain well.

'And *you* know the area well?' she asked. He was irritatingly sure of himself.

'Quite well. I do a lot of caving round here.'

Back at the car, Mills felt compelled to offer a lift.

'No, I'm fine.'

'But where are you going?'

'Into Ingleton, not far.'

She knew it was several miles and by now it was getting dark and barely possible to see down the road.

'I can give you a lift.' She unlocked the car, pushing a layer of snow away before she opened the boot.

'Put your rucksack in there.'

To her amusement he did as he was told and then removed his hat, shaking snow from his dark, curly fringe.

'My name's Fred,' he said, offering a hand.

'Mills,' she replied. It was a strong handshake and to her surprise the contact excited her.

'What were you doing up at the tunnel?' he asked as she started the engine.

Mills was concentrating on the track in front of her. It was covered in a thin layer of snow and it was not easy to see where she should go. She switched on the windscreen wipers but it was the indicator that clicked.

'Oops,' she said, laughing.

'Have you had the car long?'

'No, it's not mine. I've borrowed it for today. It's a bit different to the one I learnt on.'

'I wish I'd had lessons earlier,' admitted Fred. 'I planned to start this holiday but the weather's not been good and it's so expensive.'

Mills interspersed his monologue with the occasional "yes" and "no" but her attention was confined to keeping the car on the track. It was the first time she had driven in snow and, when she felt the wheels spin, she prayed that it would get no worse. The main road was white but the snow was wet and she recovered her confidence sufficiently to concentrate once again on what her companion was saying.

'… so I won't be able to afford it until after Easter now.'

'Oh, right.' She had no idea what he was referring to.

'Whereabouts in Ingleton do you live?' she asked as they passed the sign indicating they had reached the town.

'Just drop me anywhere. Here's fine.'

Mills waited until she had turned the car into the main street and then pulled over to let him out.

'I can get my stuff out the back,' he smiled at her. 'And thanks for the lift.'

To her disappointment he jumped out and retrieved his bag. Just as she was about to pull away he knocked on her window. She reddened as she fumbled for the switch to lower the electric window, first opening the passenger side and then her own.

'Have you got a mobile?' he asked, holding out his hand.

Puzzled she fumbled in her bag and gave it to him. He typed in some numbers but instead of making a call he handed her back the phone.

'I've put in my number; it's under F for Fred.' He grinned and dashed off before she could reply.

Mills sat for a minute while she worked out how to close the windows. Questions about her new acquaintance distracted her and it was only when she was disturbed by loud hooting from the bus behind her that she quickly moved into gear and shot off, leaving Ingleton behind.

The snow was settling on the roads now and visibility was poor even with the windscreen wipers on. The journey back past Ribblehead was all right but the road over to Hawes caused Mills some anxiety. The white flakes danced in her headlights and made it difficult to concentrate on the road. Soon it would be dark. She crawled along hugging the left-hand side of the road, away from the steep drop into the valley, conscious of another car close behind her. A van flew past her in the opposite direction and she almost stopped completely. At the next opportunity she pulled in and let the car behind overtake, pausing to take deep breaths before carrying on. At last it was the hill down into Hawes and she relaxed her grip on the steering wheel, stretching her neck and back, and leaning into the seat.

The rest of the journey was easier and once she left the Dales the main roads formed clear tracks between white fields. However, the snow did not let up and by the time she drew up outside Nige and Nina's house there were several inches covering the gardens. She parked in the street, not daring to back it onto the tiny parking space on the concrete area in front of the house. The door flew open before she pressed the bell and Nige shouted behind him.

'It's OK she's back. We were worried about you. Was it bad over there?'

'Yes, horrible.'

Mills hadn't realised how stressed she'd been until she was sitting in front of the fire clutching a mug of tea.

'You must be cold, Millie,' Nina was putting more logs on.

'No, the heater works really well in your car.' She didn't admit that she hadn't been able to work it and had been so flustered by the snow that she had been too hot most of the way.

'Was it worth the trip?' Nige asked.

Mills considered. 'Yes, I think so.' She didn't mention Fred and their chance meeting at the aqueduct. It sounded a bit cheesy.

'What are you going to do with the samples? Are you going to hand them over to Dr Lang?'

'I don't know. I don't think so. He didn't seem to care much.'

'Oh, I think he cares. He asked me what you were doing today and when I told him he seemed genuinely interested. But I got the impression he is expecting you to look after it all.'

'Why's that?'

'If you ask me I don't think he has a clue what to do himself.'

'But isn't he the expert?' asked Nina.

'Supposed to be but I have my doubts. I deliberately asked my tutees about his lecture course this term and they thought it was rubbish.'

'Seriously?' Nina laughed. 'I'm sure they didn't use the word rubbish.'

'As good as,' Nige insisted. 'Anyway, it'll be in their questionnaires at the end of term.' He looked positively gleeful.

'Anyone would think it was personal,' said Nina to Mills.

'I thought I'd get analyses done on the peat to start with,' Mills began.

'Good idea,' Nige looked enthusiastic. 'But what about the hand?' He grabbed his own wrist and flapped his hand at Nina, who sighed and raised her eyebrows.

'I've got some ideas but I've e-mailed my supervisor to ask her opinion. *And* I need to talk to Dr Lang.'

'Well don't go in too early because he won't be there. It's usually about coffee time before he appears.'

Nina was obviously embarrassed or irritated by Nige's overt animosity to a colleague and suggested that he began making supper. Once they were alone, she asked Mills whether she had any ideas about where the hand had come from.

'I can't really tell until I get it carbon-dated. The obvious theory is that it's like the Lindow bog bodies and goes back to the Iron-Age. But Sheila told me today that there was a Viking Settlement nearby which could be relevant.

'What if it isn't that old, though?' Nina asked, seriously. 'What if it's much more recent?'

Mills paused before answering. It was a question that had occurred to her while she was walking by the railway. There had been hundreds of people living at Batty Green Camp when the tunnel was being built and so it was perfectly possible that the body had been from there. But that meant that everything had decayed away, except the skin, in just over a hundred years. She didn't think that was possible.

'I don't think it is,' she replied, 'but the carbon dating will tell us that.'

Mills couldn't remember when she had last enjoyed a Sunday so much. For the last few months she had dreaded the one day of the week that stretched out without prospect of any light relief. She occupied herself on Saturdays by doing her washing and cleaning followed by a trip to the supermarket, so by evening she was weary enough to slouch in front of the television. But Sundays were empty and recently she had taken to spending the day in the department catching up on her mail and paperwork.

Sunday with Nina and Nige was a glorious expanse of non-stop domesticity. First there was the supermarket shop; not the tedious dash from shelf to shelf but a gentle trawl along each isle, investigating new lines and selecting different types of vegetable and fruit. Having a proper income helped but the young couple obviously cared about what they ate and how it was prepared. There was a brief stop at the pub on the way home, followed by tea and crumpets by the fire. Nina insisted they played Scrabble despite Nige's protestations, and quickly demonstrated that she was an expert. The day culminated in an enormous roast dinner that left them lethargic until bed-time.

Checking her e-mails before retiring, Mills found a reply from Tennessee. It confirmed that carbon-dating was the best way to establish the age of the hand and told her to contact the laboratory in Oxford. It also included a paper that described how to prepare the sample for analysis.

In the morning, accompanied by Nige, she took the peat samples into the university and began the meticulous task of drying and ashing ready for analysis. Then she went along to the departmental laboratory to arrange for their analysis. Sam was happy to oblige and carefully noted down her instructions.

'How long will they take?' she asked.

'For you, I can have the lot finished in a week.' He grinned.

She thanked him profusely and went back to check the oven where her peat samples were drying. They weren't ready, so she went down to the offices to find Terry Lang. She was still knocking at the locked door when Nige came running along the corridor dressed in a white coat, a bundle of papers under his arm.

'What did I say? He's supposed to be taking the second year practical but hasn't turned up. I've got to do it myself. Probably down a cave somewhere!'

He rushed off, leaving Mills alone in the corridor pondering his last remark. She wanted to speak to Lang urgently because she would need him to sign the order to get carbon-dating done in Oxford. If she had to wait until he appeared it would delay her investigation. The connection with caving gave her an idea, the excuse that she had been looking for. She took out her mobile and found F.

'Hi, this is Fred's phone. Please leave…'

She hesitated and then hit the button to cut him off, regretting that she had made the call. She walked slowly back to the laboratory and took the peat samples out of the oven, letting them cool before weighing them and carefully noting down how much moisture they had lost. When she had finished she put them in acid and left them dissolving while she had lunch. She had just taken a bite from a cheese and tomato baguette when her mobile burst into life. The name Fred appeared on the screen and she hesitated, she went to answer and then stopped. After several rings, to her relief, it went quiet. She waited until it rang again and then picked up his voicemail.

'Hi remember me? We met at Ribblehead. I got a missed call from a number I don't recognise. I hope that means you were trying to get me. Call me again. Please.'

Fred replaced his mobile on the desk and looked round the cramped newspaper office. Even after three months he continued to be distracted by the old-fashioned surroundings. Traffic crept past in the narrow street below and, only very occasionally, the silence was broken by the sound of a horn or a siren. He was supposed to be writing a short article about the success of the local rugby team but there was a piece of information that was nagging at him and he wanted to pursue it. He knew he should talk to the news editor but he wanted to be sure there was some truth in it first. He picked up the phone and tried Steve's number again. Still no answer.

'Hi, it's Fred. Look I wanted to have a chat about the hand… the one you had in your 'fridge? Ewa told me about it. I thought it would make an interesting story. Give me call, mate.'

He threw the phone down and opened up the article he had begun on North Ribblesdale RUFC. It was several hours before he e-mailed his few hundred words to the sports editor but the response that came back was favourable and he popped downstairs to the bakers to purchase a celebratory doughnut before making a coffee in the tiny kitchen. While Fred was out, Steve left a message to say that he would be in the pub that evening and would catch up then. A call from Mills, he concluded, as he licked sugar and jam from his fingers, would make his day.

But when the call came he was disappointed.

'Is that Fred?'

'Yes.'

'It's Mills. I thought I'd call to ask a favour.'

'Anything.'

'What? Oh, right. Yes, well you see I'm trying to contact a colleague of mine, who is at the university.'

'University?'

'The University of North Yorkshire. I know he's a caver and he seems to spend a lot of time in Ingleton so I thought you might know him.'

'What's his name?'

'Lang. Dr Terry Lang.'

'Doesn't ring any bells but I've only been based here a few months so it doesn't mean he doesn't hang out here. I'm seeing some mates tonight, I can ask around.'

'Thanks so much. If you do find him, can you ask him to ring me?'

'Yes, sure. Meanwhile…'

'You've got my number haven't you?'

'Yes, but…'

'Bye then.'

Mills sat with fingers pressed against her mouth. She had felt so stupid and instantly regretted making the call. He obviously hadn't a clue who Terry Lang was and probably now thought her a complete muppet. She took the last beaker off the hot-plate and filtered the solution. It was time to leave the laboratory and inflict herself on Nige and Nina for another evening. She stopped on the way back to pick up some groceries, determined that at least for tonight she would cook.

The pub was quiet even for a Monday so Fred had no difficulty spotting Steve and Ewa chatting to the young barman, who was a fellow caver.

'About time,' joked Steve, 'I've had a hell of a job making this pint last until you came.'

Fred felt in his pockets but Ewa stopped him.

'Don't be silly, Fred. I bought him that one. It's his round.'

They found a table and Fred, knowing they would be soon be joined by more regulars, asked Steve about "the hand".

'It was a bit gruesome but Ewa's probably exaggerated,' said Steve with a laugh.

'No, I didn't.' Ewa put her glass back on the table with a bang. 'That creep put ice-cream tub with human hand in refrigerator. Can you believe it?'

'Where did it come from?' asked Fred, wishing he could write some notes.

'God knows. He dug it up somewhere. Perhaps he found it underground.'

'So who did it belong to?'

'Do you mean whose hand was it?' Steve was grinning.

'Do you know?'

'No!' Steve exploded with laughter but Ewa was clearly not amused.

'It not funny. That guy Hunter is mad.'

'Hunter?'

'Yes.' Ewa pouted and sipped her beer.

'You should talk to him, Fred. You could get him into the papers.'

'I was thinking it might make a good story.'

'He'd love that,' Ewa slouched down on the bench and sulked.

Fred asked Steve to see if Hunter would give him an interview, thinking how professional that sounded. In his degree course at university they had practised interviewing each other but it would be the first time that he had done it for real and it was an exciting prospect.

'Give him my number and ask him to get in touch,' he suggested, and then, because he could see that Ewa was getting irritated, he said that he should be off. He wrapped his long scarf round his neck several times and pulled his jacket tight. 'See you.'

He set off in the direction of his digs but changed his mind and went back down the high street to the newspaper offices. Anyone passing later that night who looked up at the first floor would have seen the solitary figure searching back issues of the newspaper looking for any interesting crimes that had taken place in the vicinity over the last one hundred years. After all, where there's a hand, there must be a body, he argued. It stood to reason.

Steve and Ewa were still at their table but now they were surrounded by members of the caving club. Hunter was holding the floor as usual and Ewa told Steve it was time they were moving.

'I've got to ask Hunter about what Fred said,' he remonstrated.

'Another time, Steve. It can wait.' She was making for the door.

Steve moved over to Hunter and talked quietly to him. Hunter smiled and waved as Steve walked away.

'No problem Steve, I'll get onto it straight away!'

'Arrogant man,' muttered Ewa as they left.

The clouds had cleared and the sky was covered in stars. As they passed the baker's she looked up at the black lettering of the "Ingleton Mercury" silhouetted by the glow of light in the first floor window.

'It must be fun working on a newspaper,' she said to no-one in particular.

'Boring if you ask me.' Steve put his arm round her and suggested they bought some chips on the way. She shrugged him off.

'No, really. I mean, he won't be on paper for ever, will he? He could be war correspondent or in politics, couldn't he? Or on CNN news.'

'Or he could just be on the Ingleton Mercury covering weddings and funerals, for ever.' Steve was already pushing at the chip shop door.

Ewa stood outside, preferring the cold to the steamy interior of the fish bar. Steve's lack of ambition had been the cause of arguments before. Whenever she tried to persuade him to move to London with her, he refused. His mates were in Ingleton. Caving was his life. Why would he want to live in city?

They walked home in silence. Sometimes she just wanted to pack her bags and fly home where she knew her family would welcome her with open arms. Her ambition had kept her strong but the flat was cold and Ewa was tired from standing all day putting curlers in the grey wiry hair of ugly old ladies. She switched on the electric fire and started to get ready for bed.

Steve was sitting in front of the television with a can of lager.

'So what is it that makes Fred so attractive?' he called casually.

'I don't know what you are talking about.'

'I saw the way you were looking at him in the pub.' He sat watching the screen without moving.

'I'm going to bed,' Ewa called from the other room.

'Suit yourself.'

The office heating went off at night but Fred had switched on a little fan heater that he had found in the kitchen. He had been sitting for an hour looking through the microfiche that held the archives of the Ingleton Mercury when his mobile rang.

'Is that Fred?'

'Yes.'

'It's Hunter here. Steve told me you wanted a chat.'

'Right. Yes. It's about that … hand.'

'Oh yes?'

'I work on the Ingleton Mercury and I wondered if I could have an interview?'

'I'm not sure about that.'

'But we could talk?'

'Look I'm in the pub if you want to come down.'

Fred hesitated. It would be noisy and the others would be listening.

'Would you like to come to the office?'

'What now? It's ten o' clock, mate.'

'Bring some beers, I'll put them on expenses.'

Fred gave directions to Hunter and he duly appeared clutching six bottles of Guinness.

'What is this all about, mate?' he asked, settling himself down opposite Fred.

'Thanks for coming. It's just Steve told me about the hand and I wondered how you came to find it? The readers will be interested if it's local and we can do some photographs as well.'

'Look, it's a bit sensitive until we have a full picture of its origin. I'd appreciate it if you could keep it under wraps for now.'

'Is it a human hand?'

'Probably.'

'How old?'

'Look I can't tell you any more at the present time.' He stood up and turned towards the door.

'At least tell me where it was found. Was it in a cave?'

'Up at Ribblehead. Is that enough for you? I'd rather it was kept quiet for now.'

With that he picked up his bottles and left.

Disappointed, Fred resumed his search of the newspaper archives until his shoulders ached. Stretching, he checked his watch; it was two thirty, time for more strong black coffee. He would search one more set of fiches and then call it a day.

Sitting back down at the microfiche reader he opened the envelope with the dates 1945-50 neatly inscribed in italic hand-writing. He had a good system that had developed over the hours he had been searching. Without an index he had to skim over every page but he knew by now where to look. Anything of note would be on the first couple of pages and there would be comment in the editorial which would act as a check. He quickly dealt with the first few fiches and was scanning through them almost automatically. It was the editorial for June 3rd 1955 that caught his eye. *'Surely,'* it began. *'in this day and age, it should be possible for a man or a child to be out alone without risk of abduction.'* It went on to describe how in the good old days parents could let their children out to roam in the countryside without danger of them not returning. Puzzled he flicked through the rest of the paper to find what the editorial referred to. Eventually, on page four he found a small item which simply reported that a James Small had not returned home and was feared lost. His parents were concerned because, although he was fourteen, James was a 'mongol'. Confused, Fred looked up the term and discovered that it was used before the 1960s to mean that the lad had suffered from Down's Syndrome.

Curious to know whether James Small had been found, Fred continued to read the papers up to the end of 1955. This time he covered every page. Initially there were references to searches and possible sightings but very quickly they ceased and he concluded that the boy was not found. Fred leaned back in his chair and stretched. Was this what he had been looking for? A missing person, no body, assumed dead? He reached for his book and made some notes. First the name of the boy, followed by his parents' names. They would be quite old by now, probably too old, but there was mention of a younger boy who was upset by the loss of his brother. He would be in his sixties now and if he could locate him, then there could be a story. Next he checked back to find out where the boy had disappeared. '*The young man went down to the end of the farm lane each morning to see the milk collection lorry go by. A passer-by remembered seeing the boy sitting on the wall with the churns from the farm at the foot of Whernside.*'

Fred felt certain that this was significant. Out of all the papers dating back from 1927 this was the only reference to a missing person who was never accounted for – and he had disappeared close to where Hunter had found the hand.

Chapter 5

The newspaper had named the farm where James Small had spent his short life and early in the morning Fred was speeding along the road towards Ribblehead. The wind seemed to cut through his motorbike leathers and he was glad when he turned off the road as the viaduct came into view. A middle-aged man emerged from a nearby barn when Fred brought the machine to a halt in the yard.

'Morning!' the man called.

'Mr Small?' asked Fred, without conviction.

'No. Who wants him?'

'I'm Fred Marshall, from the Ingleton Mercury. I wanted to have a word with Mr and Mrs Small. I think they used to live here?'

'Ay, they did, years ago. But they retired. There was no-one to take over.'

'When would that have been?'

'In the late sixties. My dad took it over in sixty-eight. They moved down to Ingleton.'

'Were there no children?'

'There was a son but he'd become a postman and moved to Kirbymoorside.'

'Do you know his first name?'

'No. I was a baby then. And he'd be getting on a bit now mind!'

Fred thanked the farmer and climbed on the bike. Back at the Mercury offices he sat looking into space, wondering how to find James Small's brother.

'You look like you need something to do, young man.'

The subeditor was standing with a piece of paper in his hand. His hands, like the rest of his body, were arthritic and the infirmity made him look old and tired. No-one knew his true age but the consensus among the staff was that he must be reaching retirement soon.

'Can I ask you something?'

'Go ahead, sonny.'

'If you wanted to trace someone, how would *you* go about it?'

'Have you got a name?'

'Yes… well a surname.'

'Is it a common name?'

'Not particularly.'

'Good. Got a location?'

'Sort of.'

'Well, *I* would go there and ask around. Surprising who knows who.' He sat down on the edge of the desk. 'So what is this about?'

'It's like a missing person.'

'Missing eh? When did they disappear?'

'Nineteen fifty-five.'

The old man stood up and thumped the paper down in front of him.

'You get on with the sports reports, young man. You can chase missing persons in your own time.'

The old man walk out slamming the door behind him. Fred picked up the sheet of paper. He was to cover the local inter-school rugby challenge the following afternoon and write a piece which might be used as a feature to highlight sport and the young in the Olympic year. Without thinking he stuffed the note in his pocket, picked up his jacket and left the office. He wasn't sure where he was going but he wanted to get away, just for a few minutes. He ran down the stairs and out into the street. The pavement was gritty and he noticed it was brown where the melted snow was yet to dry. He was so absorbed that he almost walked into someone coming the other way.

'Freddie!' a female voice called.

He recognised the accent and stopped.

'Ewa?'

'Hello darling.' She started walking back towards him. 'How nice to see you. Are you taking break from writing those important articles?'

Was she laughing at him? Fred couldn't tell. Her blonde bleached hair blew around her face; she pulled it away with a gloved hand that left her fingers, and long red nails, exposed. Her flowing coat was multi-coloured and she wore long boots with high heels.

'So where are you off to? Anywhere exciting?' She was close beside him and he could smell her perfume on the cold wind.

'I was just getting some lunch actually.'

'And so am I! I was going to café – you shall come too.'

Fred hardly knew her and was far too polite to refuse, so he followed obediently. She walked fast with her heels clicking loudly, her hair billowing behind her.

'I have had terrible morning,' she declared to the entire room once they were seated. 'This woman, she wants perm but she wants it in two minutes! I told her at least two hours and after one hour she is demanding to know how much longer.'

'Oh dear.'

When they ordered she spoke to the café staff by name. He sat uncomfortably waiting until she had finished chatting to them. He had only popped out for a sandwich but she was ordering a special so he chose egg and chips.

'So Freddie, what are you working on at the moment?' She seemed genuinely interested.

He hesitated. He wanted to tell someone about James Small but he felt uncomfortable. 'Oh just a rugby tournament.'

She pulled a face. 'Not very exciting?'

'No.'

'But there must be some interesting things that you report?'

'Not really. I'm mainly doing sports at the moment.'

She was distracted by someone seated at another table and waved. Turning back she looked at him suddenly very intently.

'And do you have a girlfriend?'

He hesitated.

'Of course you have,' she said. 'A good-looking boy like you. Tell me all about her! What's her name?'

It just came out. 'Mills.' He was blushing, he knew.

'Meels? What name is that? Is she foreign?'

'No. She works at the university.'

'Clever girl, eh? So what does she do, this girlfriend of yours, this Meels?'

He was already regretting the pretence. 'Something complicated,' he muttered and turned round to see if the food was coming.

'And she's a caver too?' asked Ewa.

'Oh no! In fact... I was thinking of taking her underground some time.'

'Ah, I can help you then. I only start caving when I come to this country. I went down that place Great

Douk. It was good place to go for first time.' She stared into the distance. 'That was long time ago.'

'You're right; it would be a good place to start. I'll tell her.'

Their food arrived and, much to Fred's embarrassment, Ewa began complaining about Steve's lack of ambition, gesticulating with her fork as she consumed her lasagne. Intermittently she took chips from Fred's plate.

'You don't mind do you, Freddie?'

He looked around but no-one seemed to be watching them.

Over coffee, Ewa leant forward and lowered her voice. 'You know I am thinking that I will leave here altogether. Steve has no sense of adventure.'

'I think he's very adventurous when he goes underground.'

'I am sure *you* are more adventurous than he is. At least *you* have ambition.'

Fred blushed. To his relief, Ewa's mobile phone began playing a lively tune and she turned her attention to her handbag. She looked at the screen and then excused herself, muttering that she would go outside for a cigarette. Fred watched her pacing up and down the street as she spoke to her caller. Taking the opportunity to escape, he paid at the counter and made for the door. He stopped to signal to her that he had paid their bill and would have to leave. She expressed her gratitude by giving him a hug and kissing him on both cheeks while she continued speaking on her mobile. He left hurriedly.

'Darling I told you I can't get away tonight.' She was watching Fred as he strode away.

'What about tomorrow? He must go out sometimes.'

'Look, I'll ring you back later,' she said sharply and snapped the phone shut.

Lang took the phone away from his ear and looked at it quizzically.

'Is it inconvenient?' Mills asked from the door.

'No, we've been cut off,' he replied and placed it back in the receiver. 'So, what can I do for you?'

'I thought you might like an update on progress so far,' she offered.

'Sure. How's it going?'

She had prepared a short report, fearing he would be absent for another day. She handed it to him and then sat down on the sofa.

'I'll read it with interest. Just give me the bottom line.'

Mills sighed. 'Well. I'm measuring the chemical composition of peat from the ditch and I've arranged for a sample of the hand to be analysed using carbon dating. That should give us a fairly accurate age for it.'

Lang sat in silence.

'And I've checked for evidence of activity in the area but only come up with a Viking settlement, which is probably too late for this.'

The phone began to ring.

'Excellent,' he said, picking up the receiver. 'Carry on the good work.' He turned to the side and spoke softly, 'Is that you?'

Mills stood up and moved to the door. As she left she couldn't help overhearing. '*I need to see you.*'

She went back to the laboratory and unfastened the refrigerator door. She paused when she opened the plastic box to reveal the shrivelled hand inside. An artefact that could be two thousand years old preserved in the peat bog, undisturbed until now. Nervously she transferred it onto a plastic tray and cleared away the soil that was sticking to it. She brushed between the fingers and turned it over gently, noticing that it was possible to discern the lines and texture of the palm. Placing it back down she studied the nails, short and damaged, like hands that had seen hard work. Probably due to decay, she thought, searching for the scalpel blades. She opened her notebook and reminded herself how to take a sample for the Oxford laboratory. It didn't have to be large but it did have to represent the artefact. She had read that the peat would change the skin from the outside in and so she carefully cut a small section through the entire thickness of the leathery hand where it would have been attached to the rest of the body. Once the sample was safely packed in a glass vial and the plastic box was back in the refrigerator she relaxed. She pulled off her plastic gloves and threw them in the bin, washed her hands thoroughly and hung up her white coat.

As she was writing the address of the Oxford laboratory on a padded envelope, she realised that she had forgotten to ask Terry Lang for an account to pay for the analyses. She called into his office on her way to the post-room but it was locked. A message on the door indicated he had been called out urgently and would not be back for the rest of the day.

It was a clear day and most of the snow had disappeared. Even so, Fred took the road steadily and it was nearly two hours before he reached his destination. He didn't know why he had decided to set off but the way Ewa talked about Steve had made him think and he had seized the moment. Now he was turning into Kirkbymoorside he felt a little silly because he had no plan of how to trace James Small's brother. Fred started at the post office since he had been a postman but there was no recollection of anyone called Small. One of the customers suggested asking at the library since they did family history but a lady in a knitted hat pointed out that the library was closed on a Tuesday.

'You'll have to come back tomorrow, love.'

Fred wandered out into the street and stood searching for inspiration. It had been a long ride and it looked as though he would have to return another day.

'I heard what you were saying and I think the website might help.' The lady in the hat had joined him on the pavement. 'There's a website for Kirkby and you can put questions into it. I can show you if you like.' She reminded him of his Gran as she stood smiling at him.

'That's very kind of you but where… ?'

'I don't live far,' she said. 'Just down here. And don't worry,' she added as she started off down the road carrying a large wicker basket, 'my Snowy doesn't bite.'

He caught up with her as she turned off down another street and they walked together for several minutes.

'Have you come far?' she asked as she unlocked the front door to a neat little terraced house.

'Not really, Ingleton.'

'Really? Well you'll be wanting a cup of tea… and something to eat?'

'No I'm fine.'

'Nonsense, I'll put the kettle on while the computer warms up.'

Fred watched with amusement as the woman plugged in and switched on an old computer with the smallest monitor he had ever seen.

'It'll not be ready until the tea has brewed,' she said as she left the room.

Fred climbed out of his motorbike leathers, folding them neatly and placing them beside the desk. He could hear the woman talking to someone in the kitchen. The small room was neatly arranged with china ornaments covering every surface. The window overlooked a back garden that seemed to be endless.

'I told Snowy that you are a friend. I might let him come in and say hello later.' She was carrying a large tray which she placed on a low table in the middle of the room. 'Now is it warmed up yet?'

She sat down and began typing.

'Password,' she said. 'Well that's M A G G I E – my name – I'll forget it otherwise. When I forget my name I shall have to stop using it. Come here and I'll show you the website.'

She punched the keyboard and finally the word *"Kirkbymoorsidegatewaytothemoors"* came up on the screen. It was excruciatingly slow but finally the screen was complete. Maggie clicked on "interactive" and "genealogy forum".

'Now this is where you can look for people. See there are lots of entries.'

Fred could see a list of names, all people or families that were being sought out for family trees. But there were other questions too like *where are the church records archived?*

'Maggie, where *are* the church records kept?'

'In the Community Office.'

'Maybe I should go there.'

'I believe it's closed on a Tuesday afternoon but it'll be open tomorrow. I'll pour the tea. Milk? Sugar? Help yourself – and to the biscuits.'

The only hope appeared to be the genealogy forum.

'Can I put a message on the board, asking about Small?' asked Fred between mouthfuls of shortbread.

'Yes, of course dear.' She picked up the teapot and left the room.

Fred put in his e-mail and a brief message asking for information about a postman by the name of Small. Then he looked under "public services" and saw that the Community Office did indeed close at 1 pm on a Tuesday.

When Maggie returned she was accompanied by a small fox terrier that eyed Fred suspiciously and began to growl quietly.

'Now don't you be silly, Snowy. This is a friend of mine…'

'Fred,' he offered.

'There, now that's a lovely name isn't it Snowy?'

The dog lay down close to his mistress and went quiet, although it continued to watch Fred, particularly when he reached for another biscuit.

'Would he like some, Maggie?'

'That's why he came in.'

While Fred fed Snowy with shortbread he explained to Maggie why he was looking for Mr Small. Well, at least he told her that he was a journalist and was looking for a relative of a man that had disappeared a long time ago.

'He's not done anything wrong, has he?'

'No. I just wanted to interview a relative, that's all.'

'I suppose you'll have to come back another day to look at the church records.'

'Yes, if my message doesn't produce anything.'

'I could have a look for you, if you wanted. As I'm here. I'd be quite interested to see if I can find anything.'

Fred was unsure. 'I wouldn't want to put you to any trouble.'

'It wouldn't be trouble.' She laughed. 'I'd enjoy it. Now, what am I looking for… and when?'

'I suppose he would have started work in the fifties or sixties. He might have got married here, perhaps had kids. That would be a start.'

'So he would be what now? About seventy? He must've left Kirkby years ago or we'd know of him, I'm certain.'

'You're probably right.'

'Anyway it's dark now, you must be off or you'll be home late.'

He put his leathers on and stepped outside into the cold air. When she said goodbye Fred felt like a favourite grandson. He promised to phone and she would watch the website for further developments.

It was a few steps back to the square and soon he was speeding along, wondering whether his trip had been useful or not. By the time he reached Ingleton he was ready for something to eat but took the bike back to the flat and changed before walking down to the pub. Cutting across the car park by the football ground he spotted Hunter's VW van and decided to try him again for some information about the hand. Inside there were plenty of familiar faces but no-one had seen Hunter, not even Steve who had apparently been there since six.

'Ewa's got a friend coming round. She's going to colour her hair or something. I was told to make myself scarce until closing time.'

'I saw Ewa today,' began Fred.

Steve's face became tense. 'Did you?'

'Just in the café. I was having lunch.'

He looked into his beer for a long time and said nothing.

'I was asking her the best cave to show this girl I met. Ewa suggested Great Douk… for a beginner.'

'Sounds good.'

'I thought we might go this weekend.'

Steve looked up and narrowed his eyes. 'You mean you and Ewa?'

'No!'

'Who then?'

'Me and Mills… the girl I told you about.'

Steve picked up his glass and stood up. 'I'm getting another one. D'you want one?'

It was the way he said it, almost a threat. 'No, I'm fine thanks, mate.'

As time went on they were joined by friends and Fred remained after he had eaten, waiting to speak to Hunter when he appeared. He realised that he didn't even know if the hand belonged to a man or woman… or a boy. They might even be able to do DNA tests on it to see if it was someone with Down's Syndrome. That would be cool. But it was eleven and Hunter had not appeared. Someone was helping Steve to his feet and Fred decided it was time to go.

He offered Steve a hand but was pushed aside.

'Clear off, I don't need your help.' His speech was slurred and he nearly fell as he left, supported on either side by two of his caving mates. Chas stood watching, his dark eyes following their antics until the door swung behind them.

'He seems to have taken against you. Is there any reason why that should be?'

'I've no idea.'

'I'd watch him if I was you. He's not a happy man.'

Fred picked up his jacket and followed, keeping well behind the little group as they staggered along Bank Top. He made his way through to Back Gate to check if the camper van was still there, but it had gone and the car park was empty. If Hunter had been around there was no sign of him now and his investigations would have to wait.

When Nina enquired of Mills whether she had had a good day, she grimaced and explained how Lang had done his usual disappearing act when she needed his signature.

'That's typical. The guy's a moron,' Nige remarked.

'I can't understand where he keeps going. Does he have a site anywhere?' asked Mills.

'Only the one where the hand was discovered,' he replied. 'Basically he is just a skiver. I reckon he's got a young lady somewhere that he keeps popping off to.'

'He did have a phone call before he went yesterday. It sounded a bit like that.'

'There you are then, he's taking advantage of us all. You know I had to cover his practical yesterday?'

'Now then, sweetie. Don't go getting wound up about these things. OK, so the guy's a pain but you shouldn't take it so personally.' Nina wheeled herself over to the sofa and put her hand on his arm.

'The reason I take it personally is because I was told that I would have help with the first and second year teaching this term. He is supposed to be supporting the teaching not swanking around have a laugh!'

Nina grinned. 'Swanking?'

'Yes, swanking.'

'Well, Nigel, just don't over-react. He's a bright bloke and the University wouldn't have invited him if he didn't deserve it.'

'You may well say that, I couldn't possibly comment.'

'I don't mind if he's never there, so long as I can get what I want done,' said Mills. 'Can you sign the order for me to get the carbon-dating done, Nige?'

'Probably.'

'And will that give you a definite age for the hand?' Nina leant forward enthusiastically.

'I hope so. It may not be very precise but to the nearest hundred years, I'm guessing.'

'That's really interesting. And… I've also got something interesting to report. I rang the station today to see when I can start going back in. They said that they could use some help and have asked me to go through the papers for one of their current unsolved cases.'

'That's great,' said Mills.

'Yes, especially since I can do the work at home.' She turned to Nige, 'So I won't have to travel, not even get out of bed if I don't feel like it.'

'Hmm. I suppose that's one good thing.' Nige's expression gave nothing away but the silence that fell between him and Nina told Mills that he was not happy. She excused herself early that evening and went to her room to read some of the reports she had found relating to peat bodies and carbon-dating. She wasn't going to appear ignorant if she needed to speak to the scientists at the Oxford laboratory.

*

'… so I need your signature on the order for the carbon-dating and another one for the analysis of the peat.'

'Remind me why we need the peat analysis?' Lang was swinging the chair from side to side as he peered over his desk at Mills.

'Because, in due course, I want to analyse the skin sample. Then I can compare the elements with those in the peat.'

'Very good. And that will tell you…?'

'Whether the peat has interacted significantly with the hand.'

'Right.'

'What do you think?' Mills hoped he would give her advice, something she could work with.

'I think you're doing an excellent job,' he said, smiling and standing up. 'Now, I have a lecture in ten, so if you'll excuse me.'

Mills was beginning to understand why Nige found the man so frustrating. She had no proper office, a temporary bench in the laboratory and was having to impose herself on Nige and Nina's hospitality. Considering what she was putting into the project she thought the man should spend more than two minutes discussing her work. Still, she now had all the authority she needed to get carbon-dating done and she had been assured she would get the results by the end of the week.

She wandered up to the departmental laboratory and chatted to Sam about her work. He was in the middle of her peat samples and if she gave him some tissue from the hand, he would get that finished by the end of the day. At least the technician took an interest. She had just finished washing all the equipment and taken off her gloves when her mobile rang. Carefully placing the glass vial containing the skin sample on the bench, she looked at who was calling and this time she answered.

'Hello.'

'Mills? Is that Mills?'

'Yes, hello Fred.' It was the first time she had used his name. It seemed strange.

'Look, you can say no if you want to but I thought you might like to see what it's like in the caves round here. Would you like to go underground?'

She hesitated, 'I don't know. What do you mean exactly.'

'I knew it would sound odd. Would you like to come down Great Douk at the weekend?'

'I don't know. Maybe. But I haven't anything to wear, I mean protective gear, sort of thing.'

'Don't worry. I can get something for you. I just need to know if you'll come?'

'When is it?'

'What about Saturday?'

'I suppose so.'

'Good, I'll ring you later in the week.'

Mills sat for some time after he'd rung off, wondering what "going underground" involved.

Fred hadn't thought about the boiler-suit. His spare would be too big, which meant he'd have to borrow one before Saturday. He checked his watch – he had a couple of hours before he had to leave for the rugby ground. He went to close down his computer but stopped to check the genealogy forum once more, in case someone had replied. This time there was a message: *My name is Iain Small, what do you want to know?*

Chapter 6

Fred's hand hovered over the keyboard. It had taken him some time to compile his e-mail but he was still unsure whether it conveyed the right message. He didn't want to upset the man or make him think there was anything salacious in his interest in the disappearance of his brother. In the end he had simply said that he was doing an article on people who had gone missing in the Dales and he would like to speak to him about his brother James. Fred was pleased that he only had an e-mail address for Iain Small; it would have been an awkward first contact and he still hadn't developed an easy going manner when he made calls from the paper. He had even asked if he could do some training, go on a course, but the response was always the same: *'When I employed you I was looking for someone with experience. If you don't know how to do the job you'd better go elsewhere!'* The first time he'd pointed out that he didn't have experience. *'More the pity.'* was the response. He knew not to pursue it further.

He clicked on the send button and watched the message disappear into the ether. The e-mail address gave no clues to where Mr Small was living. Possibly he was no longer in the North; he may even have moved abroad. Fred finished his coffee and resolved to forget about it until he received a response. He had to cover the rugby tournament in the afternoon and needed something substantial to eat if he was going to be standing around in the cold. He was hoping to ask Ewa about borrowing a waterproof suit for Mills and if that meant another embarrassing lunch-break with the woman, then so be it. He waited until one o'clock and then went across the road, where just as he planned, Ewa was sitting in the café at a table for two in the corner.

'Freddie, darling, come and join me!' She moved her handbag so he could sit on the chair opposite. 'Sorry but I am not good company today.'

'Oh dear.' He was tempted to remain standing and make his excuses.

'Sit. Sit. I tell you, I am fed up with this place. I think I will go to London. I can get good job in salon down there. Money will be better and customers – they will give tips.' She lowered her voice. 'Up here… old ladies… they not generous.'

Fred ordered his egg and chips with beans and while he waited Ewa continued to list her sources of discontent. Soon she had reached Steve and his lack of ambition.

'Tonight I tell him, either you come with me to London or I go alone.'

Fred wasn't sure what Steve did exactly.

'Would it be easy for him to find another job in London?'

'Of course, he works for council. There are plenty of councils in London.'

Fred dipped his chips into the egg yolks while he let Ewa go on. When she had run out of steam he asked about the suit.

'As far as I care you can keep it.' Her face was flushed. 'I do not intend to go into cave again. They do not have caves in London.'

'I only need to borrow it for this weekend really.'

'For your girlfriend? This Meels?' Her expression softened. 'So what is she like, this girl. You said she is clever?'

'Well… she is at the university.'

'Which one?'

'North Yorkshire.'

'That's nice. I had friend there.' She looked past him and there was an uncomfortable silence.

Fred cleaned his plate with a piece of bread and gulped down his coffee.

'Must be going.'

'Somewhere exciting?'

'Just the rugby.'

'Well, enjoy. Come round for suit, anytime' She sounded distant.

As Fred stepped out into the fresh air, stopping to tighten his scarf, he noticed Steve standing on the opposite pavement as if he was about to cross the road. He waved but the man just turned and walked away without responding, although Fred was certain that he had seen him.

Mills was in Terry Lang's office waiting for him to return from a first year lecture. He had agreed to see her and it was his suggestion that she made herself at home if he was delayed. It gave her the opportunity to look once more at his thesis so she removed it carefully from the bookcase. She was surprised to see how meticulously it was presented and how well-written. As she thumbed through the chapters she found a section relating to carbon-dating and began to read it carefully. By the time Lang appeared she was engrossed in a detailed description of the different factors that might affect the results. She automatically closed the book and put it down beside her.

'You looked very absorbed,' he said amiably as he dropped a large file on his desk.

Mills reddened. 'I was interested in your thesis. I hope you don't mind.'

He turned away and fiddled with papers on his desk. 'Of course not.'

'I was interested in the carbon-dating. It will be really useful to have your advice when the results come in from Oxford.'

'Oxford?' He still had his back to her.

'The dating lab. I've sent the tissue from the hand there.'

'Yes, of course.' He turned round and stared at her. 'So what do you want to discuss?'

Mills was nonplussed. She had wanted to spend some time explaining where the work had got to but he was already doing that thing again. That *get to the point* thing that he did. So she would.

'I've been here for a week now.' She paused but he said nothing. 'Nige and Nina have been putting me up but I can't do that much longer, it's not fair on them. So I thought I might stay in a B&B down near the site. I wondered if you knew of somewhere down that way?'

'Me?' He looked puzzled.

'Oh, I just thought... you go caving... I just thought...' She paused. 'In fact I'm going myself at the weekend. Do you know Great Douk?' He shook his head. 'Well, anyway what with that and then I'd need transport so I wondered what the situation was regarding funding, if I wanted to continue doing this work?'

There was an awkward silence. Then he took a deep breath.

'I have funding for my work so I suppose I could find something towards your expenses...'

Mills started to thank him.

'…but I don't think it is necessary to go down to the site again. There's nothing down there now, is there? Find a hotel up here and let me know what you need in the way of expenses.' He looked at his watch. 'Must rush, got to see someone. Slam the door behind you.'

She watched him go and sighed. As she stood up to leave she picked up the thesis to return it to the shelf and stopped. There was no reason why she shouldn't borrow it for now.

Nige was in his office as she passed and so she went in and sat down.

'Hi,' he said, swinging round in his chair. 'How's things?'

'OK I suppose. I've just seen Dr Lang.'

'Oh yes.'

'I asked about getting some funding if I'm going to be carrying on with this work.'

'And?'

He said it was all right but he wouldn't pay for me to stay near the site. I think it's because I would have to hire a car.'

'He's got a big grant while he's working here but you can borrow our car whenever you want.'

'Yes but I can't impose on you and Nina any longer.'

'Of course you can. Nina enjoys the company.'

'You're very kind but it's a long way to go each day if I start to do any further work on the ditch.'

'True.'

'I'll have a look to see if I can find a B&B over there.'

'Well, at least take the car today – I can walk home.'

He threw her the keys with a grin.

Mills smiled back. 'Thanks.' She planned to go to the farm and speak to Sheila again. She would know if there was anywhere to stay locally at this time of year. Her work at the university might not last much longer and she may have to move back down to Manchester quite soon. If she was going to be doing some caving with Fred at the weekend it might be easier not to have to travel so far. But she wasn't going to say that to Lang or even Nige.

The roads were clear of snow but the tops were white as she drove over the fell above Hawes. She shivered as she remembered her return journey in the snowstorm. Today the winter sun was shining weakly and the only hazards were sheep nibbling grass shoots at the edge of the road.

She found Sheila feeding hens at the back of the farm. She looked the epitome of a farmer's wife in her flowery apron and wellington boots but Mills could tell that both came from a mail order company whose label even Fiona, her father's fashionable fiancée, would not be embarrassed to be seen wearing. When Sheila saw her she set down the pail of food and waved,

'Hello. I hoped you'd be back.'

'I thought I'd pop by.'

'I found some booklets on the railway and it describes the navvy camp really well. Come inside and I'll show you.'

Baby Richard was on the floor playing with a wooden car. In the armchair sat an old man, possibly in his seventies or eighties; Mills was not good at guessing ages.

'This is Grandad, Brian's grandfather. He always comes to me on a Wednesday.' Sheila raised her voice. 'Grandad, this is the lady I was telling you about. She's from the university.' She turned to Mills. 'I'll get those books,' she said and left the room.

'Oh aye. How do.' He was struggling to get out of the chair.

'Please don't get up.' Mills hid her awkwardness by bending down to talk to Richard. He ignored her and carried on babbling to himself as he steered the car across the carpet.

'He's been like that for hours,' remarked the old man. 'Happy as can be.'

Sheila came back with an armful of papers and Mills stood up.

'Kate looked them out for me. She did a project on them at school.' She put them on the table. 'I'll make some tea. Kate will be back from school soon and she can tell you herself.'

Mills flicked through the booklets and papers that the girl had printed off the internet until Sheila returned with a tray.

'So how are you getting on with your investigations?' the woman asked as she poured out tea and offered her a plate of biscuits.

'I've not got much further yet,' she answered. 'I'm waiting for the results of tests.'

'What sort of tests?' asked Grandad, dipping his biscuit into his tea.

'To find out how old the hand is, to see how long it has been there.'

'They reckon it's been there a long time, don't they?' asked Sheila.

'Yes but I would like to borrow these papers about the navvies just in case it comes back that the hand is more recent.'

The old man drank his tea noisily. 'Can't see how it can be recent. There's been nothing happen down here in my recollection.'

'And that's a long time isn't it Grandad?'

'Eighty-seven years since I were born here in this house.' He looked proudly round the room.

'Was your father born here as well?' Mills asked, raising her voice to ensure that he heard her.

'He was that. And his father afore him.' His breathing was laboured.

They all turned to the window at the sound of a vehicle parking in the yard. Brian was driving and Kate jumped out as soon as they stopped. She burst into the room and ran across to the old man.

'Hi Mum. Grandad, Kirsty had a nosebleed and we had to finish netball early and...' She stopped mid-sentence as she noticed Mills. 'Oh, I thought you were up the field. Dad's gone to look for you.'

'No, I've nothing more to do up there right now. In fact, I really ought to be going.' She felt uncomfortable knowing Brian was looking for her and she could see that Sheila was becoming nervous.'

'Kate, why don't you run up and tell him to come back,' Sheila asked. She waited until her daughter had gone before adding, 'I don't know why he gets so wound up about what you found.'

'He just wants to get on wi' his work,' the grandfather said, breathlessly.

'Well I better be going.' Mills wanted to avoid another confrontation with Brian.

Sheila followed her to the car and Mills thanked her again for the information Kate had provided.

'Not at all. If there's anything else we can do.'

Mills had nearly forgotten the main reason for her visit.

'Actually there is something. I was wondering if you knew of any B&Bs round here.'

'Now that's an interesting one. Lots of the farms are open in the summer for visitors but not this time of year. The nearest would be down in Ingleton I should think. I could find out for you.'

'No problem. I can pop into the tourist information down there.'

'If you're sure?'

'Yes. And I'll let you know when I've got some results on the carbon-dating.'

Sheila waved as she drove off but under the light of the lamp on the side of the house Mills could see Brian standing beside Kate and his body language was far from welcoming.

Sheila went inside and starting preparing tea for when Brian's parents arrived. The routine was always the same: after tea Brian and his father would disappear into the study to discuss the finances of the farm while Brian's mother helped wash up and the children played with Grandad.

'So, that's that. Would you like more tea before I rinse the pot?'

Her mother-in-law shook her head. 'No thanks.'

Sheila enjoyed Mary's company and they chatted about the children until the last saucer was dried and put away in the cupboard.

'So how has Grandad been?' asked Sheila. 'He's not been good this week. He just gets this wretched asthma. I expect it's the bad weather.'

'Does it usually affect him in the winter?' Sheila couldn't remember him suffering before.

'It comes and goes. It seemed better since he retired.'

Brian's father came into the kitchen, coughing.

'You should get rid of that pipe, Bill. It'll be the death of you.' Mary told her husband, shaking her head and looking to her daughter-in-law for support.

He winked at Sheila. 'I reckon I'm old enough to risk it,' he said with a grin. 'It's Dad you should be worrying about, Mary. He's right bad with his wheezing.' He went into the garden and they watched him through the kitchen window as he lit his pipe.

'Grandad met that young archaeology lass today, Mary.'

'Did he? That must have been exciting for him.'

'That reminds me,' said Sheila. 'She asked me about finding somewhere to stay down this way, temporarily. I couldn't think of anywhere except in Ingleton.'

'There's no one doing B&B at this time of year up this way. You're not wrong there.'

Fred was chilled to the bone after watching the rugby from the touchline. The play was probably very good and he had noted the names of the outstanding players, according to the coaches. He had interviewed several players and their parents. Considering he had never played rugby – his was a football school – he reckoned he had done pretty well. Now all he craved was a hot shower and a pint down the pub but something was nagging at him. He needed to get that suit from Ewa before she disappeared. What if she decided to take off for London suddenly, before Saturday? He wanted to be certain of it or the whole plan would be ruined. He wanted to take Mills to see the cave and then they could go for something to eat. If she liked the cave, he could suggest another one. He hadn't decided which one yet but he could ask Ewa again.

So he turned his motorbike down the Croft Road and into the street where Steve and Ewa shared a flat. He'd been there a couple of times to meet Steve before going off caving but in the dark he hesitated before choosing the top bell and pressing it firmly.

'Hello?' He recognised Ewa's voice.

'It's Fred. I've come for the suit.'

'Freddie! Come up, darling.' A loud buzzing followed and Fred pushed on the door. When he reached the first floor, Ewa was waiting at the front door of the flat with a broad smile. She had a towel round her head and she was wearing a dressing gown.

'You look chilly, Freddie. Come in and warm yourself. Take off jacket and sit by fire.'

Fred wanted to return another time but she insisted he came into the sitting room. A coal effect electric fire threw out a suffocating heat.

'Excuse robe,' she said. 'I am giving my hair special treatment.' She giggled.

'I came to fetch the suit. I have to get back soon,' he added wanting to get away.

'Of course, I'll fetch it right away!'

She disappeared into the hall and Fred stood examining the photographs on the mantlepiece. When Ewa returned with a plastic bag he was looking at a picture of a middle-aged woman and man.

'My parents in Serbia,' she said. 'I will be glad to see them again.'

'Are you going to visit them?'

'I want to go home, Freddie. I want to go to my country, where I belong. You cannot believe how much I miss my family.' Tears began to form and run down her cheeks and she turned away, wiping her face with her sleeve. 'Look at me,' she said, turning back. 'So silly. Now, here is suit. I hope your Meels will be very happy in it. It is for you to keep.'

'Are you sure?'

'Yes,' she smiled, 'I won't need it back home.' Then she moved towards him and gave him a hug, enveloping him in white towelling and the smell of ammonia. He was pulling himself away, as politely as he could when the door opened.

'Hello, Steve... I er... was just...' Fred waved the carrier bag at him.

'Get out!' Steve screamed at him. 'And you,' he pointed at Ewa, 'get some clothes on!'

Fred ran downstairs and out into the night. Back in his own flat he paced up and down wondering whether he had done the right thing. He wondered whether he should call Ewa but that would probably cause further trouble. The pub was obviously a bad idea since Steve could be drowning his sorrows down there so he fixed a microwave meal and turned on the television. There was nothing worth watching and by ten o'clock he decided to pass the time by making a start on the rugby tournament. As soon as he turned on the laptop he was alerted that he had new mail, a message from Iain Small: *I suggest we meet to discuss I will be in Leeds on Friday evening at Quebecs. Can you meet me there at seven?* Of course he could.

There was one other e-mail. It was from Maggie, giving her phone number and asking him to call. She had seen the message from Iain Small on the genealogy forum and wondered if Fred had contacted him. He told her all he knew and promised to update her with progress.

'Be careful young man,' she said as he prepared to finish the call. 'You don't know what he's like... his poor brother did disappear in mysterious circumstances.'

He washed the dishes and made himself a coffee. The evening had started badly but at least he had got the suit for Mills and he would be seeing Iain Small at the end of the week.

Ewa was in work before any of the girls. She had been up for hours, unable to sleep after the row with Steve. His jealousy was becoming stifling and the devotion that had attracted her at first was now driving her away. Her mind had been made up before but it had helped her to act. When she rang Hunter she told him all about the stupid row over Freddie and the suit and at first he'd been really sympathetic.

'Why does Fred want a woman's suit anyway?'

'Oh, he has girlfriend. She comes from your university. I expect he wants to show off to her.'

'Comes from here? What's her name'

'He calls her Meels.'

'Meels? Are you sure?' There was a pause. 'So what are you going to do, Ewa?'

'I don't know.'

'You can stay with me.'

'No.'

'Anyone would think that you were married.'

'You know I'm not. It's just… well… difficult. Perhaps it's best if I go to London.'

'But I will miss you. Won't you miss me?'

Ewa was tired. She could manage on her own. She would hand in her notice, work out the following week and then head for London. She might find a job but probably she would take the first flight to Serbia that she could afford.

Thursday was pensioners' day and she had a full list of shampoo and sets. She sighed as she removed her coat and hung it up carefully in the tiny cupboard reserved for staff. She boiled the kettle and set out the mugs, spooning the instant coffee into each in turn. When the first girl appeared she left her in charge while she popped along the road for milk. The newspaper office was in darkness but she hardly noticed. Her interest in Ingleton had waned and she would soon forget it for good.

To her surprise, when she told her that she was leaving, the boss hardly reacted.

'To be honest Ewa, I thought you had your mind on other matters. If you want to finish tomorrow you can. There's no need to work your notice.'

'But how will you manage?'

'We'll cope, love. But come in tomorrow; the girls will want to say goodbye.'

As she wound the series of heads with tight rollers and popped them under the drier she wondered how she would tell Steve. She rehearsed her speech as she combed out the rigid curls and sprayed each head. By the end of the day she had a headache and walked home feeling quite nauseous. She tried Hunter's number as she walked but he didn't have his mobile switched on. Once inside the flat it was a relief to see the note from Steve saying that he was down the pub. It would allow her to start packing without explanations. By the time he stumbled in late that night her suitcase was neatly stored under the bed and she was pretending to be fast asleep.

Steve left for work the next day without speaking to her. As soon as he was gone Ewa retrieved her suitcase and packed her final few things. She was leaving a lot of her possessions behind but she knew that she wouldn't be able to manage them. Looking round, she felt just a glimmer of sadness as she remembered the happier times she had spent with Steve in their tiny flat.

The rest of the day was a haze as she anxiously waited for her last customer to leave. Back at the flat she collected her suitcase, propping the note on the mantelpiece above the coal effect fire. *Dear Steve, I am leaving for ever. I am going to London to find job. I hope the rest of your life is successful and healthy. Ewa.* She had considered putting kisses but it seemed a little insincere. As she ran back down the stairs everything was blurred by her tears. As the bus carried her to Lancaster and the West Coast line, she wondered if she would regret her decision.

On the train to Leeds, Fred was rehearsing his questions for Iain Small. He had compiled a list and had planned how to introduce the subject of the man's dead brother. He presumed he was dead, of course, although even that was not certain. He would say that he was doing an article on missing persons; people who had disappeared without trace in the Dales. For that reason he had also obtained the necessary information on those who had gone missing over the past sixty years, in case he was suspicious.

The hotel was very smart and Fred was glad that he had left his bike and leathers at Settle station. Even so, he felt out of place in such grand surroundings. He need not have worried. Mr Small, when the desk summoned him down, was dressed in jeans, a high necked sweater and a leather jacket. Fred was not sure what he had expected; he hadn't thought about it much. Iain - he had asked Fred to call him Iain -

looked to be no more than sixty although Fred had worked out that he must be at least seventy. His thick greying hair looked professionally styled and his tanned face gave him a sporty appearance. He held himself straight and shook Fred's hand with a firm grasp.

'Why don't you join me for a bite to eat? Don't worry, it'll be on expenses.'

To his relief, Fred was led out of the hotel and along the street to an Italian restaurant, part of a chain that he was familiar with.

'So, what is this all about?' Iain asked, once they had ordered drinks.

Fred went through his well-rehearsed speech about the article he was writing.

'And which paper is this?'

'The Ingleton Mercury. It's very local, not a big circulation.'

'To be honest. I don't think I can help you.'

'I'll let you see what I've written if you want. You can veto anything you don't like,' offered Fred.

'No, you don't understand. I don't think I can be of much help. You see I was only ten when my brother went missing and I don't remember much.'

'There must be some things that stuck: the police, reporters, that sort of thing.'

'Not really. I expect my parents sheltered me from it. I just remember him not being there any more. That was it.'

'You must have missed him.'

'Not really. There was a gap of five years between us and you must remember he had Down's Syndrome. He wasn't expected to live as long as he did.'

'But you wouldn't have been aware of that at the age of ten?'

'Oh yes, I was constantly reminded of it by Mother and Father. How grateful we should be that he was still around.' He was speaking in a lowered voice now, almost gruff. 'He was hard work. They spoiled him. It was like he was their entire world.'

'Did you ever wonder what really happened to him?'

'I suppose so. Mother and Father were pretty knocked back by it. Mother never really recovered, the truth be told.' He fiddled with a gold ring on his left hand and played with his wine glass.

'They must have told you about the day it happened.'

'No, they never spoke of it.' He looked around the restaurant absently. 'But the kids at school talked about it. Kept reading bits out of the paper and telling me what their parents thought.'

'So what happened?'

'Nothing. He went out in the morning like he often did.'

'This was after you'd gone to school?'

'Yes.'

'Did anyone see him or see anyone around?'

'No. No-one saw anything.'

'Except the passer-by.'

'The passer-by?'

'Someone saw your brother that morning, waiting with the milk churns.'

'Did he? I didn't know that.'

'I wondered if the lorry driver would have remembered him; the driver who collected the milk?'

They sat in silence, sipping their wine.

'How did you see my message on the Kirkbymoorside website?' asked Fred.

'Through a friend of mine. We keep in touch even though I left a long time ago.'

'May I ask what you did when you left the Dales?' Fred was hoping he would remember this conversation. It seemed inappropriate to take written notes at the dinner table.

Iain seemed to relax back, taking a deep swig of his merlot. 'Oh I got out as soon as I could. I did a few years with the post office and then branched out on my own. I've been running my own estate agency down south since I was thirty-five, and still do. That's why I'm up here at a meeting with some associates of mine. I don't think I'll ever retire, can't afford it!' He raised his glass. 'Only joking. Cheers!'

Fred stopped asking questions and they chatted amiably while the pasta was served. Iain was an easy conversationalist and soon Fred was explaining how he had come to be working on the Mercury. Iain refilled their glasses and suggested a sweet. He asked Fred if he was married and the young man confided that the next day he was to have his first date with a new girlfriend. Iain knew most of the caves in the area including Great Douk, which had been close to where he had grown up. Over coffee he turned the conversation back to the purpose of their meeting.

'So why did you really want to speak to me?' he asked.

'As I said, I'm doing an article…'

'But why interview me? Why pick on my brother particularly?'

Fred hadn't meant to tell him; it was probably the wine. But it all came out.

Iain waited until he had finished speaking. 'You're telling me that a piece of my brother has been found at Ribblehead?'

'I don't know. It's all being kept very hush-hush at the moment.'

The man sat quietly for a while looking at his nails. He picked the napkin off his lap and folded it decisively before placing it neatly on the table. He looked at his watch and then opened his wallet.

'Here's my card. Keep me informed of anything you find out.' He threw three twenty pound notes on the table and stood up. 'I've got to go now. Ring me.'

Fred waited for the bill and then left. The evening had not gone the way he had anticipated and he was frustrated that there was no material suitable for an article. It was a frosty night and the drive back from the station cleared his head. He just needed to unearth some more information before he spoke to Iain Small again. As he bent over to padlock the bike to a lamppost he was aware of a figure in the shadows across the road and recognised Steve emerging into the yellow light.

'Hi Fred, can I have a word?'

Chapter 7

The desk in front of Mills was covered in the results of the chemical analyses of soil from the ditch and the tissue of the hand. Sam had worked really fast and she now had all the figures to work on. First she made sure that she had all the tables of data on her computer and then she compiled them into one enormous spreadsheet so she could plot graphs showing the values for any particular metal. Her idea was to somehow come up with a relationship between the hand and the soil it had been buried in. It wouldn't necessarily tell her anything about the hand's origin but it might show how long it had lain there or if it had been moved at any time.

She plotted some very nice diagrams to show how the concentrations of some metals changed with the acidity of the soil. That was to be expected. The peat had turned out to be very acidic at the depth where the hand was found and Mills felt that explained the deterioration of the bones, leaving the skin untouched.

She looked for the presence of certain metals that were found in pigments like woad used on the body as decoration, including copper and nickel. After two days poring over the results, she came to the conclusion that there was nothing outstanding she could report. There was no decoration on the skin of the hand and no particularly high concentrations of elements she would expect in a mining area, for example.

'…in fact nothing out of the ordinary at all,' she told Nige and Nina as they ate their fish and chips watching television.

'Never mind. You can have a break over the weekend,' said Nina.

'Yes, down a nice hole in the ground,' laughed Nige.

'I think it's a lovely idea. I wish I could try it.'

'One day,' promised Nige. 'In fact I solemnly swear that as soon as you are out of that chair I will arrange for you to go down a hole in the ground.'

'I don't know why you're so derogatory about potholes, love. Don't you have them in Wales?'

'Yes, they're called coalmines.'

'You know Mills, I'm looking forward to my day out tomorrow. After we've dropped you off Nige is going to take me to Skipton. I'm really looking forward to getting out in the countryside.'

'You'd better make the most of it, love, because that'll be it once you start on those files.'

Nina laughed. 'Mills, you should see the pile of work I've been sent! They plan to keep me busy!'

'What sort of work?' asked Mills.

'It's number crunching mainly. There are a lot of crime statistics and geographical information. You know the sort of thing – where are most crimes carried out and typically by whom.'

'Still, it must be nice to have something to do again,' said Mills.

'Oh yes, it beats doing the ironing that's for sure.'

'There's the farm where the hand was found.' Mills pointed to the right as they drove towards the viaduct. 'You can just make out the ditch at the top above the farmhouse.'

'Can't really disturb them I suppose,' said Nige. 'Not at the weekend.'

'Certainly not,' said Nina. 'Today is a holiday for all of us.'

Fred had suggested that they met him at the Hill Inn just two miles further down the road towards Ingleton. He was leaning against his motorbike, watching the car as they pulled up.

'Should I get out?' asked Nige.

'No,' said Mills, too quickly. 'It's OK, really. I'll ring you to arrange when we should meet up again. Is that all right?'

'Whenever you're ready. There's no rush.' Nina smiled conspiratorially. 'Have fun.'

Mills waved as they pulled back onto the road and then walked over to Fred. She felt ridiculously bulky in her thick clothes and waterproofs but she had read that it was important to keep warm and dry. She had worn boots but she noticed that Fred had wellingtons on. He was winding some rope and heaved it off his shoulder as she approached.

'Hi there.' She noticed that his teeth were very straight and white.

'Hi.'

'We've got to walk a short way, only about a mile. Would you mind carrying this?' He handed her a wire ladder which was not too heavy but rather cumbersome. He could see she was struggling and offered to take it from her again. Mills did not want to appear incapable and persisted, shifting it from one side to the other as it slipped from her grasp.

'Best put this on now. It saves carrying it.' He put a heavy helmet, complete with lamp, on her head. Picking up the ropes and a large canvas bag he set off and Mills followed. They made slow progress and she was too preoccupied with her load to make conversation. Fred described what they would see and do once they reached the cave and Mills began to wonder if she should have accepted his offer in the first place.

'It's a very straightforward approach,' he said. 'Easy to get into. There's a horizontal passage where you'll need to slide along the top of a ledge but it's not difficult.'

'What are the ropes and ladder for?'

'I thought I'd bring them so you could practise with them. It would mean you could try somewhere more interesting, maybe? I've been asked to help with some novices at Runscar tomorrow and I thought you might like to come?'

'Hmm.' Mills marched on up the track without responding.

'Here we are, just to the right.'

Mills couldn't see anything but Fred led her over to the cave mouth. It was wide and dark.

'Will there be anyone else down there?'

'I doubt it. No-one listed from my club that's for sure.' He dropped the ropes and delved into the bag, pulling out a red waterproof suit.

'This should fit you. It belonged to someone pretty much your size. Except she's taller.'

Without asking who it had belonged to, Mills struggled into the suit, nearly falling over in the attempt. Fred stood watching until finally he moved over and helped her force the legs past her boots.

'Thank you.'

He tied a heavy belt round her middle. 'You're beginning to look quite the part,' he said, switching on her lamp. He threw the rope and ladder in front of him and began to move inside the cave. Mills rushed forward, not wishing to be left behind.

'It's OK, I'll just put these down and then I'll come back for you.'

Mills stood looking up at Ingleborough. The flat top was covered in snow. Turning, she could see Whernside in the distance. There was not a sound.

'Are you ready then?' Fred had re-appeared and was offering her a hand. Her experience was about to begin.

Her first impression was the smell; the damp, chalky odour. It was not unpleasant but it was strange and a little unnerving. She had expected it to be dark but it took her by surprise and it was some time before she could see anything by the light of the lamp on her helmet. She was worried that she would feel claustrophobic but the flow of air prevented the penetrating darkness from overpowering her. She concentrated on what Fred was telling her and attempted to follow his instructions. Her legs were shaking a little and she trod warily, fearing that she would slip on the wet rock. As they moved slowly underground she could hear the sound of rushing water and began to anticipate the moment when she might have to duck under an icy stream.

They reached the ledge that he had described to her and she allowed herself to relax sufficiently to lie on her stomach on the ledge and wriggle herself forward until she reached an inner chamber. Down in the lower chamber were stalactites and stalagmites forming intricate patterns on the walls and ceiling of the cave. In stages Mills lost her fear of what she might have to negotiate and learnt to enjoy what she was able to see by coming underground. Fred pointed out features without using words and Mills was reminded of a film she had seen on television of scuba divers exploring the deep sea. Further on was the stream that she had been hearing as they progressed along the cave. It was falling from a fissure in the wall and splashed around the small inner chamber. Fred explained that after rain it could become quite a large pool. He pointed to a small opening that Mills was sure she would not be able to squeeze through. He went first to show her how easy it was and she followed, surprised that she could force herself through. Finally they were at a wall with no further spaces; they had reached the end of the accessible parts of the cave.

Mills was disappointed and insisted they sat for a while for her to absorb the atmosphere.

'I can turn the lamps off if you like,' he offered. 'You can see how dark it is.'

'No, please don't.' She was serious. That really would freak her out.

They travelled back as slowly as they had come but stopped in the larger chamber for Fred to show her how they would use the rope and ladder in a more difficult run. Mills found it surprisingly difficult to climb the wire ladder and felt more confident on the ropes since she had enjoyed abseiling at school. She had no sense of time at all and was surprised when Fred told her it was already four o'clock and would be getting dark outside. They packed up and carried everything back to the surface, where it was dusk and freezing outside. By the time they were back at the pub Mills was shuddering with cold and Fred suggested a hot drink.

Back in the bright lights the conversation was stilted until Mills asked Fred what he was doing in the Dales. He told her about his degree and his job at the Ingleton Mercury. Soon he was back on his favourite subject: caving.

'So are you going to come to Runscar tomorrow?'

'I don't know.' She did want to see him again.

'You're not nervous are you – I mean you did really well today.'

'It's not that. I need a lift down here unless I can borrow the car.'

'I understand.' Fred didn't sound convinced.

The pub was warm and they sat chatting for an hour until Nige appeared at the door. Mills introduced the two men awkwardly.

'Would you like a drink?' asked Fred, standing up.

'No, 'fraid not. Nina's got really cold and I think we should get back. Did you have a good time Mills?'

'Yes it was brilliant. Fred was asking if I could come back tomorrow but…'

'There's no way Nina will be going out again.'

'Oh.'

'No, I mean we won't need the car. By all means use it tomorrow.'

'Thanks Nige.' Mills knew he would need it to go shopping in the morning. 'I'll just borrow it for the afternoon then.' Fred seemed disappointed. 'Honestly, that will be quite enough excitement for me.'

They left him finishing his drink and Mills fell into the back seat.

'Had a good time?' asked Nina.

'Yes, it was good but I am tired.'

'So are we,' said Nige. 'Nina had me pushing her all round the town and then off to the pub for lunch and then along the river. At this time of year! It was freezing!'

'Yes, it was bit silly. My legs are really cold now. We must bring a blanket next time.'

'It's much warmer going into a cave,' yawned Mills. She could hardly keep her eyes open and the motion of the car soon caused her to doze, waking only when they arrived back at Priory Road.

Mills had not allowed sufficient time for the drive and she was late. She had sent Fred a quick text first thing that morning to say she would be there at about two o'clock. He had replied, indicating that he couldn't wait to see her again. It was already twenty past and she had several miles to go. She was going too fast towards a narrow bridge that crossed a beck, only stopping in time to avoid a line of cars coming the other way, including an orange camper van. She couldn't see the driver but it wouldn't be odd for Lang to be in the area. As the viaduct came into view she expected to see Fred waiting anxiously by the roadside. She stopped the car, checking her mobile, but there was no signal. There was a Land Rover parked under the arches of the viaduct. That's where he'll be, she thought and set off down the track. There were several figures dressed in waterproof suits and helmets wandering about on the moorland but they all looked too tall to be Fred. As she approached the vehicle she could read the lettering on the side; it was the local cave rescue team. Someone was leaning into the passenger window talking to the driver. Mills, unsure what to do, continued up the track until she was well away from the Land Rover but could watch the figures moving across the moor.

She couldn't do anything but stand with the weak winter sun warming her. It might not even be the cave or Fred's group, so she waited and watched. Cavers came and went. It was now three o'clock and still no sign of Fred so she was sure that he must be involved. One of the novice cavers had probably got into difficulties and he was helping. The logical thing would be to ask, so she went over to the Land Rover.

'Excuse me.' The driver looked round but now she could see that he was listening to a two-way radio. She waited until he had finished, unable to make any sense of the one-sided conversation.

'Can I help you?' he said patiently.

'I wondered whether you knew if my friend is all right. He's caving round here.'

'I can't discuss what's going on but there is an incident in Runscar.'

There was a crackle and a voice was repeating a call sign.

'Excuse me.' He turned and spoke into the radio.

Embarrassed, Mills withdrew and stood watching from her vantage point under the viaduct arch. An ambulance arrived just before four o'clock. It didn't come racing down the road with lights flashing; it just appeared like any other vehicle and drove slowly up the track, stopping by the Land Rover. She thought that things would start happening but still there was no movement except the occasional caver walking across the moor to the vehicle or down the track to the pub. Finally, the ambulance crew appeared from their vehicle and disappeared into the dusk. Unable to wait any longer, Mills retraced her tracks to the Station Inn and went inside, hoping that she would find Fred, sipping a pint.

There was a sombre atmosphere. Three men dressed in waterproofs were sitting at a table, shoulders drooped. One of them was leaning his elbows on the table, his head in his hands. Mills turned and left the bar. Outside it was dark and only a couple of vehicles remained in the car park. She climbed into the car and tried her mobile but there was still no signal.

The road was black and empty. As soon as she got a signal she tried his number again and again but there was no response. It didn't mean anything – he was probably still busy with whatever had happened. She was so bewildered that she couldn't explain it properly to Nina and Nige when they asked if she had had a good day.

'No, I… I didn't go into the cave; there was an accident or something going on. Ambulances and stuff.'

'Is Fred OK?' asked Nige.

'I don't know. I suppose so. I can't get hold of him.'

Nina wheeled herself over to where Mills was sitting.

'I'm sure it will be fine. He'll probably ring later.'

She sent Mills off for a hot bath and had supper ready when she re-appeared. They ate in silence and drank more wine than was usual. Mills went off to bed early, hoping that sleep would put a stop to the empty feeling she was experiencing. He could have rung, she thought, she only wanted to know that he was safe. But her mind was still active and at one-thirty she quietly switched on a lamp to locate her laptop, she needed to immerse herself in work now. By the time she was sufficiently exhausted to sleep, she had e-mailed a message to Oxford asking if they had any results for her yet; sent a description of her progress to her supervisor in Tennessee asking for advice, and contacted Terry Lang to say that she would not spend any longer than necessary on the project. She wasn't sure she would have anything to keep her in the Dales now.

Nina had been upbeat at breakfast and Nige chatted about his work on the way to the university. In the light of morning the previous day's events seemed strangely unreal and Mills was left feeling perturbed, unable to settle to anything constructive. Staring at her computer screen, she finally made the decision to find out what had happened. The only connection she had for Fred was through the newspaper he worked on. She checked the website for the Mercury and found a number for the editor.

'Mike speaking, how can I help you?'

'Is that the editor of the Ingleton Mercury?'

'The Sub-Editor,' he corrected her.

'I hope you don't mind. I'm a friend of Fred's.'

'I'm sorry love but he's not in yet'

'It's OK… I know… I thought he might have been involved in the caving accident yesterday. It's just that I don't know his address or anything but I wanted to…'

'To be honest love I don't know about any accident. I guess I'll hear if something's happened to him.'

Mills knew she sounded disappointed.

'Look I'm sure he's all right but give me your number and when he comes in I'll get him to give you a call. How's that?'

She thanked him and put down the phone. His cheerful manner was infectious and she began to feel more confident that Fred was actually fine and would call her soon.

She made coffee and turned back to checking her e-mails, eagerly opening a reply from the Oxford carbon-dating lab. It was quite a long message and she re-read it several times before printing it out. The results were disappointing, they said. The carbon-14 provided values that were not precise in this case; in fact the date on the hand was anywhere from 1800 to 1950. It seemed that the tissue was affected by the carbon in the peat that had interacted with the tissue.

She rang Oxford and spoke to the scientist who had sent the results. He re-iterated what she had learned from the e-mail, that the dates were a mixture of the carbon from the peat and from the hand.

'But does that mean that the hand is quite recent? Could it be less than one hundred years old?'

'Difficult to say. What we can be sure of is that it is earlier than nineteen-fifty-seven.'

'How can you know that?'

'Because of the bomb tests. From nineteen-fifty-seven onwards the figures look completely different, it would show up like a sore thumb – excuse the pun.'

When she put the phone down Mills was nonplussed. She had been expecting to hear that her find was from the first or second century AD; it was a shock to learn that it was actually only a hundred or so years old. She immediately began to wonder if the hand came not from Iron Age or Viking settlers but the more recent encampment at Batty Green, the navvy camp. It was, after all, the only major activity in the area over the last two hundred years.

She spent the rest of the day researching the history of the railway at Ribblehead, including the building of the viaduct and excavation of the tunnel across Blea Moor. She was excited to discover a newspaper article of the time which described conditions at the camp. It clearly was an extraordinary place – a town out on the moor with shops and pubs. Women and children lived with their men while they carried out the heavy work digging and laying the track. Conditions were harsh and trouble often broke out between the men, fuelled by alcohol. There had been a fight between the English and Irish navvies in 1870 which result in the Irishmen fleeing into the hills. Was it possible that the farmer had stumbled across the body of one of these men? She was by no means an expert but the hand was large by normal standards and had marks and scars that suggested it could have belonged to a working man.

When Nige came into the office she was still making notes on her computer.

'You're working in the dark here,' he said, switching on the light.

'Sorry, got a bit carried away,' she said, grinning.

Nige frowned and suggested they got back. Mills assumed that he was concerned about Nina and gathered her papers together, stuffing them into her large leather bag. For once, he didn't turn on his country and western music so they sat in silence during the short drive home. The streets were busy with commuters and late night shoppers so the journey took longer than usual. Mills spent every minute of it wondering what she had done to upset him.

Nina had the same concerned look when they eventually arrived back and Mills went to take her bags up to her room in case they wanted to speak privately. But when she went back down they were both sitting waiting for her.

Nina motioned her to sit on the sofa.

'I don't suppose you have had any news today?' she said.

'News? Oh you mean about Fred?'

'Yes.'

'No I haven't. I rang the newspaper where he…'

Nina wheeled herself over and took Mills hand.

'I spoke to the station today to find out what happened down there yesterday.'

'You did?'

'Yes. There *was* an accident at Runscar yesterday.'

Mills pulled her hand away and covered her mouth. She couldn't speak.

'It was a fatal accident to one of the cavers.' Nina spoke slowly and gently.

They must be trained to do this in the police, Mills thought.

'I asked for the name of the victim.' Nina paused and Mills waited.

'The name was Trevor…'

Mills let out an involuntary sound of relief.

Nina gripped her other hand. 'Wait.' She spoke slowly. 'Trevor Frederick Coulter.'

'So we don't know. It might not be…'

'I'm sorry, Mills. They told me that he was known to his friends as Fred. I wanted to be certain before I told you.'

Chapter 8

Mike went into the office to finish off his front page article. So far he had gleaned little information about the death of the young man that he knew so little about. He had interviewed three of his caving companions but only one had actually been at the scene. His name was Steve and he had found Fred's body lying face down in a couple of feet of water. He had attempted to revive him and the other two had tried when he called for their help but it was no use. *On Sunday, in freezing conditions, a young man lost his life to the inhospitable world below ground. The caving community is mourning the loss of Fred Coulter, 25, a quiet graduate in media studies who made a name for himself as a promising young reporter on this paper. Steve Bellamy from Ingleton was first on the scene and attempted to revive him but despite additional assistance from his club mates he did not regain consciousness.*

He had spoken to the cave rescue crew who were on duty that day and got a quote about the conditions down in the cave. They were not out of the ordinary and the nature of the drowning was a surprise to them. *The brave men of the cave rescue team hurried to the scene and attempted to revive the lad unsuccessfully. By the time the ambulance arrived they had already begun to bring the body to the surface. He was taken to hospital and pronounced dead on arrival.*

He filled in the rest of the column with details of other tragedies in the caves around Ingleton. He had a photograph of Fred in the newspaper archives. It was taken at a Christmas charity do and he was smiling, glass in hand. He was dressed in a dinner jacket and looked older than he usually did. Mike had a lump in his throat as he completed the headline: Young reporter dies in caving accident.

He was interrupted by a sound. On the landing an elderly lady was peering through the glass into his office.

He went across and opened the door.

'Can I help you, madam?'

The woman pulled off her woolly hat and fumbled with the band that was holding her frizzy white hair in a wild pony tail.

'I've come to see Fred. Is he here?'

The editor was extremely uncomfortable. The woman was standing in the middle of the office, refusing to take a seat. She struggled out of her coat and let it fall to the floor.

'I've come all the way from Kirkbymoorside to see him and I'm not leaving until I have. Where is he?'

'May I offer you a cup of tea or coffee?' he suggested.

'Not until I've seen him.'

'I'm afraid he's not… available.' He was not going to discuss his young reporter with this distressed woman without getting to the bottom of why she was here. He was apprehensive that she had something to do with Fred's wild goose chase over the missing person. 'Perhaps you could tell me what it's about?'

'It's personal.'

'Not concerning his work?'

'Well I don't know. It could be.' She had a firm expression. 'But I'm not being fobbed off with anyone else.'

'Take a seat, Mrs, Miss…'

'Maggie, everyone calls me Maggie.' She had quietened down a little, accepting the chair that Mike pushed towards her.

'Now, Maggie, is it tea or coffee?'

He returned with a mug of tea, milk and two sugars. She accepted a biscuit, admitting that she'd set out early that morning on account of her not being used to driving such long distances. Mike was used to putting people at ease and he let the woman chatter on about her car and her dog until she had calmed down sufficiently for him to ask her again why she was there.

'I have come here because Fred is not answering his phone or returning my e-mails and I don't know where he lives. He told me he worked here and so I rang but I couldn't get any sense from your lot on the phone so I have come all the way here to find out what's going on.' She paused to take a sip from her mug. 'And I was frankly worried after he told me he was going to meet Iain Small.'

'Now, Maggie. It all made sense until the last bit. Who is Iain Small?'

'James Small's brother of course. The big story Fred was working on.'

'The story being…?'

'The missing boy: James Small. Poor boy with Down's Syndrome.' She finished her tea and placed the mug carefully on the desk in front of her. 'I helped him find the brother, through our website.'

Mike sighed. 'I'm afraid that was a story that he was following entirely as a personal thing. His job was to cover sport and other topics but not missing persons.'

The woman went to speak but Mike held up a hand. 'Look Maggie, I'm sorry but Fred died in an accident on Sunday.'

He sat quietly while she digested the news. At first she looked puzzled, then angry and then as if she would start crying.

'I told him to be careful. I knew it would be dangerous. You see I checked up on that Iain Small afterwards so I knew he'd be trouble.'

He waited while she wiped her eyes with a tissue.

'If there's anything I can help with…?'

'Do you know when the funeral is?'

'Not yet no, I'm sorry I don't.'

'In that case I'll make my own enquiries.'

'If you do find out, please let me know. There was another lady enquiring…'

'Oh yes? Who was that?'

'A friend I think she said. I've got her number here. Perhaps you would pass on the information to her?'

He wrote the number down and handed her the paper.

She gathered her coat and hat, picked up her bag and pulled on her hat and looked at him intensely.

'Have a safe journey back to Kirkbymoorside, Maggie.'

'Oh I'm not driving all that way again so soon. I'm staying at the caravan site just down on the Settle road.'

Mike read through his article, correcting a few typos and then closed the file. He shut down the computer and turned off the lights. The rest could wait until tomorrow.

It was difficult for Mills to visit Batty Green without recalling the sight of the cave rescue vehicle and the ambulance. The place was deserted and she stood for a while under the arch of the viaduct thinking about Fred. The wind was so cold it was impossible to remain stationary for long so she turned her attention to the archaeology. There was a plaque to remind visitors that it had been an important historical site and should be treated with respect but there was nothing to see and she had to use her imagination to envisage the atmosphere as it would have been in the 1870s. Below the moor grass there must be so many artefacts from that period. Hundreds of people had lived and worked here. It was a small town with pubs and shops. Not just men working here but women and children. Babies had been born and died here. There must be some clues that could lead her to find out the origin of the hand.

She had read that many of the people from Batty Green had been buried in the churchyard at Chapel le Dale. Returning to the car, she drove down the Ingleton road for a couple of miles past the Hill Inn where she had last seen Fred and then turned right down the lane to the church. It was quiet and warm in the tiny churchyard as she stepped between the tombstones. She soon found that the navvies and their families did not have marked individual graves but she came across a plaque put up by the schoolchildren of the village to commemorate all of the people who died at Batty Green. She remained there for sometime, thinking about what might have been if Fred had not gone caving that morning, wondering whether it would have made any difference if she had met him in the morning instead of waiting until the afternoon.

Shivering with cold she climbed into the car and turned, not left which would have taken her back to a warm fire but right, towards Ingleton. It was her plan to visit the Mercury office to find out if there was any information about Fred's funeral. She was directed through the baker's and upstairs but the door was locked and no-one knew if the editor was due back.

As she headed back to the car park her mobile rang. She didn't recognise the number and answered with a cautious "hello".

'My name is Maggie Thomas and I got your number from the editor of the Ingleton Mercury. You don't know me but I was helping Fred find a missing person.'

'You do know that he is dead?' The words sounded peculiar.

'Yes I do and I'm so upset about it. I just knew something would go wrong. Did you know he was seeing this Iain Small on Friday?'

'No.'

'Well, what I want to know is what he said to him and whether he was any closer to finding out about that poor young boy with Down's Syndrome.'

The woman was making very little sense and seemed to be slightly hysterical but she was the first person Mills had spoken to who wanted to talk about Fred.

'Where do you live?' Mills asked.

Half an hour later she had found the caravan site on the outskirts of Ingleton, just as the woman had described it. It wasn't difficult to find the right caravan – it was the only one with a car outside and probably the only one occupied at that time of year. The door flew open and a woman of perhaps sixty, maybe seventy, appeared with a small white dog at her heels. Mills felt immediately at home with her and soon she was in the warm, feeding biscuits to

Snowy while her hostess made a pot of tea. She told Maggie everything she knew about Fred's death, without mentioning that her source was a policewoman. Maggie explained how she met Fred at the post office in Kirkbymoorside, or Kirkby as she referred to it.

'So what was it that Fred was trying to find out?' asked Mills.

'He was trying to trace a missing person from way back in 1955. A poor Down's Syndrome boy who had disappeared one morning from his home somewhere up in this direction.'

She went on to explain how Fred had placed a question on the genealogy forum and received a reply from the boy's brother.

'He told me he was meeting this Iain Small on Friday in Leeds so I've been waiting to hear the outcome.' She pulled out a handkerchief. 'I told him to be careful and what happens? He meets this man and then he's dead.'

'But he died in a caving accident, Maggie.' Mills was confused by the woman's accusations. 'There's no connection between the two things.'

'I wouldn't put anything past that man. I made it my job to find out about him once he replied to Fred's message. My friend who has lived in Kirkby all his life says he was a teddy boy. He says Iain Small was not a pleasant man.'

'What do you mean?'

'Some say he was responsible for an arson attack. That's why he left in such a hurry,' Maggie said and sipped her tea.

In an attempt to steer the conversation back to the purpose of her visit, Mills asked whether Maggie knew of any funeral arrangements.

'My dear, I hardly know the young man. I don't know his family. I thought *you* would. It's why I called, partly. You see I don't know what to do now.'

'What do you mean?'

'About this Iain Small. You see I've arranged to meet him but I'm not sure that I should now. Do you think I should speak to the police?' The woman was stroking her dog and looking anxiously at Mills, who was at a loss.

'Perhaps it would be best,' she replied. 'Before you meet him. See what they say, eh?'

'Yes, you're probably right. I'll do that.'

Mills sensed that the woman was disappointed by her response.

'I have a friend in the police force,' she offered. 'Shall I ask her advice for you?'

She beamed. 'Oh, if you would, that would be lovely. I knew I could depend on you for help as soon as I saw you.'

They parted with a hug and Mills promised to get in touch with her new friend as soon as she had spoken to Nina.

She drove back, deep in thought about what Maggie had been telling her but as she passed the viaduct at Ribblehad she swung the car off the road and up the track towards Long Witton farm. She had promised Sheila that she would keep her up to date with her progress on the hand, she told herself. However, she also had a strong desire to stand in their kitchen and, just for a short time, absorb the comfortable atmosphere of their family life.

She was not disappointed. Sheila's hands were covered in flour when she opened the door and Kate was playing with Richard on the floor.

'Come in. We're in a bit of a mess. I hope you don't mind.'

Mills didn't mind. It was just as she wanted it to be. She explained why she had called and told them how the age of the hand was not entirely clear.

'We think it dates from the nineteenth century but it could be a bit later.'

'Later?' Sheila looked worried.

'They're sure it's before nineteen-fifty-seven but the exact date is rather difficult to pinpoint.'

'Dad said if it's in the last hundred years we have to call the police.' The girl was standing up now with her arms folded.

Kate was right, of course. Mills had been so preoccupied she had overlooked the importance of the dates.

'Yes you are correct, Kate.' She was thinking on her feet. 'But I've been considering the possibilities and I believe it is most likely that the… artefact may have come from the camp at Batty Green in the 1870s. What do think?' Mills knew that Kate was familiar with the site from school and they were soon discussing life at the settlement. It was only when Brian appeared from the yard that Mills realised that it had grown dark outside.

'Do you have some news?' he asked, washing his hands at the sink.

'She's got the results of the carbon-dating,' said Kate. 'She thinks it might be a railway man.'

'It could date from the eighteen-seventies,' Mills explained, standing up. 'Anyway I must be going, it's late.'

'It was good of you to come and tell us,' said Sheila, opening the door for her and following her into the yard. 'Brian will be pleased if it means he can get on.'

Mills nodded and waved goodbye, conscious she had some catching up to do with the police.

'We were getting anxious,' said Nina when Mills finally reached the house.

Nige was busy putting coal on the fire and Nina was stretched out on the sofa.

'Are you all right?' Mills asked.

'Yes, just tired. Nige is doing dinner tonight.'

'She's been overdoing it as usual,' Nige banged the bucket down, rattled the coals with the poker and disappeared into the kitchen.

'Nonsense. I just made a few phone calls and did some searching on the web. Anyway, what have you been up to?'

She told Nina about her trip to Batty Green and the churchyard in Chapel le Dale. Then she voiced the question she had been waiting to ask.

'Did you hear any more about Fred?'

'I did.' Her face became serious.

'And?'

'Look, I shouldn't really be telling you this now but the report said that he died as a result of a blow to his head. There was a possibility that he had drowned after falling but they say that he was dead before his face went into the water. Accidental death they are saying. Of course there will be an inquest in due course.'

'But how did it happen? Did anyone see?'

'Apparently everyone was spread out as they moved along and Fred was bringing up the rear. It was only when they realised he hadn't joined them in the final chamber that they sent someone back to find him.'

'Who was that?'

'A man called Steve. He found Fred and called for help.'

Mills could feel the tears rolling down her face and stuck out her tongue to catch them as they reached the corners of her mouth. 'Was he still alive then?'

'It's not clear from the report. This Steve seems a bit confused about the order of events. I expect they'll talk to him again to clarify his statement.'

Nige came to tell them that supper was ready and stopped abruptly.

'It's OK, Nige. I'm fine. Really.' Mills wheeled Nina's chair over to the sofa and helped her into it.

While they ate, Mills told Nige about the ambiguity on the carbon-dating results that had come back from Oxford.

'Oh my God,' exclaimed Nina. 'Does that mean we have an investigation on our hands?'

'Not really,' said Nige. 'It's not on your patch for a start.'

'Not true – it all comes under Western Area.'

'And,' he continued, ignoring his wife, 'it may still be more than a hundred years old.'

'That is true,' Nina agreed.

Mills explained her theory that the owner of the hand probably came from the encampment at Batty Green.

'Still, I guess you will still have to report the age issue to Newby Wiske. Do you want me to let them know?'

'Yes, thanks.' Mills could see that Nina was eager to use her connections to help out. Nige grinned across the table at her.

'Keep her occupied, otherwise she gets unbearable!' He emphasised each of the four syllables, his Welsh accent stronger than ever.

'What will the police do?' Mills asked.

'They'll want to look at the dating report and see if there is anyone reported missing within the timescale I expect.'

Nige told them to settle back down in front of the fire while he cleared the dishes. Once Nina was comfortable on the sofa, Mills knelt down beside her.

'Did you happen to hear anything about a funeral, Nina?'

'Oh Mills, I did have a look for his family's whereabouts but his parents are separated and it's difficult. His mother is based down South and his father lives abroad. I couldn't have written down addresses, it wouldn't have looked right.'

'I know. And it isn't as if I was even a proper friend of his. After all I only knew him a few days.'

She went up to bed early, stopping in the hallway to extract from her coat pocket the piece of paper with Maggie's phone number on. The woman answered after just two rings, her voice sounded strained. Mills told her the little she knew about Fred's death and had to admit that it wasn't very much.

'Did you tell your friend about Iain Small?' she asked.

'Er, yes I mentioned it to her,' she lied.

'And what did she say?'

'That you shouldn't worry about it,' Mills replied, wishing she'd remembered to ask Nina about it.

'Typical of the police, that is.'

'No really. She felt that you shouldn't put yourself in any danger.'

'Well in that case I'll report it myself. I can't sit here worrying about it and doing nowt.'

'Are you still in Ingleton?' Mills asked, visualising the diminutive figure seated with her dog, alone on the caravan site.

'I am. I want to get to the bottom of this. I'm going to the police station in Ingleton tomorrow and I'll call you to let you know what they say.'

'There's someone to see you.' The departmental secretary was peering round the door of the laboratory. 'She's in the meeting room.'

Mills removed her gloves, pulling at the fastening of her lab coat. She washed her hands and ran along the corridor. She could see the visitor through the glass in the door. She was tall woman with neatly bobbed hair, dressed in a grey trouser suit. She was staring out of the window and turned round when she heard the door open.

'Dr Sanderson?' she asked.

Mills estimated that they were about the same age.

'Not yet. Just call me Mills.'

'I'm DC Fuller. I've been sent to have a word with you about the hand you found?'

'Well, I didn't exactly find it…'

'But it is in your possession now I believe?'

The secretary came in with a tray of coffee and placed it on the table between them, disappearing again without a word.

'Yes, it is.'

They sat down and Mills handed the DC a mug. She explained how the hand had been found and the involvement of Terry Lang.

'But I'm responsible for it now. I've got all the paperwork with the results of the carbon-dating. Do you want me to fetch it for you?'

'It would be useful to have a copy of what you have but we're not the experts and so we will be relying on you to guide us regarding what it all means.' She took a sip of coffee and Mills waited. 'You have the article stored carefully on the premises?'

'Yes. It's in our 'fridge.'

'We may need to retrieve it if the coroner requires it but for now it is probably safer here. I suppose what I really need to know is the most probable age for the hand. As you know, we only investigate bodies from the last hundred years.'

'From an archaeological point of view, the fact that there were no bones suggests that the remains were very old, Iron Age probably, but the carbon-dating makes it more recent. But there is a problem because the skin could have interacted with the peat and soil in the ditch, which messes it all up. To be honest I still think it's a lot older.'

The policewoman made some notes.

'What will happen now?' Mills asked.

'I'm not sure. They may decide to search the area for other body parts. If there are none then the case will probably be considered closed.'

Mills showed her visitor out and went to find Terry Lang. It was definitely the time for him to take an interest in the project again. He was in the staff kitchen, making coffee.

'Hi! Want some?'

'No thank you.'

'So… How are things?'

'Can we go to your office? I want to update you on what has been happening…since you haven't been around much.'

'Yes. Sure.' He sounded puzzled and Mills was pleased.

With a feeling of superiority, she spent the next half hour telling him what she had learned from Oxford. She was hoping he would be able to suggest some explanation for the strange results but, as usual, he sat and listened without comment.

'Excellent,' he said when she had finished.

She didn't want 'excellent', she wanted a conversation, a scientific discussion, a contribution from the man who was supposed to be some sort of genius.

'So, what do you suggest?'

'Keep up the good work?' He was fidgeting, as if he had another appointment and was late.

'Anyway,' Mills concluded, 'you saw my e-mail. As soon as this is sorted I will be going back to Manchester.'

'You will?'

'Yes. I have to be back before my supervisor returns. There will be nothing to keep me here once the final results are in.'

'But you'll deal with any police enquiries?'

'I can do.'

Exasperated, she stood up and made for the door. The man appeared to be completely uninterested in the project and she couldn't understand why. Pausing for a second before turning round to face him again, she asked the question she wanted to ask.

'I was wondering,' she began, 'whether you heard about the accident in Runscar cave?'

'Runscar?' He looked puzzled.

'Sorry, I just thought… knowing you go caving… I thought you might have heard something.'

She turned to open the door.

'I ought to have done,' he said. 'What was it?'

'Someone died. I just thought… you know…'

'When was that?' His voice sounded distant behind her.

'Sunday. I thought you might know what happened.'

She could sense him coming towards her, placing his hand gently on her shoulder.

'Was it someone you knew?' he asked tenderly.

'Yes,' she sobbed. 'Sorry, I have to go.'

She heard Lang calling after her as she ran from the room and locked herself in the ladies' toilet. Irritation replaced grief when she recalled the scene in Terry Lang's office; frustration with herself for making such a scene and with him for being so nice. What had he called to her? *Any time you want to talk, my door is always open.* It was all very well being cynical, she told herself, but he did actually sound as if he meant it.

Nina almost pulled Mills indoors when they arrived back at the end of the day. Nige shrugged and went straight into the kitchen to start the supper.

'Come and sit down. I must talk to you. I spoke to my colleagues about missing persons…'

'And?' Mills was removing her coat and scarf.

'They sent me some information and I started going through it but this afternoon I got a call from the station because someone had been in today to ask specifically about an old case.'

'Don't tell me…' She went to hang her coat up.

'Wait. It concerns a boy with something.' Nina was sorting through a file of papers. 'Now what was it?'

'Down's Syndrome?'

'What? Yes. But how did you know that?'

'Because the person who reported it told me about it. I was supposed to ask for your advice but I forgot.' She was waiting to go upstairs.

'Well, the reason they sent it to me was because the boy went missing from a farm very close to where the hand was found. They figured it could be connected.'

'Seriously?' Now Mills was listening.

'I looked it up. The farms are only about a mile apart. The boy disappeared from home in nineteen-fifty-five, which fits in with your dates, and he was never seen again.'

'Wow.' Mills sat on the sofa. 'That's an amazing coincidence. Maggie wouldn't have known about the hand.'

'Who is Maggie?' asked Nina, opening a file.

'The woman I told you about. She said she was going to the police in Ingleton today. She seems a bit mad but she was just worried about Fred.'

Nina stared at her in bewilderment. 'It wasn't a woman who reported the boy missing. It was his brother. And I've just arranged to go in and meet him.'

Chapter 9

Sheila grabbed Brian's arm as he ushered his parents into the kitchen through the back door, and waited until they were in the next room with the children before speaking to him quietly.

'Two policemen called this afternoon while Grandad was asleep.'

'What did they want?'

'To let us know that they are investigating a boy who went missing in the fifties.'

'It's not about that bloody hand?'

'Yes.' She sighed. 'They said that they might be coming to look for further evidence.'

'What do they mean, evidence?'

'Shh!' She looked anxiously at the door. 'You know... other bits of the body.'

'Oh God! Is there no end to it?'

'They say he lived round here. Do you know who they mean?'

'No I don't but Dad will - or Grandad.'

Bill was sitting with Kate, looking at her schoolwork.

'She's a clever one this young lass, Brian.'

'Takes after me, Dad. Have you got a minute?'

He waited until they were in the study.

'Nineteen-fifties you say?' He stared into the distance and Brian noticed how much older his father was looking these days. He had lost weight and there were bags under his eyes.

'Now I come to think of it, there was a lad. He weren't all there, childish like. Acted young for his age. I think… yes, I reckon he lived down at Kilrigg farm. There were two boys.'

'And he went missing?'

'I don't rightly know.'

'Would Grandad know?'

'Oh aye, he'd remember summat like that.'

There wasn't a chance to talk to him until they'd all had tea. The women were washing up and the children were helping Bill build a bridge made of Lego.

'I remember,' Grandad said. 'There were a young mongol lad down at Kilrigg farm. Old Small lived there then. Yes, he had him and another lad. He were retarded they called it then. Wandered off and were never seen again. At first they reckoned he must have fallen down a hole somewhere hereabouts and we all helped search for him but it were useless. In the end it were assumed he'd been taken off by Gypsies.'

'Travellers?'

'It happened in early summer, just before the horse fair in Appleby. Loads of them coming through here then. The police never found anyone like but round here they were pretty sure he'd been picked up by them.'

'Stolen by the Gypsies? Sounds like a tall tale to me. Why would they do that?'

'Who knows, lad, who knows. There's folks around now, them paedophile rings. Maybe there were summat like that then.' He was affected by a bout of coughing that left him wheezing and exhausted.

'I think it's time to be going,' announced Mary, gathering up her belongings and indicating to her husband and father-in-law that they should be off. The children hugged them and stood by the door waving as the headlights disappeared down the track.

'Did you find out who it was?' Sheila whispered.

'Aye, some young'un at Kilrigg farm.'

'So what will they do now I wonder?' she asked.

Brian shrugged and disappeared into his study, shutting the door behind him.

'Thank you for allowing us to come round this evening, Mr Bellamy.'

The two young detectives were perched uncomfortably on the tiny sofa. They were both built like rugby players and Steve pondered absently whether the frame would withstand their combined weight.

'May we have a word?'

'Yes, of course.'

'It's just that we have a few details we want to confirm with you before we ask you to sign the statement.'

'OK.' Steve wasn't sure about offering them coffee. Would it seem too informal?

'You gave us a very clear description of the layout of the cave system and we've made a diagram of where we think everyone was at the time when Mr Coulter was injured.'

The more senior of the two handed Steve a hand-drawn picture with stick men distributed along the crawls and in the chambers.

'Would you check that it is correct, as far as you can remember, please sir?'

'Well, this is Chas in the end chamber with the two new members of the club. I was in this section, in front of Fred, who was bringing up the rear. He knew what he was doing and it's an easy run down there. That's why we took the novices.'

'Good. Thank you, sir.'

Steve returned the diagram to the officer.

'Now, I'd like to go back to the point when you found your friend.'

'Right.'

'What position was he in?'

'Lying in the water. I told you before, he was lying face down in the water.'

He would always remember the sight of the body, stretched out with his face disappearing in the pool.

'And how was he dressed, exactly?'

'He had his suit on, his helmet and he was wearing gloves.'

'Are you sure about his helmet, Steve?'

'Yes. The torch was still on as well.' It was reflecting in the water; he could see it now.

'And there was no-one else around?'

'No.'

They rose to their feet in unison.

'In that case, sir, we'll leave you in peace.'

It was too late to offer them a drink now, Steve thought. He showed them out, shutting the door quietly behind them and going into the kitchen for a beer. He returned to watching the figures on the silent TV screen but his mind was replaying the scene in Runscar.

He fell asleep after his third beer, waking only when his phone rang.

'Steve, that you? You sound peculiar.'

It was Ewa. When she had rung before Steve had been terse, still stinging from being abandoned so suddenly. Tonight he missed her as much as ever but felt morose. He explained that the police had just left and described in detail the events of Sunday. Ewa immediately burst into tears and had to ring off until she was able to call back.

'Would you be that upset if it had been me instead of him?' Steve asked.

'Don't be so stupid!' she yelled at him. Then her voice softened. 'I was thinking. I will come back this weekend. There may be things we need to do.'

'Such as…?'

'I don't know.'

'Where will you stay?'

'At flat of course! I can't afford to stay anywhere else. Don't worry, I sleep on the sofa. Do you know if there is service for Freddie? I would like to go to service.'

'There may be,' lied Steve.

'Then I will come.'

'And even if there isn't a service, we could have a memorial caving trip.'

'Are you sure?'

'They've done it before.'

'OK, I come. Will you meet me at station?'

'Of course I will.'

Steve put the phone down with mixed feelings. His heart was pounding at the thought of Ewa back in Ingleton even if she was doing it because of another man – a dead one.

The early morning sun was casting shadows on the walls of the tiny interview room as Nina waited for Hazel to collect Iain Small from reception. She wheeled herself behind the table, hoping her chair wasn't too obvious. Because she was still officially signed off she knew that she shouldn't even be there. Something to do with insurance they had said. But she and Hazel had worked together for several years and she was a good mate. No-one will need to know, she had said. Besides, he had only reported a missing person, one that had disappeared fifty years ago.

The man looked young for his age. He was dressed casually but was still smart and Nina noticed the Rolex on his wrist. She introduced herself and he responded politely, but without any warmth, as if he was uneasy with the situation. She put it down to the fact that he was talking to young women officers and dismissed it as typical reaction from a member of the older generation. It was meant to be a friendly chat with a concerned relative but to her surprise it soon became a serious complaint of how the police had mishandled the case of the missing boy.

'I've gone over in my mind for years what happened when Jimmy disappeared. Was there any organised search? No, it was the neighbours and local farmers who were out on the fells. Was there any publicity? Posters? Radio? Television? Nothing. Just because he had Down's Syndrome didn't make him less important. My parents were devastated by their loss. They never recovered from it. And what did the police do? Nothing!'

Hazel looked at Nina, her mouth tight and then she stared down at the table.

'Mr Small. I am sure the force did all they could at the time.' She indicated the file in front of her. 'I have all the details of the case and I can assure you they did explore all avenues.'

Nina could not help but feel sympathy for the man. The grey file was less than a couple of centimetres thick. She would not have felt re-assured. Glancing at Hazel for tacit permission she leaned across the table.

'DC Fuller is right Mr Small. In the fifties there were far fewer facilities at our disposal. Opportunities in the media like 'Crimewatch' were not available and the communication networks were far less effective.'

Small opened his mouth but Nina kept going.

'Now we are reopening the case we will be able to bring everything to bear and be sure that we have covered every technical aid at our disposal.'

Hazel smiled at Nina gratefully.

'Mr Small,' she said, 'if you can give us your account of what happened?'

'But you must have my statement from when it happened. Or has that been lost?' His tone was still belligerent but the ferocity had waned and his eyes had taken on a morose demeanour.

'You were how old? Ten?'

'Eight, nearly nine.'

'It would be helpful to have your recollection as an adult, even after all this time.'

Nina took notes while Hazel asked the man about his brother and the degree of his disability. It was clear that the boys had not been close and he didn't try to hide the fact that Jimmy was an embarrassment, the source of teasing and bullying for the younger brother at school.

'So what exactly happened on the day Jimmy went missing?' Hazel asked.

'It was a Saturday and I was helping my father with the sheep. Jimmy used to wander off all the time and we never worried. He'd always be back at dinner time. It was only when it got to the afternoon and he hadn't appeared that my mother got in a state. She sent me off to look for him.'

'Where did you go?'

'Just down to the lane.' He was rubbing his hands together and pulling at his tie, as if to loosen it. 'He usually went down to meet the wagon that picked up the milk churns. He used to sit on the platform and wait for the wagon, then come back for his dinner. Except this time he didn't.'

'Would he have gone along the lane by himself?'

He leaned back in his chair. 'I've often thought about that. I don't think he would unless he was with someone.'

'Someone he knew? What about a stranger?'

'I don't know. He was very trusting of people.'

'So what about this wagon driver, the one that picked up the churns?' She turned the pages of the open file.

'He worked for the local dairy. Jimmy knew him. We all knew him.'

Hazel read from the file. 'He says here that the boy wasn't there that morning.'

'Did he? Well then that's probably true.' He sighed and leaned heavily on the table. 'Look, do you think you are going to get to the bottom of this after so long?'

'It's possible, Mr Small,' Nina interjected. 'The first thing is to take a sample of your DNA.'

'What for?' he asked sharply, pushing back his chair as if ready to leave.

'Just as a record, in case we… need it.' Nina had agreed with Hazel that at this stage it would be unfair to make any connection between the dismembered hand and the man's brother.

'I know that you've found something… something that might belong to Jimmy. That's why I came here in the first place.'

'Really?' Hazel closed the file and gave him her attention.

'Look, I know that you have found a dismembered hand near the farm.'

'How did you learn about that?' asked Nina.

'There was a lad, a journalist, he was making enquiries. I met him and he told me about it. And now this old woman keeps e-mailing me about it.'

'Do you know where we can contact them?'

'I can give you their e-mail addresses. That's how they got in touch with me, through the internet. I just want to find out what happened to my brother.'

'In that case, Mr Small,' Hazel said, 'you won't mind giving us a DNA sample.'

She led him down the corridor while Nina waited self-consciously for her lift, acknowledging passing colleagues who paused briefly to ask how she was before rushing on up the stairs to the offices. Hazel came down with a coffee and stood imparting the latest gossip about the goings-on at the station.

'*Inspector* Turner is keeping everyone on their toes.' She remarked with a knowing smile.

'I imagine he's enjoying his position.'

'Actually Mitch is OK but we do miss you Nina. I hope you can come in sometimes. It was nice to have you sit in this morning.'

Before she could answer Mills appeared in the doorway and Nina introduced her to Hazel.

'We've already met,' she said. 'I saw her at the university about the… er… hand?'

'Hi,' said Mills.

'Off we go then!' said Nina. 'See you soon, Hazel. Mills, give us a push will you?' She signalled to her friend to get moving.

'What's the matter?' Mills asked as soon as they were outside.

'Just keep going. I didn't actually tell her that I knew you.'

'Is it a problem?'

'Not really but I should have mentioned my personal connection to her.'

They were on the main road before Mills asked about the meeting with Iain Small.

'What was he like? What did he say?'

Nina took a deep breath. 'I think it's probably best if I don't discuss it with you, Mills. You do understand, don't you?'

'Of course.' Her voice did not disguise her disappointment.

'I'm sorry.' Nina leant across and rubbed her friends arm. 'I just want to work out what's important before I talk about it. At the moment it could be a murder enquiry. And by the way, the forensic guys will need to have the hand or part of it for DNA.'

'Right.'

They travelled in silence for a few minutes.

'Look, I have to ask,' began Nina, 'how did you know this woman called Maggie? How did she know about the missing boy?'

'It was Fred. She helped him get in contact with the brother, the one you saw today.'

'And why was Fred involved?'

'For the newspaper I suppose.'

'I guess finding the hand would be an interesting story.'

'Oh he didn't know about the hand. I didn't tell him about that.'

'But he did know,' said Nina seriously.

'Well, I don't know how. It wasn't me, honestly.'

'You know, Mills, I'm wondering if you should pay your friend Maggie a visit. I could just come along for the ride. What do you think?'

Mills grinned. 'What now?' She slowed down at the next junction and took the road out of town, heading for Ingleton. It was not late but the afternoon was growing grey and cold. The caravan site looked deserted except that Maggie's Corsa was there, as before.

'How are we going to get the chair in there?' asked Mills, looking at the tiny steps outside the door to the caravan.

'Can't do it,' she replied. 'We'll have to ask her to come somewhere I can access. Is there a café in the town?'

The door opened as Mills approached and Maggie welcomed her with a broad smile.

'Am I glad to see you, dear! Have you some news?'

When Mills explained Nina's predicament she immediately agreed to join them, telling Snowy to stay and be a good boy. In a few minutes they were drinking tea and nibbling parkin. Maggie related how she had rung the police station without even querying who her friend was and why she was there. Nina said nothing but let Mills ask the questions. It was soon clear to her that Maggie was ignorant of the existence of the dismembered hand and her harassment of Iain Small was purely down to Fred's interest in his missing brother.

'So they said they would look into it and I left them my details. I said I'd be back in Kirkby by the weekend.'

'It can't be much fun in the caravan,' Mills observed.

'It's not me, it's Snowy. He's getting bored. He likes a garden.'

Mills and Nina grinned at each other.

They took her back to the caravan and promised to keep in touch. As they left, Nina asked Mills whether she had Maggie's phone number.

'Yes. Why?'

'Just in case we need to speak to her again. That's all.' It was like when she began jigsaw puzzles as a kid by picking out all the edge pieces. She was collecting the bits, even if nothing fitted together yet.

Ewa felt a pang of recognition as she stepped off the train at Darlington. Steve was standing awkwardly on the platform. He hadn't seen her yet and looked unusually smart in the new jacket she had had such difficulty persuading him to buy. She called to him and was touched to see his face change into a broad smile. He came over and went to kiss her rather diffidently, so she pecked his cheek and gave him her bag to carry.

'So how's London?' he asked as he swung the car out onto the road.

'It's fine.' Her tone gave nothing away. She did not want him to know how hard it had been to find a job, that she was in a tiny corner shop where the old ladies were not only fussier than they were up here but also unfriendly and seemed unable to understand her accent.

'Found somewhere to live?'

'Oh yes.' Her bed-sit was small and dirty. The house was full of men who smoked and drank. She would lock herself away in the evening and pray that she would find a job that paid enough for her to move on. Coming back to Ingleton was difficult for her but not as hard as it would be to leave again. She was glad it was dark and the beautiful countryside that reminded her of home was hidden behind the flashing headlights.

'I thought we'd eat at the pub tonight,' said Steve. He was concentrating on the road and Ewa was able to study his profile.

'That's nice,' she replied.

'I just thought you'd want to catch up with everyone.'

He drove them straight there, although it was early, and they sat with their drinks in the empty bar making small talk while they waited for a familiar face to appear. The barman came over to join them for a while and Ewa, once again, was forced to put a gloss on her new city life. At last a figure all too familiar to Ewa appeared.

'Hello Hunter!' called Steve.

The barman went to draw him a pint and the new arrival chatted with him for a few minutes before carefully carrying his full glass over to their table.

'Well, fancy seeing you here, Ewa,' Hunter said with a grin, pulling up a stool and settling himself down. He sipped his beer and exhaled loudly.

'What brings you back up to the Dales then?' he continued.

'She heard about Fred,' answered Steve. 'Wanted to show her respects.'

'Bad business.' Hunter picked up his glass and held it suspended half way to his mouth. 'I expect there'll be an inquest.' He took a gulp and then another before replacing the glass on the table.

'I suppose,' agreed Steve. 'The police were round again yesterday.'

'What did they want?'

'To go over it all again. Just what I'd told them before.'

'I guess they have to get all the details, mate. Always the same when there's been an accident.'

'When is funeral?' It was the reason she had come, wasn't it? Neither of them answered her.

'There will be funeral, won't there?'

'Of course,' said Steve, 'but it might be delayed because of the inquest.

'No. The inquest won't be for ages. The funeral will go ahead before that. Once the PM is over.'

'PM? What is PM?' She was irritated by Hunter showing off as usual.

'PM, short for post mortem. It's when…'

'I know post mortem!' she snapped.

Hunter offered to fetch more drinks and when they were alone Steve asked if she was feeling all right. She pretended it was because she was hungry and he suggested they order their meal. In the past, on special occasions, she had chosen her favourite steak dish with a stilton sauce but when he suggested it she experienced a wave of nausea.

'Just fish, please… and few chips.'

By the time their meal was served they were surrounded by club members. Ewa's women friends were mainly like her – girlfriends of cavers. She had only been away one week so they were not even aware that she had left Ingleton. It suited her not to have to explain her new life to everyone. Instead they discussed the accident and whether Fred's funeral would be held in the area. The consensus was that his family lived down South and so all they could do was to commemorate his life in their own way. There were outings dedicated to cavers' memories and it was agreed amongst the women members that something should be done for Fred. At first their men ridiculed the idea as sentimental but when Chas arrived he took the women's side and no-one was willing to contradict him. Very soon there was agreement to have a day's caving in Fred's memory with Chas being left to decide the date and venue.

Hunter dragged Steve and Chas off for a game of pool and Ewa was left with two of her friends.

'Is it true you've moved out of Steve's flat?' one asked.

'Yes.'

'So where are you living now?' asked the other.

Ewa sighed and explained as succinctly as she could. She was watching Hunter as he came back in from the pool room.

'Will you excuse me?' she said and walked across to the door marked "Toilets". There was a corridor past the "Ladies" and the "Men's" that led round a corner to a door marked "private" that led to the landlord's sitting room. She waited there and soon Hunter joined her. As he reached her he put his hand out and leant on the wall, trapping her very effectively, so she couldn't escape when he kissed her.

'Stop it.'

'What's the matter? I thought you'd come back to see me?'

'No. That is not why I come back. I need favour.'

'Anything.'

'My suit for cave. Fred borrows it for girlfriend, Meels. She works at university. Please find her and ask to give back to me.'

'I don't know who she is.' The smile had vanished.

'I think you find her. She has weird name. She is in university. Tell her to give suit to you. I can collect it… when I meet you.'

He stroked his chin in silence.

'Look. If I see her I'll tell her to ring you. OK?' He went to kiss her again.

'I told you. It is over.'

'You know it will never be over. If it was going to be over it would have happened when I went to the States.'

'It did.'

'So what were we doing in the last four months?'

'I don't know. I was stupid, really stupid.'

'No you weren't. You know you can't resist me.'

He was grinning in a stupid, irritating way and trying to kiss her again. There was the sound of the door to the bar opening and they stood still until the door to one of the toilets had slammed.

'I must go.' Ewa tried to move.

'But when are we going to get together again?' Hunter asked. 'Are you free tomorrow?'

'I do not want to be free with you again. Leave me alone now, please?'

'Should I tell Steve that's what you want?'

'You do not tell him anything. Please. You must not.'

'Well, why don't we discuss it over a drink tomorrow? You can tell him you're seeing the girls from the shop.'

'Perhaps.' She turned to leave and he grabbed her wrist.

'I'll call you tomorrow, don't ignore me or I swear I'll arrange that chat with Steve.'

She pulled her hand away and almost ran back into the bar. Steve was still in the pool room and waved as she passed the door. She smiled at him but kept moving, sensing that Hunter was close behind.

She felt a hand on her shoulder and turned

'Don't forget, I'll see you tomorrow,' he said and walked back into the pool room.

Steve didn't reappear until closing time and was unusually quiet as they walked home. Once in the flat he switched on the television and settled down to watch the football.

'I stay here until Saturday?'

No answer.

'If you like I stay Sunday.'

'Whatever.'

'Just until memorial.'

Silence.

'For Freddie.'

Steve snapped the television off with the remote. His face was twisted, as if in pain. 'Look, I don't care what you do,' he spat out the words. 'You do whatever you want. But don't expect to come back here, that's all. Why don't you just go and stay with lover-boy? I'm sure he'd be pleased to find you a bed.'

Chapter 10

There were two messages waiting for Mills when she reached the department. The first was a memo from the departmental secretary to say that the police had rung and would be there in an hour or so. She sighed and put it in her bag. The second was typed on a single sheet of A4: *Fred borrowed a caving oversuit of mine, could you get it back to me please?* It was followed by the name "Ewa Prodanovic" and a mobile phone number. She had forgotten all about the suit, which was still in the boot of Nige's car. She would have to call the girl later to apologise but now she had to pack up the plastic box and deal with the forensic scientist who was coming to take the dismembered hand away for examination.

Mills was disappointed when a young police constable finally arrived, just as she was going for lunch. He was not from forensics but simply acting as a courier, so she was unable to quiz him about what tests would be used on her precious artefact.

'Will I be able to have it back when they are finished with it?' she asked.

'I don't know miss.'

'But I will get to know the results of the tests?'

'Can't say miss.'

'Do you know who I should contact?'

'No miss.'

'Isn't there even a paper to show I've passed it over to you?'

'Oh, yes miss, I nearly forgot.' He put the box down on the bench and fumbled in his pocket, producing a crumpled sheet requiring her signature.

When he had gone she considered what to do now that the object of her work had been effectively confiscated. It occurred to her that she might as well go back to Manchester, just as she had threatened Lang she would do a few days before. She retrieved the message from her bag and called the girl's number, figuring that she had better arrange to get the suit back before she left. The voice at the other end soon took a friendly tone when she explained who she was.

'Meels? Oh it is so nice to hear you. I am so, so sorry about Freddie. You must be so sad.'

'I just rang about the suit. I'm sorry, I should have returned it but…'

'No, no, there is no problem. I wanted to speak you because there will be caving event. What do you call it? A memorial for poor Freddie. I want suit but then I think maybe you come too?'

'I don't really know how to… Fred was just teaching me. I don't think…'

'Of course you must come, Meels. I can help you and my friends. Please will you come?'

'When is it?' She was going back to Manchester so it probably wouldn't even be possible.

'This Sunday. It must be soon because I go back to London on Monday.'

'I'll think about it.'

'No, please come. Freddie would have wanted I am sure.'

'Look, I'll bring the suit down this afternoon and we can talk about it then.'

'Promise?'

'Yes, I promise.' It was the last thing she wanted to do but she couldn't find a polite way of saying no to the woman. She had simply wanted to return the suit.

She would give it back and then she would say no to the caving trip.

She sought out Nige and described the events of the morning.

'I was thinking that I could kill two birds with one stone by visiting Long Witton Farm to let them know that it's currently a police matter and then taking the caving suit back down to Ingleton.'

'So you'll need the car.'

'If it's not a problem. I won't be too long.'

'No, you go ahead.'

'Thanks, I'll fill it up while I'm out.'

'Even better.'

In her hurry to get moving she almost collided with Dr Lang, who was leaving his office further down the corridor.

'Hi there, everything cool?'

'Yes fine. The police picked up the hand this morning. I'm just tying up some loose ends and then I'm going back to Manchester.'

'Loose ends?' He was ushering her back into his office and indicating for her to sit down. She obeyed reluctantly.

'I'm going to the farm to let the owners know what's happening.'

'Good idea. I could come with you.'

'But then I'm going on to Ingleton to return my caving suit to the person who lent it to me.'

'Oh I see.'

Then it occurred to her. 'Did you by any chance give my address to a woman called Ewa Prodanovic?'

'Prodanovic?' He shook his head.

'She's a caver down in Ingleton.'

'No, don't know anyone of that name.'

She stood up. 'I'd better be off then.'

'This police investigation, Mills. It may come to nothing. If it does I'm sure we'll be able to continue our work.'

'If *we* get the opportunity I would be happy to continue the work. But at the moment there is nothing for *us* to do, is there?' She left him with a fixed smile.

Her frustration and irritation with Terry Lang evaporated as she approached the Dales. The morning had been cloudy but now the sun was breaking through and there were patches of blue appearing. She drove more slowly, soaking in the calming atmosphere of the fells. She would have liked to have stopped right there, put on her walking boots and set off for a few hours alone. Perhaps she would... later. Now she had some calls to make. She put her foot down gently and concentrated on the road.

The police car parked in the yard was visible from the track. Mills was unsure whether to drive up to the farm and was slowing down to turn round when Sheila saw her and waved.

'Have you come to see the police?' she asked.

'No. I wanted to let you know what was happening, but I guess you already know.'

'They want to start digging up the top. They've taken Mr Small up to have a look where his brother's hand was found.'

Mills was shocked. 'Do they know who it is?' she asked.

'I don't know... I assumed... because he came... oh dear, have I said something I shouldn't have?'

'Perhaps they'll tell us when they come back down?' suggested Mills.

'Yes... happen. Why don't you come in and wait?'

While Sheila made tea Mills asked how long the police had been there.

'They've only just arrived. That Mr Small was here first. He's a real gentleman. Did you see the car he drives?'

Mills looked through the window at the Mercedes parked in the yard.

'Well apparently the police had gone to the cave first thing this morning,' she continued.

'The cave?'

'Runscar, it's just down the way. There was a young lad died in there Sunday last.'

'Yes. I heard,' Mills took a breath.

'They didn't say anything to me but I heard them talking like and one of them said that there would have to be a thorough investigation with forensics.'

Sheila chattered on while Mills sipped her tea in silence. She was going over the suggestion that Ewa had made and she had so abruptly rejected. Perhaps it would be the right thing to do, to say goodbye in the way he would have liked. After all, they were due to have another trip together before the accident happened.

They were interrupted by a sharp tap on the back door. A large middle-aged man in a black mackintosh came into the kitchen, followed by an older man in an expensive-looking leather jacket and woollen scarf.

'We've finished for now madam but we'll be sending a team in tomorrow or Monday to make a start on the ditch.'

'Thank you, inspector. This is the archaeologist I was telling you about. Did you want to speak to her?'

He turned to scrutinise Mills. 'No, it's not necessary at this time. I'm sure we know how to contact you, miss?' It was a question more than a statement.

'I expect so,' she said.

'I'd like to stay and chat if I may?' It was the man in the leather jacket.

'Righto then, Mr Small, I'll leave you here and crack on.'

Sheila went to see the inspector out while Iain Small introduced himself to Mills. She was careful not to reveal that she already knew of him through Maggie. She was grateful that Nina had refrained from telling her what had happened at the police station when she had interviewed him.

He explained very briefly that the police thought the hand might belong to a relative and asked her to give him the details of how it had been found and what tests she had made on it. She found it difficult to explain scientific results when all the time she was conscious that the object she was talking about was possibly part of his missing brother. He listened politely without a word, nodding at her explanations and conclusions.

'May I ask,' she said, 'whether the police are sure it's your… relative?'

'Not certain but it seems very likely. They'll do a DNA test and they are looking for any other… remains.'

Sheila offered him tea but he excused himself and left, saying that he would be back to the farm if there were any further developments. The police would let him know.

'He comes from Kilrigg Farm, just a bit further along the dale,' Sheila told Mills as soon as she returned. 'His father farmed there until nineteen-sixty-three. He was ever so interested in talking to

Brian. They were nattering about the farm for the best part of an hour before the inspector arrived. I reckon he'd like to meet Brian's dad and Grandad because they must have known each other. Brian's dad would've been at school with him.' She sighed. 'Can you imagine losing a young child like that without ever knowing what had happened? It doesn't bear thinking about, does it?'

They sat for a few more minutes before Mills set off for Ingleton. Following Ewa's precise instructions, she found the flat easily and struggled up the stairs with the suit.

'I will make tea. You like tea? I have Earl Grey.' Mills watched the tall blonde woman bustle about in the tiny kitchen, finally handing her a mug and ushering her into the cramped sitting room.

'So, you are at university?'

Mills nodded.

'What you study?'

'Archaeology.'

'Very interesting, archaeology.'

'Yes.' Mills remembered what she had wanted to ask. 'How did you know where to find me?'

'I know…' She frowned, then smiled. 'I know because Freddie told me all about you… Poor Freddie.'

'Oh.' Mills could not remember ever having discussed her work with Fred in the short time she had known him but the woman clearly was a close friend of his, so perhaps she had.

'Had you known him long?'

'Freddie? Not long. Few months. Such sweet boy.'

They sat with their tea in an uncomfortable silence and Mills was conscious of Ewa studying her.

'So, Meels, will you come to caving event to remember Freddie?' She was smiling, her head on one side as if willing Mills to say yes.

'I'm sorry. I really don't think I can face it.'

'If you are frightened we will help you. I have friends, they will help.'

'Thank you but it's not that. I just don't think I could cope with it, not so soon after… you know.'

After a short silence Ewa sat up straight and sniffed. 'You are right. It is not good idea. I think we must find other thing. What do you think?'

'It would be nice to do something,' offered Mills.

'What you do in England to remember someone?'

Mills had to smile. 'I don't know. A service I suppose… or some charity event.'

'Event? What event?'

'Anything. Jumping out of aeroplanes?'

Ewa looked confused.

'Or a sponsored walk?'

'A walk? Where a walk?'

'Anywhere. It doesn't have to be far.'

'Like Three Peaks Walk?'

'I don't know. What is that?'

'Three peaks here. Ingleborough, Whernside and other hill.'

She leapt up and took a book from the shelf behind her. She flicked the pages until she found what she was looking for and handed it to Mills. The three peaks walk was twenty-two miles long circular route, starting at Horton-in-Ribblesdale and going from Pen-y-ghent to Whernside to Ingleborough and back. It passed right by the aqueduct where she had first met Fred.

'That would be perfect,' she said.

Ewa gave her a hug and stepped back, beaming.

'We go next weekend. I tell friends and we go Saturday. I come back to Ingleton on Friday. I am sure I can find somewhere to stay,' she added softly.

'This isn't your flat?'

'No. It belongs to Steve. He was boyfriend but I live in London now. We are finished.' She seemed wistful.

'But you'll be here on Saturday?'

'For sure. I'll call you on Friday, yes?'

Mills thanked Ewa as she left. Her idea had provided a way of remembering Fred without the prospect of going underground, which frankly had filled her with dread.

As she drove past the caravan site, it occurred to Mills that Maggie might like to hear about her meeting with Iain Small. She pulled over and rang her mobile number.

'Maggie! Are you still in Ingleton?'

'No, I'm back in Kirkby now, love. How are you?'

'I'm fine. Look I just wanted to let you know that I had a chat with Iain Small this morning.' She waited for Maggie to respond.

'I've made it my business to meet that man,'

'Really?'

'Yes. I want him to answer a few questions.'

'He's very pleasant, Maggie. Quite charming.'

'Hmmm. We'll see about that.'

'Do you want me to come along?'

'No dear, there's no need for that. I'll be fine. Snowy will be there to protect me.'

'I'm sure you won't need any protection, Maggie...'

'If you say so. I'm not giving him my address here, just in case. We're meeting on neutral territory.'

Mills tried to keep her amusement from her voice. 'Right, Maggie. Let me know how it goes won't you?'

'Yes. Thank you dear. I will.'

'…And, Maggie, if someone wanted to use the caravan…'

On the journey back Mills was preoccupied with her plans for the next week. She would stay and do the Three Peaks Walk before returning to Manchester. If the police released the hand back to the university she could return and help Dr Lang with the study but it could be that the project was over before it had hardly begun. Her supervisor would be back from Tennessee in a few weeks and life could be normal again in no time. The prospect was not appealing.

'How long will it take for the DNA results to come back?' she asked Nina as they sat eating that evening.

'Depends what priority they put on it. It could be weeks. Although I suppose it might get overtaken by events if they find a body to go with it.' She was carefully spooning rice pudding into bowls.

'I saw the police at the farm today. And I met Iain Small.'

Nina looked up. 'Where?'

'At the farm. He was meeting your lot there.'

'Was he?'

'He seemed a nice guy.'

'Yes.'

'Nina, I know why he was there. They think the hand might belong to his missing brother, don't they?'

'Sorry, I shouldn't really discuss the case with you, Mills.' She kept her head down, concentrating on handing out the pudding.

'But I know about him. It won't make any difference.'

Nina ate in silence and Mills looked at Nige, who shrugged.

Mills toyed with the rice. She had never really liked it, especially when it was thick and stodgy. She took a mouthful and then rested the spoon back down in the bowl.

'I only wanted to know if you do think it was his brother.'

'I'm sorry but I can't say.'

The emotion that she had been feeling since talking to Ewa finally came to the surface and she could feel a lump in her throat.

'I'm sorry. I just wanted to know because if it is I might as well go back to Manchester now.'

She got up from the table, excusing herself and fled to her room.

Mills avoided Nina and Nige at breakfast and left, saying she would be working at the university all day, even though it was Saturday. She spent the weekend getting her notes in order and writing a full report on the discovery of the hand and her scientific analysis. When she reached the section entitled 'conclusions' she sat staring at the screen. The page remained blank. Until she had the DNA results from the police she would have to leave a big question mark over its identification.

Monday morning she carried a copy of the final draft down to Dr Lang's office and left it on his desk with a note to say that her work was finished. She didn't care that he wasn't there; in fact she was relieved. She didn't want to have to discuss it with him any more. So she was surprised when, that evening, she received an e-mail from him, thanking her for her comprehensive report and agreeing it probably would have to end there. He wished her well in the future and thanked her again for her contribution. When she showed the message to Nige, he laughed.

'So what was *his* contribution?'

'Nige!' Nina glared at him and he pulled a sheepish face.

'So what are you going to do now?' It was the first time in several days that Nina had conversed with Mills.

She had been thinking about it and now she had a plan.

'I'm going to stay until next weekend, if that's all right. And do the Three Peaks Walk. Then I'm back to Manchester.'

'You're going to do the Three Peaks? I've always wanted to do that!'

'We could push you!' joked Nige.

'Don't be daft! But when I'm better…'

'Yes, of course we'll go then.' His voice was flat and Mills sensed that Nige had less confidence in Nina's full recovery.

Maggie had fallen asleep watching the television, overcome by the bleary heat of the gas stove. She was woken by Snowy's insistent barking and his claws catching her leg as he jumped from her lap in his eagerness to reach the door. Behind the curtain a silhouetted figure emerged from a large car. She switched down the sound and waited for a knock at the door.

The man stood at the bottom of the steps illuminated by the light from behind her. He was neatly dressed and smiled politely if rather nervously while Maggie attempted to stop Snowy barking. She finally managed to drag the dog back into the caravan, indicating for the man to come inside.

'Do sit down Mr Small.'

'Thank you, Maggie. And do call me Iain.'

She noticed the smart cut of his hair and automatically looked down at his nails. She liked a man with well-kept hands. She offered him coffee, despite herself, and while she boiled the kettle, Snowy sat bolt upright at his feet growling quietly.

'Thank you for coming, Mr Small,' she said when she had brought in the tray with the cups of coffee. 'You probably wondered why I asked you here.'

'Well, Maggie, you did make it pretty clear that you were concerned about your young friend.' His tone was light but Maggie wasn't going to be taken in.

'Fred, his name was Fred. And I know you met him because he told me.'

'Yes, he wanted to discuss a personal matter with me.'

'Your brother.'

He looked surprised and she knew she had him at a disadvantage.

'Milk?'

'No thank you.'

He took the cup and saucer from her, holding them away from him, as if concerned that he would spill the coffee on his beige chinos or his leather jacket.

'Yes, he told me about your brother,' continued Maggie. 'What did Fred ask you?' She watched him carefully but his expression did not change.

'I don't believe it's any of your business, Maggie.'

Her heart was beating faster but she continued to smile at him.

'It *is* my business, Mr Small. I want to know what happened to my friend.'

'I repeat, what that young man and I spoke about is private and personal. If you want to ask him, then please do so.'

'I can't.'

'Why not? Does he not want to discuss it either?' He smiled and placed his cup and saucer back on the tray before rising.

'Because he can't.'

The man looked puzzled.

'What do you mean?'

'He died last week, Mr Small.' Maggie tried hard to keep the emotion from her voice. 'He died in a cave.'

He wound the scarf round his neck slowly, as if grappling for what to say.

'I'm sorry to hear that but it's nothing to do with me.'

'Are you sure, Mr Small?'

Maggie was on her feet and they stood glaring at one another.

'Look, did you invite me here to accuse me of something?'

'I just think it's odd that Fred arranges to meet you and the next thing he's dead.' The tears were just behind her eyes but she felt angry and wasn't going to let him leave without finding the truth. 'I think he found something out about your past that you were uncomfortable with.'

'I think you're an over-emotional old woman. I'm going.'

Snowy was growling as they raised their voices. Small turned to leave.

'I know about your dealings with the police in the past. I know about your police record. Arson, wasn't it?' Now she was feeling confident again.

He didn't turn round but she saw his body stiffen.

She continued. 'I heard someone was hurt... badly... really badly.'

Without responding he moved to open the door and suddenly Snowy was tugging at his trouser leg. As he turned back towards her, Maggie could see his face was contorted with anger.

'You leave me alone, you old witch.' He kicked out and the dog flew across the floor yelping. 'Or you'll regret it!' He slammed the door behind him and a short while later she heard the roar of a powerful engine disappearing. Shaking with anger and tears, she picked up Snowy and held him close to her while she rang the police.

Chapter 11

When the message finally came it wasn't through the forensics science service but from the familiar voice of her friend on voicemail.

'Mills? It's Nina. They've got the results. It's a man but not Iain Small's brother. I thought you'd want to know.'

She immediately rang back to get the details.

'Nothing more to say. The DNA didn't match. It isn't his hand after all.'

'So what happens now, Nina?'

'Not sure, to be honest. They were looking for a body but they may decide to call it off now.'

'Will they let me see the report?'

'I don't know if they'll release it at this stage.'

'Can you find out if there are any more details? Please?'

'I'll ask.'

Mills could hear the smile in Nina's voice. 'And thanks, Nina. You're a real friend.'

'I know.' She laughed.

That evening Nina was waiting for her waving a sheet of paper.

'I asked them to e-mail the info from the lab. It doesn't make much sense,' she added, 'but they were quite excited by the DNA. It matches a rare group which means that it could possibly belong to a Traveller.'

'You mean like a Gypsy?'

'Maybe. It's just a possibility. Look it's here, something to do with chromosomes.' She handed a page to Mills.

Over forty percent of Roma men carry Y chromosomes of haplogroup H-M82 which is otherwise rare outside of the Indian subcontinent.

'How does that affect the date of the hand?'

'It doesn't,' said Nina. 'There have been Travellers attending the horse fairs in Appleby since the sixteen hundreds.'

Mills sat down on the sofa, scanning the document. She was still wearing her coat and gloves. Without looking up she said, 'This might tie in with my idea about it originating from the railway camp at Batty Green. There were Irish navvies – they could have been Travellers, couldn't they? That would mean it is over one hundred years old, d'you see?'

'Talking of batty, that friend of yours from the caravan was causing problems with our Ingleton colleagues again last night,' Nina said. 'They've got her down as a bit of a loony now.'

'I'd better give her a call,' Mills said, folding the paper carefully and putting it in her bag.

'She'd better be careful it doesn't get her into trouble. Stalking is an offence you know.'

Mills wasn't sure if Nina was joking or not but decided to ring Maggie to warn her. She had to concentrate hard to make out what the woman was saying. She was speaking very fast and barely pausing for breath. Finally Mills was able to calm Maggie down sufficiently to understand that she had met Iain Small.

'But Maggie, he wasn't even there when Fred had his accident!'

She would not be dissuaded and when Mills refused to ask Nina to use her influence, she announced that she would return to Kirkbymoorside and speak to the police there. Concerned for the smart, unassuming man she had met at Long Witton Farm, Mills told Nina about Maggie's irrational hatred of Iain Small.

'Don't worry,' she said. 'They have her measure and won't do anything about it.'

'I wonder if he knows the hand is not his brother's.' Mills said. It was not a question; she knew better than to quiz her friend again.

But Nina smiled and took her hand. 'Mills, I'll find out what I can. In fact your inquisitiveness has really been a help – I got onto the station to ask if I could get more involved and they agreed for me to go in again tomorrow to get up to speed on the case notes.'

'Seriously?'

'Yep.' She grinned. 'Nige is really against it, so will you take me? We don't have to tell him.'

Mills hesitated, but only for a second. 'Of course I will.' She guessed that it was easier for Nina to feed her with information now that it was unlikely to be a murder investigation.

They discussed the news with Nige over supper.

'You mean it's an archaeological artefact once again? Dr Lang will be glad to hear it. Does that mean you'll carry on with the work?'

'Don't know,' answered Mills. 'It's tempting to leave it but it could still be of interest – perhaps from when the railway was built.'

'Hardly ancient then?'

'No,' she conceded. 'And I should really get back to Manchester.'

'Not before you've done the walk though,' said Nina.

'No. I do want to do that.'

Next morning Mills took Nige into work with the excuse that she needed the car to get to the farm in Ribblesdale. Nina was waiting when she arrived back at the house. Her hair was shining and she was wearing her favourite red wool suit. Together they manoeuvred her into the car before Mills dismantled the wheelchair and heaved it into the boot. Nina was anxious to be out of the car and inside the building as soon as possible.

'It's nice to see you Nina.' Mitch's new role suited him. He appeared self-assured and charming. 'You know everyone.'

She smiled at the team. It seemed so normal to be back with them again.

'The agenda for this morning is to review what we have on the dismembered hand,' he continued. 'We've got the DNA back and it's not the lad who went missing. We informed his family as soon as we received confirmation. The age of the hand is ambiguous and so we have to treat it as suspicious until we learn otherwise.'

'So what happens now?' It was Hazel.

'Simple. We continue to look for a body until we know it's over a hundred years old.'

There was a groan from the team.

'I know.' Mitch was smiling. 'It's cold and wet but it's got to be done. Let's hope the scientists find the answer sooner rather than later.'

When the meeting was over it was Nina's chance to ask Mitch about the DNA results.

'It means that there is a very good chance that the body was that of a Traveller. Not so surprising. We believe there were a number of Irish Travellers visiting the horse fair, as they still do today. It probably makes it quite old and out of our hands, so to speak. We haven't found any records of a Traveller or Gypsy missing in the area over the past hundred years anyway.'

'So what's to be done now?'

'Not a lot, I'm afraid Nina. There are some reports to be done if you're happy.'

'That's fine. Can I do them at home?'

There was a pause. Nina knew they couldn't get her upstairs and so they would either have to let her take the work home or organise a desk on the ground floor.

'Yes, of course. I'll pop up and get the files.'

When he returned he stood looking about him, uncomfortably. 'Look,' he said, 'I'm going down to see the lads at the site this afternoon. I'd offer to take you along but…'

'Don't worry, Mitch, I understand.'

'I'll get Hazel to keep you up to speed,' he offered.

A thought struck her. 'Millie can bring me down!'

'Millie?'

'Sorry, Mills Sanderson – she's been doing the archaeological investigation. What time shall we meet you? About two? At the farm?'

When Mills picked Nina up she had a pile of paperwork in the back of the car. She explained that she had spent the morning on the internet, researching the Irish navvies who worked on the railway at Blea Moor. She was now even more convinced that the hand belonged to a railway worker murdered by a hoard of English navvies during a fight in eighteen-seventy.

'We'll tell the Search Team Leader when we get down there,' Nina said.

'Who's that?'

'Mitch Turner. He was taking the meeting this morning.'

'But we can talk to the guys who are working on the ground, yes?'

'I don't see why not.'

When they reached Long Witton Farm Nina told Mills to leave her in the car and find out what was happening. She watched her friend disappear into the house and then reappear with a young woman carrying a child. She pointed up the hill and Mills set off through the gate while the woman made her way over to the car.

'Would you like to come into the warm?' she asked as Nina lowered the window.

'It's a bit difficult with the wheelchair…'

'That's no problem. I'll pop Richard in the playpen and then I'll come and help.'

Nina sat patiently while Sheila extracted the chair from the boot and constructed it expertly, finally helping Nina into the house.

'That was impressive,' said Nina when she was inside.

'I do it every week for Grandad – my husband's grandfather – he comes over on a Wednesday while my mother-in-law has her hair done and gets a bit of shopping.'

They chatted about the children and Nina's pregnancy until Mills arrived with Mitch, who had to duck under the doorway when he came into the kitchen.

'How's it going?' Nina asked.

'Not well. It's been three days now and they've found nowt.'

'What's the plan?'

'I asked for a body dog to join in the search but I'm not sure I'll get it. Another day and I reckon we'll be calling a halt.'

Nina sipped her coffee and listened to Mills enthusiastically describing her theory that the hand belonged to a navvy.

'If that's true, they'll be calling off the search. We're only interested in bodies less than a hundred years old,' Mitch said.

When Sheila offered Mitch a flask of coffee for the lads Mills volunteered to take it up to them.

'I would like to see how they're getting on,' she said.

'Would you mind if I have a quick word with my colleague?' Mitch asked when Mills had gone.

'Of course not,' said Sheila, 'Richard will be fretting at being left on his own for so long.' She went into the next room and Nina could hear her chattering to her son.

'It's about the young lad found in the cave down the road,' Mitch's voice was low and he bent down so his face was level with Nina's. 'The pathologist's report is not looking good. They don't think he drowned. The knock on his head was a heavy one. They can't be sure but it looks like he was hit before entering the water. I've got to arrange for a specialist SOCO team to go down there; it's not an easy place to get to and the lighting is appalling.'

Nina wondered why he was telling her. 'Is there something you want me to do?'

'No. I just thought you would like to be kept informed.' He smiled at her and straightened up. 'We miss you at the station, you know. We'll be glad to have you back.'

'Thanks for the coffee!' Mitch shouted through to Sheila and she returned with her toddler in her arms. Once again, Nina wondered how she would manage when her baby came if she wasn't walking by then.

'We'll be glad when it's all over,' Sheila admitted. 'Brian goes on and on about getting it all filled in and forgotten. He reckons it's upsetting everyone, even his grandfather – and he hasn't farmed here for years.'

When Mills returned, Mitch thanked her for her help.

'I'll let the Chief Inspector know about the Irish navvy link. It would explain the unusual chromosome thing and seems logical. At that stage I'm guessing we'll call off the search and give the hand back to the university.'

'And what will you do now?' asked Sheila, looking at Mills.

'Write up my conclusions and go back to Manchester, I suppose,' she answered. 'The findings are interesting because it suggests that body parts can be tanned in peat even over quite short time scales *and* the bones can disappear quite quickly if the soil is acid enough.'

Nina, who was watching Mitch could see he was impressed.

'Well come and see us before you go back,' said Sheila. 'Kate would be interested in what you've found and I'm sure she'd like to say goodbye. She'll be at home next week. It's half-term.'

Nina watched her friend and waited.

'I'm off after the weekend. But I'll try and pop in before I go.'

In the car Nina sensed that her friend was thinking about her return to the city. She found the silence intolerable and grasped at the distraction.

'I've not seen the railway camp,' she said. 'Will you give me a push round it?'

'There's nothing to see,' said Mills when they reached the arches of the viaduct. 'The camp was over there and the tunnel is up there but it'll be difficult to go much further.'

It was a bad idea. The wind was cold and the rough track made it hard work for her friend to push the wheelchair. Nina's legs were cold within minutes.

'Tell me about the navvies. What happened? Why were they fighting?'

'I think it started with a pub brawl which ended with an Irishman being killed. The men involved, who were English, were arrested and this caused some sort of riot. The English navvies chased the Irishmen and their families off the camp.'

'Were any of them killed?'

'Don't know… maybe…They disappeared into the woods apparently.'

'Have any other bodies been found?'

'Don't think so. I suppose it all seems very far-fetched.' Mills sounded dejected.

'Look on the bright side, Mills. At least the body is historical and not the result of a recent crime.'

'True.'

Mills was very quiet on the way home. Nina wanted to tell her what Mitch had said about Fred's death possibly not being an accident. But it was police business and she knew she should not share it with a member of the public, even her friend. And then something happened that eliminated it from her mind temporarily. The red light was flashing on the answer machine when they arrived back at the house.

'Nina? It's Mitch. We've got something. It looks as though we've found the rest of the body. Can you let your archaeologist friend know? We might need her help. It's too late today – it's nearly dark now – but if she could be down here in the morning I'd be grateful. We didn't need the dog after all.'

Chapter 12

Mills packed her fieldwork tools in the boot and was out of the house at seven-thirty the next morning. Nina agreed that she would not be able to do anything down there, dependent as she was on her wheelchair. Even so, Mills felt awkward about leaving her at home as she set off while it was still dark. The roads were quiet and she had left town and was heading for the Dales long before the rush hour had begun. It developed into a perfect sunny morning and Mills felt a growing excitement as she turned up the track to Long Witton Farm and parked alongside several other vehicles, including two marked police cars. There was a uniformed constable standing by the gate that opened onto the moorland; he looked cold and bored.

'I'm Mills Sanderson,' she explained. 'Your inspector asked me to come?'

He opened the gate and made a note of her name on his pad.

'They're on top of yon hill,' he said, unnecessarily. She had already seen the small band of figures in the distance.

Mitch introduced her to the others in the group and explained that he was now acting as the crime scene manager. They were mainly scene of crime officers but there was also a pathologist examining the body.

'We've asked for an archaeologist from forensics,' he said, 'but since you are familiar with the site I thought you might…?'

There was a pile of rags in the ditch but when Mills looked more closely she thought she could see some bones less than a metre away.

'What would you like me to do?' she asked.

He appeared uncertain. 'Just any comments you may have. Obviously we have to wait for forensics before you can go nearer but with your expertise we would appreciate your help when he arrives.'

'When is that?'

'Oh quite soon, I'm sure.'

While she waited, Mills occupied herself by taking measurements of where the body had been found. She used her global positioning system to identify the spot to within a few metres but also took photographs and made sketches of the place in relation to where Brian had discovered the hand. They were about thirty metres apart but that wasn't surprising if the digger had disturbed the body and possibly even torn the hand away from it. She was impatient to see how much the body had deteriorated. Once she was finished she told Mitch that she would see if she could rustle up some coffee for them and walked back down to the farm.

'I suppose there's no question that the body belongs with the hand – if you see what I mean?' Sheila was preparing the flask of coffee while Mills warmed herself against the Rayburn.

'The police seem pretty sure.'

'I still can't get my head round it,' Sheila continued. 'When they came down last night, well… Brian nearly threw a fit and Kate was so overexcited. Dear me. Mary rang me this morning and said that Brian's Dad is in a right state over it.'

Mills carried the coffee out to the police team and hung around watching the two scenes of crime officers at work, wishing she could climb down into the ditch to take a closer look. Mitch wandered over to her, looking at his watch.

'I'm sorry. I thought he'd be here by now.'

He smiled at her and she shrugged.

'So, have you been in archaeology long?'

If it was a chat-up line it was a strange one, she thought, as she answered self-consciously. But he listened and asked questions that certainly sounded as though he was genuinely interested. When she asked him what would happen to the body once the forensic archaeologist arrived he admitted that he knew less than she did and insisted she describe what she would do.

'I suppose I would want to clear the soil away from the body pretty carefully because I don't know its age. If it has been preserved in the peat it could be hundreds or even thousands of years old. I would want to work at it systematically and ensure nothing was damaged.'

'Well, that would be the same approach that our forensic people would take except in their case they want to ensure that no clues are obliterated when they handle the body. But the Chief Inspector wants to get it removed as soon as possible so we can identify it. I think we want the same thing really, to find out how old it is and who it is.'

An hour later Mills was beginning to get very cold and was relieved when she saw Sheila climbing up the slope with a large thermos flask.

'I wondered what will be happening about the …' Sheila waved towards the ditch while looking directly at the inspector. 'Only my daughter will be back from school and I don't know what…'

'I'm sorry. We're waiting for the forensic archaeologist. I don't know when…'

Sheila looked at Mills as if for assistance.

'They can't do anything until they've done a proper examination,' she said, putting her hand on Sheila's arm. The woman smiled but she looked worried and Mills guessed that Kate was not the only member of the family to cause her concern.

When she had gone, the two SOCOs joined the sergeant to chat, warming their hands on mugs of hot soup. He invited Mills to join them and tried to involve her in the conversation but she continued to feel like an outsider as they discussed other occasions when they had worked with the inspector.

Finally there was a cry from below and she turned to see a young man striding up the hill. He was wearing a long khaki coat and wellington boots, a bright red scarf trailing behind him. He was carrying two large carrier bags as well as the rucksack on his back.

'Hi, I'm Phil,' he offered his hand to Mills, who took it while looking round desperately for Mitch.

'You need to talk to the inspector,' she said. 'He's over with the others by the ditch.'

'I'm from the forensic team,' the young man explained. 'I'm rather late actually, had a puncture on the bike.'

'You cycled here?' Mills was puzzled.

'Cycled? Cycled?' He looked baffled and then a huge grin broke out on his face and he guffawed.

'No, motorbike – like with an engine.'

She pointed him in Mitch's direction to cover her embarrassment and followed him over to the ditch. Soon he was down beside the SOCOs, pulling off his gloves and unloading his plastic bags.

'You can give me a hand if you want,' he called and Mitch indicated for Mills to join him.

At first she stood and watched as he moved carefully round the pile of rags and made notes but once he started to examine them more closely he called her over. Mitch was nodding encouragingly, so she lowered herself into the ditch.

'Not much to see yet, just some clothing and a small bone here.' His long body was doubled over and his knees were almost meeting his chin so his voice was muffled. 'The search team did a good job; sometimes it's a real dog's breakfast by the time I get to see the body.'

She knelt down carefully by his side, watching him gently scrape the wet soil away from the grey cloth.

'See here, we've got the skull but there's a lot of damage to the bone. It's what happens in peat.'

He leaned back on his heels and wiped mud from his cheek with a grin. 'Sorry, can you see?'

She could now. He had exposed the top of a skull, the peat had stained it a dark brown but she could see a matted clump sticking out at the top.

'Is that hair?' she asked.

'No, there's a bit of skin left but I doubt if there'll be any hair to speak of. Do you want to give me a hand by brushing the soil off this piece of cloth?' He handed her some gloves and a tiny stiff brush.

Gingerly she began removing small clods of peat away from the material. To her it looked almost like sacking. She wanted to ask Phil what it was but she didn't like to interrupt him while he was concentrating on the head. Occasionally Mitch would peer down and ask how it was going, until after about an hour he announced that he had to be off but he didn't want to go leaving Mills on the site. Phil insisted that it would speed things up if she stayed to help and eventually the inspector agreed reluctantly.

'I'll leave a lad down there overnight,' he said, pointing to the bottom of the field. 'But I hope we'll be able to move the body tomorrow, eh?'

'Maybe,' muttered Phil.

They worked together until it began to get dark. Mills was full of admiration for the young man and the systematic way he worked. By the time he covered the remains with a tarpaulin there was a fully exposed skull. When he helped her back out of the ditch she realized that the others had left and they were alone on the moor.

'Thanks. I couldn't have got on so fast without you,' he said as they made their way down the hill.

They stood by the cars as he loaded his bags into the boot of a people carrier. Then he studied his watch. 'Gosh, is that the time?' He brushed his hair back from his forehead. 'Will you be here tomorrow?'

'I can be.'

'Good. I usually start about ten.'

Inside the farmhouse Brian was watching the cars disappear down the track.

'At last they've gone.'

'There's still the young man on the gate,' Sheila called from the kitchen. 'I'm going to take something out to him in a minute.'

'Can I go Mum?' called Kate.

'No, you know you're not to go out there while the police are working,' Sheila sounded uneasy, Brian thought.

He sat by the fire, watching his daughter working at the table. She was using a variety of felt tip pens, carefully selecting each in turn, using it briefly and then replacing it as she chose the next colour. The tip of her tongue protruded from between her lips as she concentrated on the drawing. Richard tottered over asking to be picked up. Brian placed his hands under his son's armpits and hauled him onto his knee. He heard the door go and strained to hear his wife as she went across the yard but the fire was crackling and Richard was laughing as he tried to climb over the arm of the chair.

'Why can't I go out there, Dad?' asked Kate without looking up.

'Because it's tea-time, love. So you'd better tidy up and lay the table for your mother.'

'Grandad didn't come today.'

'I know.'

'Mum had to go over and look after him while Granny had her hair done.'

'Did she?'

'She said it was because Grandad's ill.'

'Really?'

Brian waited until he heard the back door open and wandered into the kitchen, with Richard in his arms.

'Sheila? Kate says Grandad's ill.'

'His asthma is worse and he said he didn't want to come over. He was disappointed that he wouldn't be seeing the children this week. I wish you hadn't told him about the body, it seems to have really upset him.'

'Should I go over and see him?'

'I really don't know. Perhaps once it's all over.'

'When do they say it will be gone?' He had lowered his voice to almost a whisper.

'They don't know yet.' She pulled a resigned face and then peered into the next room. 'Now then Kate, have you laid that table yet?'

Anxious to resume the work, Mills arrived at nine but she wasn't the first. To her surprise Terry Lang's orange VW van was already in the farmyard. She went over to the constable on the gate and asked whether Dr Lang had been through.

'Oh no, miss. I couldn't let him through without the Inspector's say so. He's not here yet.'

Mills could barely suppress her amusement and went across the yard, assuming that he'd found refuge in the farmhouse.

Terry Lang was seated comfortably at the kitchen table. He looked surprised to see her.

'Sheila here has been very hospitable,' he said, waving a piece of toast in her direction.

'Would you like some tea, Mills?' Sheila was dropping teabags into a large brown pot. 'I'm making some for your boss.'

'How's it going?' asked Lang. 'Nige told me about the body. Thought I should come and see it for myself.'

'We'll have to wait until Phil arrives.'

'Phil?'

'He's the forensic archaeologist I was assisting yesterday.'

'Right.' Lang was concentrating on spreading a thick layer of marmalade on his toast.

Mitch appeared at the back door just as Sheila was pouring out the tea.

'Excellent timing,' he said and introduced himself to Lang, who remained seated.

'Terry is my project manager,' explained Mills, who had spent some time deciding how she would describe him. 'He is responsible for the work I have been doing on the hand.'

'Are you an archaeologist?' Mitch asked, smiling politely.

'Yes, I am.'

'He is an expert in bones,' added Mills.

'Excellent,' said Mitch. 'I can show you what we've found. Mills was assisting our forensic guy yesterday.'

'He asked me to come back today,' Mills said quickly.

'Fine. The more the merrier although we'd better wait until he arrives.'

They had only just climbed up to the ditch and were standing looking down at the tarpaulin when there was the distinctive sound of a motorbike roaring into the farmyard below.

'That's probably Phil now,' Mills said.

The three of them stood in a row waiting for him to appear below them and watching his progress up the hill. In addition to his heavy coat and woollen scarf, he had added a multicoloured knitted hat pulled down over his ears.

'Is that your camper van?' he asked when he was introduced to Lang.

'Yes, d'you like it?'

'Brilliant.'

The two men stood chatting until Mitch looked at his watch, then at Mills. 'Will you be assisting us today?' Phil asked. 'Mills and I will be glad of some help if you're free.'

'Absolutely!' shouted Lang striding over to the ditch and looking down. 'Awesome!'

Mills didn't know what she had expected but Lang seemed perfectly capable of working on the remains. He took the opposite side to her, clearing the mud from the clothing, while Phil continued to expose more of the skeleton. By the end of the morning it was possible to distinguish the outline of the body, including what looked like legs, shrouded in cloth, bent away to one side.

Mills stood up, stretching her arms and rolling her shoulders to release the tension that had built up from working in almost freezing conditions. Phil was out of the ditch in a single bound and offered her a hand up. They looked down at the remains. It was a real body now and Mills could believe it was a navvy from the railway, killed as he tried to escape a bunch of half-crazed men wielding clubs and knives chasing him up onto the moor.

'Any idea how old it is?' asked Lang as they made their way down to the farmhouse.

'No,' replied Phil. 'The decomposition suggests hundreds of years but the conditions are rather unusual. I've seen one like this before and it was actually not as old as it seemed.'

'How did you know?' Mills was interested to learn how they would establish the age of their body, and how long it would take to do so.

'The clothes. We've a marvellous lady who is an expert in fabrics. She virtually takes one look at a garment and can date it to within a few years.'

'Phil, before we go in,' said Mitch, 'can I ask you what will happen now? Can we move the body today?'

'Possibly. I want to loosen the rest of the remains this afternoon but it could be moveable by the end of the day.' He paused, rubbing his chin. 'If we could have some floodlights we might finish it off today.'

'Sounds a bit risky,' said Mitch, 'and it gets very cold up there after dark. I think we'd better assume it will be finished off tomorrow. Will you arrange the necessary?'

'What? Oh, I see. Yes, I'll get the van to come and pick up tomorrow afternoon. That will give us plenty of time to finish off.'

'Good news!' announced the inspector when they went into the warmth of Sheila's kitchen. 'We'll be moving out tomorrow.'

'And will that be the end of it? I do hope so,' she said. 'My husband wants to get it all covered up and forgotten.'

'I don't blame him,' said Mitch, 'but we will need it left as it is for a while, in case we have to look for a weapon.'

After lunch Mitch asked if they would examine the clothing in case there were any articles which might identify the body such as coins or papers.

'Rather not, mate,' said Phil as he jumped into the ditch, 'better leave that until we get him back to base.'

'Him?' Mitch looked suddenly interested again.

'Don't read anything into that. I call them all he until I know otherwise, not sure why.'

By four o'clock the wind had grown quite strong and the light was fading fast. Phil suggested they called it a day and Mills agreed willingly. Her hands were so numb that she struggled to remove her gloves and gratefully accepted Phil's help as she tried to scramble up the side of the ditch.

'Which way do you two go home?' he asked.

'I'm go back via Hawes and Leyburn. Is that the way you go?' Mills asked Lang.

'Yes.'

'I thought I'd stop for a cuppa in Hawes,' Phil continued, rubbing his hands together, 'fancy joining me?'

Mills wanted to but not if Lang was there too. Before she had a chance to decline Lang shook his head.

'No thanks, I've got to go in the other direction tonight.' Without any further explanation he started off down the hill.

'Mills?'

'Yes. I need something to warm me up.'

'Good. I'll see you in the café at the top of the town as soon as you get there. D'you know where I mean?'

'Yes.' She had seen the place where bikers usually stopped.

Lang set off and Mills followed, noting that he turned right onto the road towards Ingleton. She turned in the opposite direction and was soon overtaken by Phil, who waved as he disappeared round the bend ahead.

It was quiet in Hawes and the café was nearly empty. Phil was already seated at a table by the window.

'I ordered you a mug of tea. I'm going to have my supper here although it's a bit early – are you eating?'

'No, I'm fine.' So there's no-one at home making his tea, Mills thought.

'Still cold?'

'No, I'm nearly thawed out, thank you. The car heater is quite effective.'

'The bike's not so good. I still can't feel my hands.'

Mills found out as much as she could about Phil while she watched him wolf down pie, chips and beans. He had studied at Oxford and after doing his doctorate he had spent time working on mass graves near Belgrade. It wasn't something he wanted to talk about.

'When did you join the forensic service?'

'Two years ago. I thought I'd had enough of the forensic work but it seems to keep pulling me back.' He wiped his plate clean with a piece of bread and popped it into his mouth. 'So what about you?'

She told him about her time in university and how she worked in Manchester now.

'How can you bear to be stuck in a city like that? I wouldn't be able to stand it. Not to be able to walk in the hills whenever you want. High rise flats. Horrible.'

She agreed but felt she had to defend it. 'But it's a fantastic place to study.'

'Depends what you want to do. I'd rather be working on something that is relevant to people now.' He didn't sound pompous and Mills couldn't help but agree that his job was more relevant than hers.

'Whereabouts do you live then?' she asked.

'In Arkengarthdale.'

'Where?'

'Don't you know it? It's across the tops beyond Swaledale. Quite small but perfectly formed. I've got a cottage there – you must come and see it some time.'

'I'd like to.' She felt she had looked at him for too long and turned away. 'It's dark. I'd better be going.'

'See you tomorrow then?'

'I'll try.' She knew Nige needed the car to take Nina to the antenatal clinic.

'I can pick you up if it's a problem.' She wished he would stop looking at her. Before she could respond, he added, 'Or Mitch, he'll be coming your way. Do you want me to ask him?'

She agreed gratefully.

They left the café together.

'Drive carefully.' He smiled affectionately.

'I will.'

She thought about him all the way home. Three years as an undergraduate, then a PhD plus two years in the forensic science service. He must be at least twenty-eight. No there was the time in Belgrade. Possibly twenty-nine or thirty! Would a five year gap be a problem, she wondered.

Chapter 13

Nina was waiting for Mitch when he arrived to collect Mills. She had coffee waiting on the table and offered him toast, which he declined. Mills had overslept and they could hear her rushing about upstairs. Nina had let her doze because it gave her the opportunity to quiz her boss about the young lad who died in the caving accident.

'It's up in the air at the moment, Nina, but we've got some interesting evidence to assess. We're a bit short of analyst time at the moment.'

'I can help.'

He looked surprised.

She knew he would be difficult to convince of her ability to resume normal duties but she had to do something. It was driving her crazy to be so useless. She needed something to get her teeth into.

They both looked up as they heard Mills on the stairs.

'Please?' begged Nina.

'OK.'

They were sitting in silence when Mills opened the door.

'Sorry, I was checking my e-mails,' she announced.

'That's a big bag,' commented Mitch.

'Just some overnight things. I'm doing the Three Peaks tomorrow so I thought I'd stay down there.'

'Where will you stay?' asked Nina.

'I've just got a message from Maggie, she says I can use the caravan in Ingleton.'

Mills felt quite uncomfortable during the journey down to Ribbleshead. Mitch began by asking her what she thought about Nina returning to work in a wheelchair. He seemed to think once she had the baby she would decide to stay at home and give up the force. Mills wanted to defend her friend but wished to remain polite which meant they sat for much of the journey in silence. Later he tried to make conversation again, this time asking how she came to be working in forensic archaeology. Not wishing to admit that she knew nothing of the subject, she explained about the studies she had made on the hand before the police became involved. The change of topic put them back on a professional footing and the conversation relaxed. When Mitch mentioned Phil she was tempted to ask how well he knew him, but that was definitely not professional.

Mills could see the motorbike parked in the farmyard and was up the hill and in the ditch before Mitch could catch her up. The ground was still frozen in parts and they worked without conversation until they stopped for coffee. It was too cold to sit so they stood around, stamping their feet and warming their hands.

'So how's it going?' Mitch asked.

'It's going better than I thought considering the frost. We'll have it out in good time.' Phil smiled at Mills. 'We make a good team, don't we?'

'Well, I've got to get going,' said the inspector. 'There's another job in the area that needs my attention.' He looked at Phil. 'Can I have a word?' His jaw was tense as he turned and strode a few paces away. The two men spoke for a few minutes and then Mitch walked quickly down the hill, stopping only to speak briefly to the man on the gate.

Left on his own with Mills, Phil was more talkative than he had been in the morning. He explained what he was doing to expose the rest of the body and allowed her to assist him with superficially cleaning the peat adhering to the ribs, spine, arms and legs.

A few minutes later he gave a low whistle. 'Hey, look at this.'

'What is it?'

'He's been shot.' He was pointing to where the bone was shattered above the knee joint.

Her mind was racing. When did they start using guns? How did this affect her theory about railway navvy?

'Can you tell what sort of gun?'

He laughed and she was immediately self-conscious.

'I'm no expert but it may be possible to tell something from the way the bone has splintered. It'll be easier when we get the body back to base.' He looked at his watch. 'Talking of which, we've got a couple of hours before the van arrives.' He was so intent on the task in hand that Mills was reticent to ask about lunch, so she was relieved when Sheila arrived with some food for them. She peered gingerly over the edge of the ditch and made a squeaking sound.

'Oh my goodness, I didn't think..., I didn't expect...' She turned away and Phil bounded over to her.

'I'm sorry if it upset you,' he said. 'I should have warned you.'

'It's all right. It just startled me. I didn't expect to see a real... body.'

'Well, you'll be pleased to know that it's being moved soon. The van is arriving mid-afternoon.'

'That's a relief. We all just want to fill in the ditch and forget about the whole episode. It's affected the whole family.'

Mills handed Phil a sandwich as they watched Sheila make her way down the field. As she went through the gate into the lower field a small group of sheep walked towards her.

'She reminds me of my Mum a bit,' he said. 'When she was younger.'

'She's really nice.'

'Yes, like my Mum.'

Mills wanted to hear more about his mother but instead she bit into her sandwich and watched the last sheep disappear from view.

'Where's your boss today, Mills?'

'I don't know. I expect he's busy. He usually is,' she said. It was a great relief to her that he hadn't re-appeared.

She carried on with the meticulous work helping Phil loosen the final pieces of the skeleton from the peat. The cloth was attached in parts but much of it had separated. It was impossible to tell what it was but Mills instinctively felt they were not female attire. She knew that it was possible to tell the sex of a skeleton and was tempted to ask but didn't want to appear foolish.

'I'll go down and see if the van is coming. I can ring from the house. Will you be all right up here, Mills?'

'Of course.'

When he re-appeared, Mitch was with him and they were in deep conversation as they made their way across the moorland.

'Phil has asked if you can help at the laboratory but I've had to say no, Mills. In view of the nature of the injuries and the lack of any date of death, I don't think it would be appropriate.'

Phil grinned sheepishly at her and shrugged his shoulders. She smiled back to show her appreciation of his efforts. Mitch peered down at the skeleton, which was now lying almost completely intact at the bottom of the ditch.

'Can you tell if it's male or female?' he asked.

'From the pelvis and the skull I'd say it's definitely male,' Phil replied. 'We can confirm it in the lab.'

'I see that the skeleton has both its hands intact.'

'Yes, it is odd,' remarked Phil.

'I've been thinking about that,' said Mills. 'The skin of the hand must have somehow been detached as it changed chemically.'

'Really?' The inspector looked sceptical.

'Yes. Like a glove peeling off a hand.'

'Well don't look at me,' said Phil. 'I haven't seen anything preserved like that. It's not my area of expertise.'

Soon a team of three arrived to collect the body. Mills watched the woman take a series of photographs as the two men and Phil, gently manoeuvred the body onto a plastic sheet. They stopped at intervals while the camera flashed until finally the skeleton, with soil and rags attached, was coaxed gently into the black bag. She noted how carefully they carried their prize down the hill, leaving her standing alone by the empty ditch. It was as if there had never been anything there. She gathered the tools into Phil's bags and was waiting when he returned alone.

'Good. All done.'

'What happens now?'

'Too late to start anything today. We'll begin some tests on Monday.' He studied his watch. 'Look, I'm finished now. Are you going back with Mitch?'

'He was going to give me a lift down to Ingleton.'

'You can wait for him if you like but he might get delayed. He said he was going to a cave hereabouts.'

Mills continued walking and waited a few seconds to regain control of her voice.

'Do you know why?'

'Got divers down there. Crime scene,' he said. Some lad died down there a couple of weeks ago.'

They were almost at the gate. There was no guard now the body was gone. No longer a crime scene here, she thought.

She wanted to say that the kid was a friend but that might shut him up and she wanted to find out what he knew.

'What happened?'

'I don't know. He just wanted to ask me about the injuries. There was some head trauma that seemed suspicious.'

Mills moved mechanically to the farmhouse and knocked. She handed Sheila the flask and thanked her for her hospitality over the past weeks. She invited Mills in but she refused and wandered back into the yard without thinking how she was getting to Ingleton.

'So do you want a lift?' Phil asked.

'Yes, but…'

'Don't worry.' He went to the back of the bike and produced a helmet. 'Where is it you're going?'

It was not the first time she had been a passenger on a motorbike but it was her first experience of travelling through the open countryside on such a powerful machine. The undulating road sent them rising and falling until she began to feel quite ill and was grateful as Phil slowed for instructions on how to reach the caravan site.

To her surprise Mills found the site in darkness. Maggie's message had simply said that the key was hidden under the gas cylinder. Without the lights on the bike they would never have found it.

'This is a bit bleak,' said Phil, leading the way inside. 'When was it last used?'

'I rather assumed Maggie was still here. I saw her last week. It was warm then.'

They tried to light the propane heater but they couldn't work out how to turn the cylinder on.

'Well at least the lights are on electricity,' Mills said, hoping she sounded cheery.

'What about food?'

'Oh, I'll manage. I expect I'll meet Ewa at the pub later.'

'You can't stay here, you'll freeze. I can give you a lift back home.'

'No, I've got to be here early tomorrow. It's the Three Peaks. I've got to go.'

'Well, come to my place. I've got loads of space… and it's warm.' He stood looking at her. 'Well?'

'I don't know…' It had seemed such a good plan but the caravan was no longer the cosy place it had been the previous week when Maggie was in residence.

'Come on,' he said, taking control. 'It's a no-brainer. We'll go back and I'll make us something hot to eat before we get hypothermia. I can get you back here early tomorrow.'

What could she say? Less than an hour and she was sitting in front of a log fire sipping red wine and stroking a gentle grey lurcher with intelligent brown eyes.

'Do you like mushrooms,' Phil called from the kitchen.

'What's not to like?' she called back.

'Just tell Earl to go away if he's bothering you.'

'He's not bothering me. How old is he?'

'I've no idea. He found me just over a year ago. Just appeared one day when I was out walking. Couldn't locate the owners, probably Travellers.'

After dinner he showed her round the rest of the cottage. The rooms were small but they were cosily furnished with a mixture of styles that combined to make a lived-in home.

'This is the guest room,' he announced proudly as they entered the last room upstairs. 'I'll put a hot water bottle in for you – it hasn't been used since I moved in.'

'When was that?'

'Nearly two years ago. Sad or what?'

Mills felt mixed emotions, trying to decide whether he saw her as special or just didn't normally entertain.

'Can I use your phone?' she asked when they were back downstairs. 'I must get in touch with Ewa – she's arranging tomorrow's walk. I can't get a signal here.'

It was difficult line. Ewa was in the pub and there was a background of lively chatter.

'Steve and I can give you lift to beginning at Horton, Meels.'

'No, it's all right. I can get to Horton myself. What time are we starting?'

'Steve! Steve! What time Meels says.' There was a pause. 'What? What? OK. OK, no problem.'

Suddenly her voice became clear again. 'Meels, are you there? OK. Steve says meet at eight o' clock at café; it is start of walk. Yes?'

'Yes that's fine. I'll be there. Are there many coming?'

'I ask them tonight. I am sure many will come.'

'Everything OK?' Phil asked as she settled back down by the fire.

'Yes… I think so.'

The rest of the evening they chatted and watched television together, always under Earl's watchful gaze. When the news finished, Mills yawned and said she should be going to sleep as she had an early start.

'Do you mind taking me down to Horton?' she asked. 'I told Ewa that I'd be there at seven-thirty.'

'Will it be light by then?'

'I don't know but it will be a long day. I've never walked so far before. Have you done it?'

'No. I was wondering… if I could come with you, if your friends don't mind.'

Of course she wanted him to come but it didn't seem right when it was Fred's day. And Ewa might not like it. She explained that it was awkward because it had been arranged by Ewa. But she didn't say why it had been arranged.

'Perhaps you could ask her when we get there? I won't be offended if she says no. But I will want to meet you when you get back to join in the celebrations.' He was leaning back on the sofa with the dog lying across his feet. He looked so relaxed, Mills doubted if anything would offend him.

'Wake up, Mills.'

At first Mills couldn't place the voice and was disoriented. The room was dimly illuminated by a light in the hall and she could see a figure in the doorway.

'Phil?'

'It's time to get up. I've cooked some breakfast so hurry up before it burns and Earl gets it instead!'

She could smell bacon as she made her way to the bathroom. It didn't take her long to climb into her walking gear and pack her rucksack ready for the journey. Downstairs the lurcher was still curled up in his basket. Phil was shovelling bacon, egg and fried bread onto two plates.

'Sit down. Tuck in.'

Usually Mills would avoid a cooked breakfast at seven in the morning but she had slept so well and felt so relaxed that she wolfed it down with brown sauce and toast.

'Ready for the cold?'

It had snowed overnight, leaving a covering on the fells but not enough to settle on the roads. Mills was glad she was dressed for the hills as they sped along in the half-light, her eyes watering in the biting wind.

There was just a single car parked in the public car park in Horton-in-Ribblesdale. As Mills climbed off the bike, the front passenger door of the car opened, casting a beam of light across the gravel as Ewa got out.

'Hi there Meels!' she called and turned back, as if urging the driver to emerge.

Mills waited for Phil to switch off the engine and then indicated for him to come over to meet her friend.

'Ewa, this is Phil. He gave me a lift down.'

They shook hands in a formal way.

'So where are the others?' Mills asked brightly.

'I think no others,' Ewa said with an exaggeratedly glum face. 'I ask them but they all busy.'

'So it's just the two of us?' Mills looked over at the waiting car.

'No, Steve is in car. He's… he's… cold. I go get him.' She returned to the car and opened the driver's door.

'Sounds like they might welcome an extra body,' suggested Phil.

Mills followed Ewa with the intention of asking if Phil could join them but as she got near she could hear raised voices and retraced her steps slowly. If those two were going to be her only companions it was becoming increasingly attractive to have Phil along as well.

'I think we'll just assume that you're coming!' she said to him quietly as they stood together in the half-light.

At last Steve emerged, struggling into a jacket and pulling on a large rucksack. Ewa introduced him and kept up a cheerful chatter to cover the fact that Steve was clearly not happy. However, he obviously knew the route and led off at high speed. It was fine for Phil with his long legs, thought Mills, but she wasn't sure that she would be able to keep up the pace for over twenty miles. The group walked quickly across the road and through the farm to begin the ascent of Pen-y-Ghent. The cold air formed clouds as Mills breathed heavily on the first uphill section of the day. There were patches of snow remaining but mostly it had thawed leaving the ground sodden. She didn't want to talk and was happy to maintain the pace in order to keep warm until the sun appeared. They must appear a miserable band, she thought, strung out in a line, almost invisible under layers of thick clothing, hats, scarves and gloves. Steve was leading the way, never turning or communicating with Ewa who was following close behind him. Phil remained with Mills and whenever she turned round he was always a few metres away, looking as cheerful as ever. The climb up the first peak was hard work but rewarding. There were bigger patches of snow as they reached the summit and in the low morning sun the view across to Widdale was spectacular.

'This is beautiful,' declared Ewa. 'A very fitting way to pay tribute to poor Freddie.' She sounded out the words slowly and Mills wondered whether she had consulted her dictionary especially. Steve was already climbing the ladder stile and they set off in pursuit.

'Too cold to hang around for long but if he carries on at this rate we'll be back in time for lunch,' murmured Phil as he waited for Mills to clamber down the stile.

'If we keep this up I'll be dead before lunch-time,' Mills replied but to be honest she felt pretty good so far, except for the cold which seemed to be getting worse.

They moved more slowly downhill where the thaw had left the ground boggy and Mills was quite relieved when they emerged onto a farm track. While she stamped her feet, Phil consulted the map.

'There's a bridge up ahead called "God's Bridge",' he said. 'The road goes right along to the viaduct from here. That's Nether Lodge.'

'Quite the tour guide, aren't you?' teased Mills.

'I like to know where I'm going,' he replied, 'unlike our friend up there at the front.' He indicated Steve, who was about a hundred metres ahead of Ewa.

'Do you think we'll be able to stop for a minute when we get to the viaduct?' Mills asked. 'We'll be a third of the way round and we're making good time.'

'We can do whatever we want, Mills.'

'I think I'll ask Ewa.'

She ran to catch the girl up, nearly slipping on a patch of ice, and tapped her on the shoulder. 'Hi.'

'Meels. Are you OK? I think we walk too fast. Is hard work.' She kept moving at the same pace, looking ahead and breathing hard.

'Is Steve all right.'

'I guess so.'

'I suppose he's upset about Fred, being with him when it happened?'

'Perhaps. And perhaps he is angry with me.'

Mills walked along with her, wondering what to say.

'He is angry because I do this.'

'What, the walk?'

'Yes. He think I'm stupid, foolish girl. He say that no-one else want to do stupid walk.'

'I did.'

'Yes but you were special friend.'

'Not really.'

'Yes, I know. He told me that.'

'So why is Steve angry?'

'Because he thinks I was special friend too.'

Mills could think of no response and walked in silence beside her until a suitable period had passed and she could change the subject.

'Do you think we could stop for a few minutes at the viaduct?'

'Of course. It is nearest place to the cave where... We should stand for a few minutes and say prayer.'

'Yes, of course.'

Phil, who had remained a short distance behind, quickly caught Mills up when she slowed down.

'So what was the verdict?'

'It's a bit complicated. We're going to stop at the viaduct but…'

'What?' Phil asked with a laugh.

'Well, it probably sounds a bit weird but Ewa wants to pray.'

Phil looked amused. 'She doesn't strike me as a typical muslim lady.'

Mills would have found it funny if it wasn't such a delicate subject.

'No. You see, the reason for this walk is to commemorate a friend, mutual friend, who died in a caving accident a little while ago. And the cave was nearby.'

'Runscar,' said Phil after a pause. He was looking serious now.

'Yes.'

'Mitch. He didn't want to discuss it in front of you. I couldn't understand why.'

'The case?' They were standing facing each other now.

'It's probably best not to discuss it now.'

'Why not?' His expression changed as she raised her voice. He looked almost hurt as he took her arm.

'I'm sorry Mills but it's Steve. He was there when it happened. He could be a suspect.'

She opened her mouth but didn't know what to say. Her mind was going through so many options at once. 'OK,' was all she managed as they walked on.

'I think the plan to stop at the viaduct is sensible,' he called after her as she speeded up. 'Look at the dark cloud over there. Looks like more snow.'

She turned round and saw the weather closing in from the north.

'I don't think Ewa meant a permanent stop; just a break,' she said as he caught her up.

It felt colder as soon as the sun went in. Their faster pace brought them level with Ewa who obviously welcomed their company. She chatted to Mills, who was pleased not to have to continue her conversation with Phil. She was trying to determine in her own mind what his comments had meant. Did Mitch really suspect Steve of being involved in Fred's death? She shivered and looked sideways to catch Phil watching her.

'Would you tell Steve that we're stopping at the viaduct?' she asked him.

He increased his pace and was soon out of earshot.

'Ewa, was Steve with Fred when he died?'

'No. No he find him. When they say that he is missing, Steve go back to search him.'

Mills watched Phil catch Steve up and walk alongside him. They seemed to be chatting amiably.

'That must have been upsetting for him.'

'Upsetting?'

'Sad, distressing, making him unhappy.'

'I guess so. To me his is just angry.'

'Perhaps he felt he could have done something. Prevented it happening?'

'Perhaps. I say to him you must not feel guilty but he is worse.'

'It will take time.'

'Hmm.'

They caught the men up at the main road and the four stood huddled together by the Station Inn. A few flakes of snow fell and immediately melted on the tarmac.

'I think it would be foolish to carry on in this,' Phil said. No-one responded. 'It's going to get worse, look at that sky.'

They all turned to stare in the direction of Hawes. Mills, noticing the dipped headlights of a police car coming down the road, glanced round to see who had noticed it. Steve was staring at it biting his bottom lip.

'Well I think we should keep going. If we're going to do it, we'd better get on with it.' Steve said angrily.

'I agree with Phil,' Mills said, surprising herself. 'It would be silly to carry on.' She was remembering the first time she had met Fred not far from this spot. The snow had come out of nowhere when she had been by the aqueduct and so had Fred. She didn't want to go to the same place again. Not now. Not with Ewa and Phil, especially not Phil.

'Do you think so Meels?' Ewa's face was white with cold, she was rubbing her hands together and breathing into them even though she was wearing woollen mittens. 'Surely Freddie would have carried on?' she asked unconvincingly.

'I don't think so,' answered Mills.

'Well I'm off. See you.' Steve turned and set off up the track, which was hardly visible under the thin layer of snow.

Mills noticed that the police car had parked in the pub car park.

'I suggest we go inside and see if we can get a hot drink and something to eat,' suggested Phil.

'But how we get back?' Ewa asked.

'I've got an idea,' said Phil, 'come on, I'm frozen.'

Mills led Ewa to a seat near the fire while Phil went to ask for coffee.

'Was cold in caravan last night?' asked Ewa.

Mills admitted that she had stayed with Phil. 'We went to look at it. It was quite difficult because it was dark. Fortunately it's the only one with a garden shed next to it so I was able to recognise it. It took ages to find the key because she had left it under the cylinder.'

'Cylinder?'

'Propane gas – they use it for cooking.'

'I see.'

'Anyway, in the end I stayed with Phil.'

'He seems nice man.'

'Phil? Yes he's very nice.'

'He your boyfriend?'

'No, not really.'

'You work with him?'

'Yes, well no, not exactly. We met over work.'

They watched him chatting to the landlord, who disappeared into the kitchen. He then started a conversation with two men who were leaning against the bar. The way they turned and greeted him convinced Mills that they were from the police car.

Phil finally returned with three coffees and sank down, holding his hands to the fire.

'Well?' asked Mills, 'What was the clever idea you had?' She suspected that it concerned his friends at the bar.

'I just got us a lift back to Horton.'

'Would it be in a police car by any chance?'

'How did you guess?' he asked with a grin.

'Can you drive Steve's car, Ewa?' Mills asked.

'Of course – I drove this morning. I have keys, see? But what about Steve?'

'I'm sure he'll be all right.' Phil said. 'If he's a caver, he can manage a bit of snow.'

Soon the two men came over to introduce themselves. Mills noticed how attentive they were to Ewa and she suspected that the driving technique was designed to impress her. She was relieved when they arrived back at the car park in Horton safely.

'Are you sure you'll be all right, Ewa?' Phil asked once more.

'Yes. I go to Steve's flat and wait for him there.' She hugged Mills and gave Phil a kiss on both cheeks.

'I don't know about you,' Phil said, 'but I need a nice hot bath. Let's get back home.'

Ewa didn't know how Steve got back to the flat that evening. She cooked a meal for the two of them but when he wasn't home by seven she ate her share. Eventually he arrived, cold and tired but still angry. She couldn't tell whether he was cross with her, himself or someone else. He refused to speak but sat with his head in his hands until she begged him to tell her what the matter was.

'Do you want me to leave?' she asked finally.

He lifted his head and looked at her.

'Yes, that would be best. You go.'

She went to the bedroom and sat on the edge of the bed. She couldn't get a train that evening and she didn't know where to spend the night. When she had packed her bag, she went to say goodbye but he ignored her. Sadly she pulled the front door behind her and stepped out into the night. She had just a few pounds in her purse and was too humiliated to contact her old friends. There was one person she knew where she could spend the night, so she called up his name on her mobile phone with fingers that were numb with cold.

Chapter 14

Nige was in the kitchen when he answered the phone. He ran upstairs and handed it to Nina who was lying in bed listening to the radio.

'It's Mitch.'

She struggled into a sitting position and pulled the duvet up to her neck.

'Mitch? How are you?'

'I'm fine Nina. Sorry to bother you but I just wanted to check something. It's about the young caver. I got your report and I'm going to move on it. I think we all agree that there's sufficient evidence to bring Steve Bellamy in for questioning.'

'Right.'

'Can you get in to the station tomorrow to sit in on the interview?'

'I don't see why not. I can get Nige to drop me off on the way to work. By the way, how did the work go on Friday? I haven't seen Mills since.'

'We got the body out. She helped our guy finish off. I had to go over to Runscar.'

'Did she get to Ingleton all right?'

'That I don't know. She and Phil had gone by the time I got back. In fact did she say she was going to a caravan site? It's a strange coincidence and probably nothing. I heard that there's been an incident …'

'What incident?' She put her hand out for Nige.

'What's up?' He sat on the edge of the bed holding her free hand in both of his.

'There's been a fire. I'll find out more and get back to you. I just thought that she mentioned staying down there overnight.'

'She was. She was going to stay there on Friday night. I haven't heard from her since. I just assumed… Oh my God, what if…'

'Now then Nina, you know better than to jump to conclusions. I'll get back to you as soon as I have anything.'

He rang off. Nina sat, still holding the phone to her ear.

'What's wrong?' Nige was stroking her arm.

'I don't know yet. Help me get up. We're going to Ingleton.' She rang her friend but her phone was off so she left a message begging her to ring back immediately.

Nina wanted to set off for Ingleton straightaway but Nige managed to persuade her that they should wait for Mitch to ring back. She had little choice since she depended on him to drive, like everything else. She vented her frustration by attempting to dress herself unaided which resulted in her sitting on the bed in tears while Nige helped her on with her socks.

They sat in silence at the kitchen table waiting for the call. When it finally came Nina grabbed the phone, glaring at Nige.

'Mitch?'

'Nina.'

'What's happened?'

'I'll tell you what I know. There was an explosion at the caravan site last night, in the early hours, about two-thirty. It was a propane gas cylinder going off. We don't know if it caused the fire or was caused by the fire but the result was that a caravan was burnt out.'

'Was anybody hurt?'

She could hear him breathing heavily.

'They have found a body.'

'We'll go down, now.'

'There's no point, Nina. There's nothing to see. I'd rather you stayed put in case I need you to…'

She knew what he meant. He might need her to identify the body. She put the receiver down and burst into tears.

Mike had been almost the first on the scene, although the explosion was heard right across Ingleton. Some had put it down to fireworks but Mike knew it was bigger than that. Peering at the illuminated hands of his alarm clock, the newspaper editor had made a mental note: two-thirty-four precisely. He dressed quickly and had just finished scraping the windscreen when he saw a blue flashing light pass the end of his road. He jumped in and followed at speed. Afterwards, when he was relating the occasion to his friends, he recalled that he was going too fast round the bends; if anything had been coming the other way…

The glow of the fire had been visible long before he turned into the caravan site. There was barely anything left of the van; it was a twisted mess of metal and plastic. He pulled up well away from the police car and hovered quietly in the background until the fire engine arrived. Not that they could do much. Eventually he was spotted by one of the police officers who asked him for some identity.

'It's OK, constable,' shouted his sergeant. 'It's Mike from the Mercury.'

'It's all right lad, I'll keep out of yer hair.'

He waited until the flames had been extinguished and the body had been taken away before he approached the sergeant.

'Do we know how it started?' he asked casually.

'No. 'Appen it was a faulty cylinder. Didn't imagine anyone was staying here at this time of year.'

'Are you sure about that? I had a visitor recently who said she were staying on the site.'

'Is that right?'

'Ay, and I reckon you may have met her too. She was dead set on complaining about your lack of action as far as I remember.'

The sergeant looked puzzled.

'I think she was called Maggie. Oldish woman, went by the name of Maggie.'

'Oh no, not the woman with the little dog.'

'I don't know about any dog, she just came to see me about my lad who died in the caving incident.'

The young constable interrupted with a message for the sergeant.

'Thanks for the info, Mike. I'll need you to make a statement in due course. Got to get on now.'

'Righto. I'll get out of your hair.' Mike knew they wouldn't be able to do much until daylight.

The next day he was back at the scene of the fire soon after breakfast. He chatted to the young constable on duty there and offered to fetch him a bacon sandwich. He was back within twenty minutes, by which time his sergeant had appeared with three plain clothes colleagues and a photographer.

'Not an accident then?' Mike asked.

'Not clear at this stage. We are continuing with our enquiries. You can quote me on that.'

'Do you know if it is her?'

'What, the old dear? No idea. The body's a mess. Burnt to a crisp.'

Mike lowered the sandwich without taking a bite. 'When will you have identification?'

'As soon as I can get on with my work, Mike.'

He took her hint, wandering away until he could survey the scene undetected.

The caravan had been totally destroyed by the blaze and the remains of the cylinder was lying about fifty yards from the ruins. At this stage the police are unable to issue a statement but investigations are under way to establish the identity of the body. However, the Mercury has information that points to a terrible arson attack resulting in the death of a defenceless old lady and her dog. When she spoke to our reporter she was trying to alert the local police about her concerns...

The young police constable had just re-appeared from the bushes, where he had presumably been relieving himself. Mike went down to head him off.

'Excuse me, constable. I wondered if I could ask you something. Your sergeant said it would be OK to request information.'

'Oh ay.'

'The caravan, do you know who the owner is?'

He pulled the notepad from his pocket.

'It's a lady who lives here in Ingleton, a Mrs Threlfall.' He shut his notepad.

'Thank you, son.'

'Constable! Get back here at once!'

'That's the sarge, I'd best be off.'

'That's all right, son,' muttered Mike under his breath, 'I've got what I need.'

It didn't take him long to find her and she was perfectly willing to tell him all about the disaster of her lost caravan. When he asked her if anyone was staying there she said no, it was not let out in the winter.

'Not even to friends or relatives?'

'Not at present.'

Clearly the police had not mentioned the details of the tragedy to her. After a second cup of tea and hot buttered scone he had established that she had a cousin called Maggie who lived in Kirkbymoorside. She had a snappy little terrier called Snowy.

…a terrible arson attack resulting in the death of a defenceless old lady and her dog, Snowy. When she spoke to our reporter she was trying to alert the local police about her concerns regarding the death of a local lad in a caving 'accident'. Did she know something that put her in danger? Could the police have acted to prevent her tragic death…

Mike leant back in his chair, rubbing his chin. He couldn't erase the picture of the agitated woman, standing in his office telling him about the man called Iain Small. He picked up the phone and called the photographer.

'Can you get over to the caravan site. Get some shots of the burnt out van before the police take it off for forensics.'

'What's the story?'

'Not sure but it could be big.'

'Wake up now, young lady! Your breakfast is ready.'

Phil was standing beside the bed with a tray and she recognised the delicious smell of bacon and coffee. She sat up, taking in Phil's room with its heavy dark furniture.

'How are you this morning?' He placed the tray on a dark oak chest at the bottom of the bed.

'I feel wonderful, thank you.' She smiled and he came round to give her a kiss.

'Oh and here's Earl to say hello!'

The dog walked over to the bed and laid his head on the cover beside her.

'I think he's after a bit of bacon.'

'What about you?' she asked.

'Oh I had mine ages ago. We've been out for a walk. It's a lovely day.'

'I'd better get up too, then,' said Mills.

'No, no, no. First have your breakfast and then… well, I'll see you downstairs. No rush.' He grinned and left the room; Earl stayed to share her bacon.

Mills found Phil in the kitchen.

'Mills, I thought we could walk down to the pub for lunch. Work up an appetite.'

'Sounds good but I was thinking I should ring Nina. I haven't got a signal. Can I use your phone?'

'Sure, go ahead.'

The phone only rang once before she heard Nina's voice.

'Hello?' Her voice sounded anxious.

'Nina?'

'Who is it?'

'It's me. Mills.'

There was a scream at the other end. 'Nige, it's Mills! She's on the phone.'

Mills waited for her to calm down.

'Nina, what's happened? What's the matter?'

'Oh Mills, we thought… I thought… They said… Here Nige, you tell her.'

There was a pause. Mills thought she could hear wailing.

'Mills? Are you OK?'

His gentle Welsh burr was reassuring.

'I'm fine. I was only staying over with Phil. What's the matter with Nina? Is she crying? Is it the baby?'

'Yes, well no. It's fine. She thought you were dead that's all.'

'Dead?'

'Because of the caravan. She thought you were in the caravan. It blew up.'

'You're kidding!'

'No. Someone was killed and she thought it was you.'

'I'd better come back.'

'No, it's OK. It's not a problem now we know you're safe. Nina's fine now.'

Mills sighed. 'I'm going out for lunch but I'm sure Phil will bring me back straight after.'

'OK. We'll be here.'

The way down to the pub followed the beck in the bottom of the dale. The trees were white with frost and the ground was frozen. They passed no-one as they made their way talking and laughing. It was only when they passed a derelict barn that Mills was reminded of her phone call to Nina and the hysterical response it caused. Had she said that someone had been hurt in the fire at Ingleton? The caravans had all been deserted when they went down on Friday but could someone have arrived for the weekend.

Her mood soon changed once they were in the warmth of the "CB". It was full of customers enjoying Sunday lunch in an atmosphere that instantly relaxed Mills so she was able to enjoy Phil's company. Their conversation was easy and flitted from their mutual interest in archaeology to a discussion of their favourite television programmes as children. But once the bill was paid – Mills tried to insist on sharing the cost but without success – and they were on their way back she asked Phil about the 'accident' at the cave.

'Is Steve really under suspicion?' she asked, unsure what the correct term should be.

'He was one of the cavers present that day. That's all.'

'You mean it could have been any of them?'

'I don't know, Mills. All Mitch said was that they were concerned about the nature of the head wound and were treating the death as suspicious.'

'But why would anyone want to hurt him? He was such a nice guy.'

'It may be nothing. You know what the police are like, always suspicious.'

'What d'you think will happen?'

'Not sure. It may mean further tests on the… body. Look, are you comfortable talking about this?'

'It's not a problem. The important thing is to know the truth.'

'You're right there.'

They walked in silence, retracing their steps until they were turning up the narrow green lane to Phil's cottage. The lurcher greeted them at the door then turned back to the fire, where he curled up on his grubby rug.

'Just time for a cuppa before I get you back home, Miss Sanderson. That's if you want to go?'

'Better had.' She didn't want to outstay her welcome.

The reception that met them when they arrived back in town was overwhelming. Nina was in tears as she explained how she had thought Mills had died in the fire. Nige had been on the internet to find out more but there was no mention of the body found in the caravan.

'Does it say who owned the caravan?' asked Mills.

'No. Just that there was an explosion.' Nige answered.

'Explosion?' asked Phil and Mills together.

'A gas cylinder went up.'

They looked at each other but said nothing.

'I'm making tea if that's OK with you,' announced Nina wheeling herself into the kitchen. Mills followed.

'He seems very nice, Millie.'

'Thank you.'

'You know what I mean.'

'Yes.'

'Did you have a nice weekend?'

'Yes.'

'You gave me a fright…'

'I know and I'm sorry. I should have called you when I decided not to stay at the caravan. It was so cold and we couldn't get the gas to work.'

'Oh no, you don't think it could have been leaking?'

'No. There was no way we could even budge it. Anyway there's nothing to say it was that caravan. Was there?'

'No, of course not. Now, does he take milk and sugar?'

Nige and Phil were discussing the merits of ground penetrating radar to search for bodies when Mills carried the tray in. She took pleasure from the fact that they were getting on so well. She wanted her friends to like him. It was late by the time she followed him outside to see him off.

'Busy looking at the body tomorrow I suppose?' she asked.

'Yep,' he said, putting his arms round her. 'So when will I see you next?'

'I don't know.' She would be making her final arrangements to return to Manchester this week.

'Well, I think we should definitely get together on Thursday.'

'You do?'

'Yes.' He gave her a final kiss and climbed onto the bike. 'I'll give you a call before then.'

She watched him turn the corner before moving back inside with a shiver. Her phone had been off all day so she popped upstairs to switch it on – in case he called later. There were two messages. The first was from Dad. He rarely had anything to say but generally rang once a week. She suspected that Fiona told him to do so. Anyway she would ring him tomorrow.

The second message was from Maggie. It was garbled but from what she could gather, the woman had heard the news and was worried about Mills. Her voice was verging on the hysterical and insisted she ring her as soon as she got her message.

'Maggie?'

'Mills? My. I've been so anxious.'

'You heard about the fire?'

'My cousin rang me. She was concerned for me but I told her I wasn't staying there. Then I thought of you. My word, I am so relieved!'

'Was it your cousin's caravan?'

'Yes!'

'So who was staying there?'

'No-one.'

'But I thought there was someone killed.'

'No, I don't think so. Lucky you weren't there or it might have been different.'

'Yes… I suppose so.'

'To be honest I do wonder if… no, I shouldn't say.'

'What?'

'If it was arson. I wondered if someone thought I would be there.'

'You mean deliberately set fire to it?'

'Yes. And you know who knew I stay there.'

'No. Who?'

'Iain Small, that's who. There I've said it now.'

'Maggie, I don't think that's possible really, do you?'

'I'm just saying, who else knew I stayed there? In fact that's why I met him there, so he wouldn't know where I lived.'

When Mills went back downstairs she checked with Nina about someone dying in the fire.

'Did I say that?' she asked. 'Maybe, but if I did it was in confidence. Please?'

'OK.'

Changing the subject abruptly Nina asked if she would be meeting Phil again.

'I'm seeing him on Thursday.'

'Ahh!' Nige was grinning.

'What?'

'The fourteenth,' Nina replied. 'The fourteenth of February?'

'Oh, I didn't realise.' She was blushing. 'It's Valentine's Day.'

'Ingleton have had that mad woman from Kirkbymoorside on the phone again!' Hazel was calling to Mitch as he bounded up the stairs to the office.

'What is it this time?'

'The same thing really. She's saying that Small is trying to kill her.'

'He'll not be the only one,' Mitch muttered as he struggled out of his coat. 'Look, I've asked Nina to come in today for the interview. Have they got Bellamy?'

'Yes, Guv, he's downstairs.'

'Good. We'll start as soon as she arrives.'

'She's here. I've just taken a coffee down for her.'

'In that case I'll be five minutes. And I want you in there as well.'

Steve Bellamy was sitting hunched over the table, head in hands.

'Would you like a cup of tea, Mr Bellamy?' Mitch began. He always started off friendly and worked systematically, avoiding any serious confrontation unless strictly necessary. He had studied his boss at work and decided at an early stage not to follow his example.

The lad refused a drink with a shake of his head.

'I think you know why we're here, Mr Bellamy?'

'Yes. It's about the accident.' His voice was quiet and Mitch asked him to speak up.

'It's about Fred.'

'That's right. You were the first to find him?'

'Yes. I've been through all this.'

'I know, but bear with me. We have some additional information so we need to check it out. All right?'

'I suppose so.'

The lad seemed distant. He heard the questions. He answered them. But all the time he seemed distracted. He jiggled his knees up and down and looked round the room as he answered.

'…so when you found him, he was in the water?'

'Yes.'

'So what did you do?'

'I pulled his head out of the water and tried to find a pulse. I couldn't find it but I thought he was alive. I tried to clear his airways, I did everything I could think of and then I called the others.'

'How long did you spend doing all that.'

'Not long.'

'How long?'

'Few minutes I suppose. No, probably no more than a minute.'

'Did you know Fred well?'

'I wouldn't say well.'

'But you were mates.'

'Not really mates.'

'A friend? An acquaintance?'

'We went caving in a group. That's how I knew him.'

'You have a girlfriend?'

'No.'

'No? I thought you did. Let me see.' He deliberately referred to his notebook.

'Ewa Prodanovic.'

'It's Ewa, with a vee,' replied Steve.

'Is that a foreign name?'

'She's from Serbia.'

'Right, sorry. Eva, then. Is she your girlfriend?'

'No. Not any more.'

'I'm sorry.'

'Where is she? Is she here?' Steve was looking round anxiously.

'What's the matter, Steve? Worried she might have shopped you?'

'No!' He looked pained. Mitch thought he resembled a small child who had been caught pinching sweets.

'What's the matter, Steve?'

There was no reply.

'I'm terminating the interview at…' He looked at his watch. 'Nine forty-five.'

The three detectives drank coffee while they reviewed progress so far.

'There's something worrying the lad, that's for sure,' said Hazel.

'Yes, you're right.' Mitch said. 'He seemed quite rattled when we mentioned the girlfriend. Thanks for the information, Nina.' She said nothing. 'Hopefully his solicitor will advise him to do the right thing.'

Back in the interview room, it was Hazel's turn.

'Steve, there's obviously something worrying you.' She looked at the elderly duty solicitor, who returned the stare.

'Is there something you want to say?'

Their suspect looked at the grey-haired man sitting next to him and then across to Hazel.

'You think I did something to Fred, don't you?'

'Did you?'

'I tried to help. But maybe I did it wrong. Maybe I did something wrong. Did I?'

'Did you hit him hard on the head?'

Mitch looked at Hazel with a surprised expression.

'No, of course not. I put my fingers down his throat. Would that have done something wrong?'

'No.' Hazel looked angry and Mitch felt disappointed.

'Tell me about Fred,' she continued.

'Like what?'

'Did he have any particular friends?'

'Don't know.'

'A girlfriend?'

'I suppose.'

'Who?'

'Some girl from the university.'

'Were you jealous of him?'

'No. Why should I be?'

'Because you'd lost your girlfriend, Ewa.'

'No I hadn't.'

'But you said she wasn't with you anymore.'

'She was then.'

'So why did you split up?'

'I don't know.'

'Was it over Fred?'

Mitch let her continue but wondered where it was leading and threw a quizzical look in her direction.

'Perhaps Fred was interested in Ewa?'

'No!'

'So Ewa was interested in Fred.'

No answer.

'So you were jealous of Ewa's interest in Fred and decided to get rid of him?'

'No!'

'Right. Let's stop there for a moment.' Mitch was unhappy with the way the interview was going. 'I think it might be a good idea for us to have a chat with Ewa Prodanovic.' He carefully pronounced her first name correctly but struggled over her surname. 'Where can we find her?'

'I don't know!' The three of them stared as the young man burst into tears. When he had pulled himself together, Mitch smiled at him and asked gently, 'Where is she, lad?'

'I don't know. I followed her to the caravan site and that was the last time I saw her!'

'Hazel. Get the lad a cup of tea. I'm adjourning the interview to let him gather his thoughts. Nina, can I have a word?'

She followed him down the corridor and into an empty office. He held the door for her and closed it quietly.

'This girl Eva, Ewa whatever. You said that Mills Sanderson knows her?'

'Yes.'

'Would she know how to get in touch with her?'

'Probably.'

'Do what you can. There's a phone here. Let Hazel know if you need owt; she'll be along the corridor with the lad. I've got things to do.' He turned to go.

'Guv?'

'Yes, Nina.'

'Do you think there's a connection between the caravan fire and this girl?'

'Could be. It's up to you to find out.'

Nina spent the next two hours on the telephone. She left a message with forensics then tried the morgue but they were busy. Eventually her friend rang back and she asked her about the girl from Serbia.

'Is there anything about her that is distinctive, Millie?'

'Like what?'

'Anything. Tattoos, piercings, teeth, hair…'

'She has long blonde hair, really blonde, bleached blonde. Why do you want to know?'

'OK. What else?'

'She's quite tall and speaks with an Eastern European accent. Is she missing?'

'Tattoos?'

'I wouldn't know. Her ears are pierced, I suppose. Nina, what is this all about?'

'It may be nothing. We just need to find her. Do you have a number?'

'Of course. Why didn't you say?'

Nina noted down the mobile number before asking Mills when she had last seen the girl. Finally she asked the question that had been worrying her.

'Millie, listen. Did Ewa Prodanovic know Maggie? Did she know about the caravan?'

'I don't think so.'

'Are you sure? You didn't take her there or tell her about it?'

'I suppose I might have mentioned it… in passing. Why?'

'I'm sorry. Police business.'

There was a pause.

'We just want to locate Ewa so she can help us with our enquiries.'

'What enquiries?'

'Sorry Mills.' She replaced the receiver and stared at the pale blue wall opposite. She tried Ewa's number but it was off. But she had little time to brood before the phone disturbed her thoughts. The pathologist was finally returning her call. She requested as much detail as he could give her on the body from the fire but he had little to offer. Eventually she stopped him.

'I'm going to describe a possible victim, would you tell me whether it is possibly the same person?'

'I'll try.'

She repeated what Mills had told her about Ewa and waited.

'Well… it's always difficult but it could fit. She is certainly in the right age range. It's not impossible. Is she missing?'

'Not sure. I'll get back to you.'

'Well, if you're getting more information it would be helpful to find her dental records. If she's from

Serbia there might be something distinctive that we could work with.'

Nina wrote a few notes and then picked up the phone and tried forensics again. This time there was someone in the office. They could tell her little, except that it was definitely arson. Diesel everywhere.

'Anything to identify who was staying there?'

'No. Not even enough left of the mobile phone to give a clue.'

Nina finished the conversation quickly and dialled another number.

'Julian? It's Nina. Yes, thanks. Fine, really. I'm at work. Yes. Can you do me a favour? I've got a mobile number here. Could you find out where and when it was last used? Thanks. I'll be right here.'

She waited fifteen minutes by the clock on the pale blue wall until he rang back.

'Yes?'

'Have you got a map handy?'

'Where was she?'

'In Ingleton.'

'She lived in Ingleton. Whereabouts?'

'Can't say. It's not accurate enough there. Works better in towns where there are more masts. Do you want me to find out who she was ringing?'

'No, not now.' It was beginning to feel like a wild goose chase. Mitch would be expecting results and she wanted to show that she was fit to be back at work. Come on girl! Needing coffee she glided down the corridor towards the tearoom, where Hazel was gossiping with a member of the admin team.

'Hi, Nina. How's it going? Mitch said he wants to start again soon. Have you got anything?'

She didn't want to admit that she had failed. Smiling, she accepted a coffee and made non-commital noises until the girl from admin left.

'There's a possibility that the body is Ewa Prodanovic but we don't even know if she's missing. The only connection with the caravan is what Steve Bellamy says and if he's right, he was probably the last person to see her alive. She's not answering her phone but we know it was last used in Ingleton on Saturday night. That's not surprising because she was staying there with Bellamy before returning to London.'

'Sounds like we need to talk to him some more about his girlfriend.'

'Ex-girlfriend. From what Mills told me at the weekend, they weren't even on speaking terms on Saturday.'

'DC Fuller! DS Featherstone!' They could hear their inspector's booming voice coming down the corridor towards them.

'In here, sir,' called Hazel.

'Some proper evidence at last,' he announced. 'The caver's head was bludgeoned before he entered the water. Whoever did it deliberately replaced his helmet and left him lying face down in the rock pool. Premeditated murder.' He spooned coffee from the jar and poured water from the kettle into the mug. 'Got anything, Nina?'

Nina took a deep breath. 'Nothing conclusive, sir. The body in the caravan could be his ex-girlfriend – she made her last call in Ingleton on Saturday night but we're not sure she's missing yet.'

'If he's cool enough to treat the young lad like that, he could have followed her to the caravan and set fire to it. If he thought she'd been cheating on him with the lad.'

'Are we charging him, Guv?'

'I think we are.'

Chapter 15

Mills watched Nige helping Nina into the car for her first full day back at work and then set off on foot to the university. The sun had finally emerged and it was almost spring-like. She checked her mobile to ensure there was enough signal and the battery was still adequate. She had a feeling that Phil would call. Noticing there were fewer cars than usual as she stood at the traffic lights, she remembered Sheila saying that it was half-term and that she had promised to call in and see Kate before she went back to Manchester. It was extraordinary how things could change in a few days. She had been so keen to get away and continue her work in Manchester. Now she would be glad of any excuse to stay on, or at least to visit the Dales again.

'So, what's new?' Terry Lang was sorting through his mail in the entrance hall.

'Oh, quite a lot actually. I'll come and see you.' She consulted her watch. 'Ten-thirty?'

He looked surprised and slightly irritated.

'OK.'

Mills turned and grinned as she stood waiting for the lift. She planned to clear her stuff from the laboratory and spend the rest of the day on her report. It was nearly finished and she had only been hanging on for the final results on the hand to complete her conclusions. She didn't have to wait long. Her mobile was vibrating and she could see it was Phil's number.

'Hi, it's me,' he said.

'Hi.'

'How are you?'

'I'm fine. Have you got any further with the body?'

'Well, that certainly is getting to the point!' he was laughing. He had such an infectious laugh.

'Well?'

'Why do you think I'm ringing you? Because I missed you?'

'I miss you but I want to know what's happening!'

'OK. Here it is. The experts say that the clothing is thirties.'

Nineteen thirty?'

'Yes.'

'Oh. So it's a police matter then?'

'Yes, 'fraid so.'

'Do they know who it is?'

'No. Not yet.'

'Will they match it up with the hand?'

'Yes, they've sent DNA. There were shotgun pellets lodged in the skull.'

'Really? Well. That's my investigation over then.'

'Don't say that.'

'Well, it's true. It isn't even a navvy from the railway.'

'Might not be so far away though.'

'What d'you mean?'

'I shouldn't say but it looks like the Traveller theory fits. There are aspects of the clothing and teeth that suggest a member of the Gypsy community. It ties in with the fact that no-one was reported missing in the area. Look, sorry but I've got to go now. I'll call you later.'

'Righto, speak to you soon.' Mills sat in front of her computer and sighed. She spent the next half an hour completing her report with the final result that the body associated with the hand was only fifty years old. She made the best of it, discussing how bodies could deteriorate to a mere skeleton and yet parts, like the mysterious hand, preserved. She assumed that the final part of the story, confirmation that the hand belonged to the body, was a matter of course. She printed out the report and bound it in the departmental office, returning to find Terry Lang looking for her.

'Ready for that chat now? Only I've got to shoot off soon.'

She gave him the report and explained how the body had been identified as originating in the fifties.'

'Wow, that messes up your theories,' he said, leaning back in the chair. 'Still, worth a go I guess. So you'll be back to Manchester now then?'

'Yes, I suppose so.'

'Probably the best plan.'

'You think so?'

'Yeah. Big university like that. Much better than hanging out here, don't you agree?'

She didn't respond and he left, thanking her for her help in case he didn't see her again.

'Why do I get the impression he wants to see the back of me?' she asked when she saw Nige in the cafeteria.

'Because he's ignorant and he's worried that you'll rumble him, probably.'

'Don't be silly.'

'It's true. He's useless. He can't teach. He does no research. He's avoided giving a seminar since he arrived in October. If you ask me I think he's a fraud, a complete charlatan!'

Mills laughed.

'I asked Jake to make some enquiries out in the USA,' he continued. 'See what he can find out about Dr Lang on his home territory.'

'And what did he say?'

'Nothing yet. I'm waiting to hear.'

'How is Jake?' Mills had avoided the question in the past but now it wasn't so difficult.

'He's fine. He sends his… his regards.'

'Please send him mine.' It felt strange saying that without that feeling both familiar and painful.

'I will.'

'And how was Nina when you dropped her this morning?'

'OK. She was looking forward to being back but I think she'll get very tired.'

'I'll go back early and cook tea if you like.'

'Thanks, that would be excellent. I think there's some sausages in the 'fridge.'

'Oh I think we can do better than that on such an important day.'

'Important?'

'Nina's first day back, you idiot! I'll stop off at Morrison's.'

Mills could tell that Nina was tired but was more tactful than Nige, who insisted she put her feet up on the sofa as soon as he brought her home.

'Busy day?' Mills asked, once she was settled.

'Pretty tiring, actually,' she admitted as soon as Nige had gone upstairs. 'I suppose you'll hear soon enough. Steve Bellamy was arrested for Fred's murder.'

Of course she had known there was some suspicion over Fred's death but she hadn't expected this. Steve was clearly a difficult character but why would they think him capable of that?

'But how?'

'I can't, Mills. You know I can't.'

'But poor Ewa. She's obviously still attached to him. She was so down on Saturday.' Then she remembered Nina's questioning. 'Is that why you wanted to find out about her. Have you had to question her as well?'

'We'd like to but we can't locate her.'

'She's probably gone back down to London.'

'Maybe. Don't know where to start though.'

'You could talk to her friends in Ingleton. It shouldn't be difficult to find where the cavers hang out.'

'That's true.' Nina sat in silence for a few seconds. 'Are you busy tomorrow, Mills?'

'No.'

'Fancy a trip to the Dales?'

'Actually that would be good. I have to pop in and say goodbye to a friend.'

Nina looked disappointed. 'Not Phil?'

'No, Kate. She's the little girl at Long Witton Farm. I promised I would see her before I leave and it's half-term.'

'Good. That's a plan then.'

'Anyway I've got get to get back in the kitchen and check on the dinner. I told Nige I'd do something special for your first day back at work.'

Nina smiled. 'I'm going to miss you when you go back to Manchester you know.'

'Me too.'

They set off early in the hope that they would catch Sheila and Kate at home. The wind was not so cold but there was rain in the air and it was a dull morning. The radio was on quietly in the background as they chatted about the body at the farm and what the forensics team might discover on further examination. Suddenly Nina leant forward and turned up the volume.

'*... police have issued a statement that confirms the fire was set deliberately and there was a body retrieved from the burnt wreckage of the caravan. At this stage it is being treated as murder. Finally, there is good news on the football front...*'

Nina turned it off and looked across at Mills.

'Now we'll have to deal with the press as well. I wonder if they've managed to identify the body yet?' She made a call on her mobile and asked for Inspector Turner.

'Mitch? I heard the news on the radio. Have you got an ID yet?'

There was a long pause while Nina listened intently.

'Look, I'm on my way to Ingleton now. I'll go there now. Is it on the main street?'

There was another pause and then she put the phone away.

'We're to go the hair salon and speak to the girls there. They may have a contact address in London.'

'Shall we go to the farm first?' They only had a few more miles to go and soon Mills was turning the car onto the rough track. The rain had started to fall more heavily, and by the time they had extracted Nina and were settled inside it had become a steady downpour. Kate was seated at the kitchen table carefully shading a drawing with pastel pencils.

'School project,' explained Sheila as she made coffee.

'It's an environmental project,' the girl explained. 'We have to choose something and write about it for next week.'

'So what did you choose?' Mills asked.

'Lapwings. They need protecting you see. I'm doing a picture.' She turned it round to show them her sketch of birds in flight over a meadow.

'A talented artist, young lady,' said Nina, moving over to the table and lining herself up next to Kate's chair.

'Any news about the body?' Sheila had taken Mills to one side, her voice almost a whisper.

'No. I'll let you know if I have anything I can tell you.' She thought it would be best to say nothing, since she was unsure how much she was supposed to know herself.

'When I told Brian's grandfather about it he was quite upset. I suppose it would shake you up to know it had up been there all that time. I wondered whether the police will be wanting to ask him about it?'

'I probably shouldn't say but they say that it would have been buried in the thirties, so it wouldn't have been when he was running the farm anyway.'

'No, that would be Brian's great-grandfather.'

Worried that she had already said too much, Mills suggested that she speak to Nina.

'I'm sure she'll be able to put your mind at rest.'

Nina spent a long time talking to Sheila while Mills sat with Kate, who showed her the rest of her sketches and work she was compiling for her project. There were poems and extracts from books, describing the bird that had been such a common sight in the past.

'Grandad says he remembers there being lots more round here.'

There was a cry from the corner of the room where Richard had been playing happily. Sheila ran over and picked him up.

'Did you hurt yourself?'

The lad was in tears and clung to his mother.

'It's probably time we were going,' announced Nina, looking across at Mills.

'Yes, we'll leave you in peace… and thanks for everything.'

'Don't forget what I said, Sheila,' added Nina. 'Let me know if Mr Ryman is asked to answer any questions. I'll try and be there.'

'Thank you so much, Nina. I'd be very grateful. He seems so worried about it all. And with his asthma…'

Nina sat quietly in the car with her eyes closed. Mills had the windscreen wipers on full as the rain drove almost horizontally at them. In Ingleton, Nina looked weary as she pulled herself out of the car into the wheelchair. Mills struggled to manipulate her through the entrance of the hair salon and inside with the help of the manager. When they told the woman the purpose of their visit, she looked concerned and explained that she didn't have a forwarding address. She called across to the girls working on their clients, who shook their heads. As they turned to leave a young woman came over. She had a protective cape over her clothes and large silver clips in her hair.

'I couldn't help hearing,' she said. 'You were asking about Ewa?' She was not local and Mills thought her accent was from Liverpool.

'Do you know her?' Nina asked.

'She was my flatmate for a while, until she moved in with Steve. Did you want her address in London?'

'You have it?'

'She gave it to me in case any mail came. It does sometimes. Do you have a pen?'

Nina noted down the address, thanking the girl and asking for her name and phone number as well.

'Well,' she said when they had settled in the empty café and placed their orders. 'I'll give the info to Mitch. Let's hope they can find her.'

It was the first opportunity the two friends had had for a while to sit and chat, just the two of them. They caught up on the news; Nina found out a bit more about Phil and was pleased to learn that Mills would like to move back closer to the Dales again. Nina, in turn, admitted to being anxious about coping with the job and the baby with her disability. By the time they were served with their food they were chatting like the good friends they really were.

'Excuse me.' The girl from the hairdressers was standing beside their table. Her hair was neatly bobbed and she was wearing a tweed coat but Nina recognised her by her heavy use of eyeshadow and lip pencil.

'Hello. Do join us.'

'No, I'm not stopping. I just wanted to tell you something that might be important. My boss told me you're the police, see.'

'That's right.' Nina was fumbling for her card.

'It's just that I did see Ewa this weekend just gone.'

'That's right, she was up here. When did you see her last?'

'On Saturday night, in the pub.'

'What time?'

'About eleven. I was going to say hello but she was with a bloke and I was occupied myself.' She giggled.

'A bloke? Who was she with?'

'Don't know his name. She's been involved with him for ages. I think he must be married or summat. Always very secretive. Anyway it was definitely him.'

'Do you have a name for him?'

'He rang the flat once. He called himself "Hunter" but I don't know if that's a nickname.'

'And you don't have any contact details for him?'

'No. Look I'd best be off. You've got my number, yeah?'

'Thank you,' she glanced at her notes, '...Lorraine.'

Mills watched her walk briskly out of the café and down the road, waiting for Nina to break the silence. She was deep in thought.

'Nina, presumably you'll have to find this guy, Hunter?'

'What? No, not unless we can't find Ewa. We'll wait until the address in London has been checked.'

The wipers beat monotonously on the windscreen. There was no relief from the downpour and when they were home Mills lit the fire and sat drinking tea while Nina rang Mitch.

'No, don't leave,' she insisted as Mills stood up. 'You've heard it all anyway.'

She related what Lorraine had told her, spelling out the address in London. Then she listened for a while and said, 'Really? Did he know?' Another pause. 'Mitch, can I ask you something about the body at Long Witton Farm? I was wondering if we are going to question the farmers who were working the farm at the time? We are? Then can I sit in? Really? Well that's even better. Thank you. Thank you, Mitch.' Finally she put down the receiver.

'They're sending someone round to where Ewa lives now. He'll call me back when they've spoken to her.'

'Was there something else?' Mills asked.

'Yes but...' She paused. 'Mills, would you happen to know if Ewa was... is... pregnant?'

'No. Why?'

'Nothing. I just wondered. And, guess what? I get to interview Sheila's father-in-law and his father.'

The sound of a key in the front door announced that Nige was home. He complained that he had been trying to call all day and was worried about Nina. When he accused her of over-exerting herself Mills withdrew to the kitchen and made more tea. When she returned, he had his arm round her and she was gently chastising him for being an over-anxious father-to-be.

'I presume you had a bad day, Nige?' Nina said, kissing him on the lips.

'Yes, *re-a-lly* bad.'

'Students?' asked Mills.

'No, Terry Lang.'

Nina raised her eyebrows, saying nothing.

'What now?' asked Mills, always happy to have a moan about her supervisor.

'Oh the usual but, I tell you what, there is definitely something funny about him.'

'What now?' Nina sounded exasperated.

'I asked Jake to do some digging for me.'

Nina shot a glance at Mills and she responded with a smile and a slight shake of her head.

'And?'

'Definitely something not right, a bit fishy. You see this guy Lang is supposed to have been a bit of an expert on bones, yes? And he is supposed to have done some work on war graves, right? I got Jake to check. But when I asked him this afternoon if he could give a seminar on his experiences he downright refused.'

'Perhaps it brings back bad memories,' suggested Mills, thinking of what Phil had said.

'Bollocks!'

'Nigel! That's enough!' Nina seemed genuinely upset by his outburst.

'I've got his list of publications from the departmental file this afternoon. I found he'd presented a paper at the annual conference of the Society for American Archaeology two years ago.'

'So?' Nina sounded irritated.

'So when I asked him about Puerto Rico he said he didn't know!'

Mills giggled. 'Why Puerto Rico?'

'It's where the conference was held. I told him I was thinking of going on holiday.'

'You're mad,' muttered Nina, on her way to the kitchen.

'Anyway I've got a plan,' continued Nige. 'I've asked for a copy of his CV from the office. Then I can do some more detailed investigation.'

'You better get in here and start investigating these potatoes if you know what's good for you Nigel Featherstone!' Nina's voice was loud and sharp.

Nige pulled a face and grinned. 'Better do as I'm told,' he said as he left the room.

After dinner Mills went up to her room. She told herself it was to give her friends some space but admittedly she was hoping that Phil would call. She set up her laptop and wrote some e-mails until at last her mobile burst into life.

'Phil? How are you? I was hoping you'd call.'

'I wanted to make sure you're all set for Thursday.' His voice was stronger and richer on the phone.

'I'm looking forward to it.'

'When can I fetch you? I can get over early.'

'Any time, I've not got anything to do here.'

'All right for some! I'll leave work early afternoon so I should be with you by four easy.'

'Right.'

'So what have you been up to?'

She chatted for a little while and then casually asked how work on the body was progressing.

'That's been going very well. In fact I meant to tell you. The hand and body definitely match and the date is now deemed to be around nineteen-thirty or certainly between nineteen-thirty and nineteen-forty. The unusual blood type indicates a Traveller and Lancashire and Cumbria forces are looking for anyone reported missing in their area.'

'What about the lead shot?'

'Not much use without something to match it to.'

Mills could hear Nina from below asking her if she wanted coffee.

She finished her call and went downstairs.

'Millie, I am so sorry. I didn't realise you were on the phone.'

'It was only Phil.'

'I guessed that.'

'He just wanted to check the arrangements for Thursday.' She followed Nina into the kitchen and watched her preparing the cafetière.

'Going somewhere nice?'

'Just his local pub but it is really nice there and they've got a special menu on.'

'Sounds lovely.'

'What will you and Nige be doing?'

'Nothing special. We're an old married couple remember?' She handed Mills a mug.

'What about Ewa? Is there any news?'

'That's what I wanted to tell you. It's about the caravan fire. They've identified the body... the one they found inside. It was Ewa. When they searched her flat they found a photograph of her wearing a crucifix identical to the one found on the body.'

'That's why you asked if she knew about the caravan.' Mills could see Ewa's animated face, hear her cheerful laughter. Poor Ewa. Poor Steve. 'What's happened to Steve? Does he know? Is he still at the police station?'

'Yes.'

'But why?'

'He was the last person to see Fred alive.'

'No, I mean is he a suspect? What reason?'

'A motive? They're fairly sure it was over Ewa. He's a very jealous character, Millie.'

'But there was nothing going on between Fred and Ewa, was there?'

'He thought so and he had guessed she was pregnant.'

'Pregnant?'

Nina took her hand. 'He's been in custody since Monday. They were running out of time. Anyway, that's what I wanted to tell you... he's been charged with murdering them both.'

Chapter 16

Nina chose her clothes with care, taking longer than usual to apply her makeup. She had woken feeling more energetic than usual and Nige had noticed how easy she was to get downstairs.

'There you are, then,' she had said. 'I *am* getting better.'

Mitch was late which gave her time to finish breakfast and tidy the kitchen before giving her husband a goodbye kiss and shouting cheerfully up to Mills. Her friend had been quiet, saying little as they ate, disappearing to her room as soon as breakfast was over.

The wing mirror reflected Mitch struggling to fold the wheelchair. He cursed as he caught his finger between the arm rest and the seat. Nige, who had been watching from the window, came out to help and finally they were ready to leave. She pulled a face at her husband as the car pulled away from the kerb and he hid a smirk behind his hand in an exaggerated way. The pinch mark still showed on Mitch's hand as he reached over to switch on a local radio station. Nina assumed he was monitoring what the media was saying about the double murder charge. Half an hour later, after they had been subjected to inconsequential banter punctuated by dated pop songs, a phone-in programme began and thankfully he turned it off.

'I'm leaving the questioning to you today Nina,' Mitch announced after a period of silence.

'Thank you. Is there anything in particular you want me to cover?'

'No. I don't expect to get anything out of it. The old codger will probably be gaga. Just confirmation that he has no recollection of anyone being murdered.'

'Mitch!'

'You know what I mean. He's not going to say he knows anything about a body on his property, is he?'

'I thought it would be useful to have a list of farm workers and anyone passing through.'

'Of course. You know what to do.'

When they drew up outside the neat bungalow, Nina noted with satisfaction that Mitch made a relatively proficient job of constructing her chair. They were soon settled in a pleasant room, sipping coffee and chatting to Sheila's mother-in-law, Mary Ryman. There was no sign of her husband.

'I'd best go and fetch Grandad then,' she said. 'His breathing is none so good today so he's been resting.'

They sat in silence listening to the clock ticking away the minutes.

'OK?' asked Mitch.

'Yes,' replied Nina as the door opened.

'Mr Ryman?' Mitch stood up and moved out of the way so Mary could manoeuvre the second wheelchair into the room. The old man looked pale and weak. 'I'm DI Turner and this is DS Featherstone, sir.'

Nina smiled and raised her hand in a friendly wave towards the old man. 'Hello again, Mr Ryman.'

He didn't answer but looked at them quizzically.

Mary Ryman made as if to leave the room.

'Would you like to stay, Mrs Ryman?' she asked.

'If I may?'

Nina looked across at Mitch and he nodded.

'So, Mr Ryman. As you know there was a body found on Long Witton Farm recently, which appears to have been buried there in the nineteen-thirties or forties. Obviously we wish to get to the bottom of this and so far we have not been able to identify the body.'

The man nodded at the end of each sentence. He had a full head of white hair and watery blue eyes. She found it difficult to imagine that he could have any possible involvement with the body even if he had been old enough.

'So what do yer want to know, lass?' he asked slowly, his face unchanged and serious.

'Obviously we want to identify the body and so it would be helpful to have a list of any individuals who worked on the farm in that period, even if they were only there for a short time. I assume your father was running the farm at the time?'

'Ay.'

'Did you have any farm-hands, hired help?' she wasn't sure what they would be called and looked across at Mitch who was smirking.

'Let me think.' The old man sat for a minute staring at his hands. 'We generally had help from neighbours but a few summers we had passing help,' he said at last.

'What do you mean by *passing help* Mr Ryman? Would that be itinerant people?' She looked across at Mitch.

'Ay.'

'People going to the horse fair for example?'

'Ay.'

'Any names in particular?'

'Names? Names? Eighty year ago? Nay.'

'But you may have had a Traveller or Gypsy working for you one summer in the thirties?'

'Happen.'

The old man seemed totally unmoved by the questioning but Nina noticed that Mary Ryman had been watching him anxiously throughout the interview. Now she fetched an inhaler from the mantelpiece and offered it to him. He took it and breathed deeply as he held it to his mouth.

'So, Mr Ryman, can you remember any Traveller or Gypsy working on the farm who disappeared suddenly or unexpectedly?'

'Happen. You couldn't rely on them. Here today, gone tomorrow. Once they were paid, they were off.' He was breathing more heavily now and pausing between sentences.

Mitch was sitting with his eyes closed.

'How old were you at that time, Mr Ryman?'

He sat looking about him. 'What, in't thirties? Maybe ten.'

'You were eighty-eight last year, Grandad,' offered Sheila.

He used the inhaler again. 'That's what I said. I were born in nineteen-twenty.'

She made a quick calculation. 'So you were about ten?'

'Yes.' He leant back in his chair, pulling at his shirt collar, his breathing becoming more laboured.

'Have you finished?' Mary asked. 'He's in a bad way.'

'One last thing,' Nina continued. 'You said your neighbours helped on the farm. Are they still around?'

Mary answered for him. 'No, they've long gone. Dead and gone. You won't find any of 'em alive now. He's the last of 'em.'

The old man was getting worse and when Mary excused herself, Nina heard her on the telephone. She returned, taking the old man's hand and told him she had called the doctor.

'She said to call her next time Grandad was took bad,' she said. 'We left it too late last time and he had to go to hospital. We don't want that, do we Grandad?'

The old man appeared exhausted by the effort to breathe and Mary was getting more flustered and anxious.

'Well, we'd better be off,' announced Mitch. 'I want to catch up with the local sergeant before we go back.'

Nina didn't want to abandon Mary and suggested to Mitch that she stay for the doctor to arrive, unless he needed her to accompany him? She guessed he would find her a hindrance and was soon alone with the Rymans, hoping that something might come from her extended stay.

Mary was too anxious to engage in conversation. She sat bolt upright on the sofa watching Grandad as he lay limply gasping for breath. Nina had been positioned at an angle that allowed her to look out of the window onto the road, so she watched for the doctor's car. There was a camper van parked across the road and, as she gazed out, two young men emerged from the house opposite. She recognised one of them as the new lecturer from Nige's department, the one he and Mills disliked. He looked pleasant enough as he stood chatting to the other man, who was strikingly tall with very dark hair, combed back and tied in a pony tail. His dark beard gave him a wild but rather interesting look.

Her daydream was broken by Mary leaping up to answer the doorbell. There were voices in the hallway and a young woman appeared carrying a large bag.

'Should I leave?' Nina asked.

'No. I just want to listen to Mr Ryman's chest and take his blood pressure,' she said smiling and turned to attend to the old man.

Mary bustled round making tea, even though it was declined by the doctor.

'I think he should pop back into hospital so they can keep an eye on him,' the young woman said briskly, folding up her stethoscope and putting it away in her bag. 'It's not really an emergency. Would you be able to get him there Mrs Ryman?'

'Yes, I can get Bill to take us, like he did before.'

While Mary was seeing the doctor out, Nina rang Mitch to collect her.

'I'd best go and pack a bag,' Mary announced when she returned. 'It's a good job you let me wash those new pyjamas of yours.'

By the time she had the suitcase prepared, Mitch had arrived.

'Take care, Mrs Ryman. I'm sorry that Mr Ryman is not well. I hope it wasn't our fault?'

'No, of course not. He was having trouble before you arrived.'

As Mitch was easing Nina's wheelchair through the door, she spotted the man with the pony tail walking towards the town.

'Do you know that man?' she asked Mary.

'Oh ay, he's one of them cavers. Always down some pothole or t'other.'

'Would that be the caving club where they lost that lad recently?'

'Ay. And that young hairdresser.'

On the way back, Nina agreed with Mitch that the visit had got them nowhere. She asked if she should visit other families around Long Witton Farm to find out more.

'Sounds like a pointless exercise. The local force can do a routine visit but I can't see it helping if they've all moved on. Best wait to see if we have a missing person lead from Lancashire or Cumbria first.'

Nige was waiting when they arrived at the house. He had the wheelchair out of the boot and constructed before Mitch was barely out of the car. There was just time for Nina to thank Mitch before she was whisked inside the house and the door slammed behind her.

'I'll make you some tea. You must be frozen. Why did he make you stay out so long?'

'It's only five o'clock, Nige. What's the matter with you?'

'I thought you'd be here when I got back. I was worried.'

She wanted to hug him but part of her was cross with him trying to smother her. She let him make her tea and sat contentedly in front of the fire, describing her day.

He went back into the kitchen, insisting that he would prepare the evening meal while she rested. Nina tried to dissuade him. It was fish and she knew it would prove difficult for him but he refused her offer of help. As soon as Mills appeared she begged her, in a low whisper, to give Nige a hand. Consequently a complete disaster was averted, and Nina was able to congratulate the chef without sounding insincere.

'I made an interesting discovery today,' he announced at dinner.

'Oh yes?'

'Mm. I got hold of Lang's file.'

'How?'

'Best not know, really. Anyway, it appears that he was working in Bosnia before he came here. He was excavating at a site where victims of the Sebrenica massacre were buried, in a place called Kamenica.'

'Interesting.'

'Very, because Mills says that Phil has never met him and he was working out there as well.'

'At the same time?' Nina asked.

'Quite recently.'

'But possibly not at the same place,' Mills said.

'Possibly not.'

'It's not surprising they didn't meet, Nige. There must be several places where victims were buried.' Nina pointed out.

'I suppose so but I'll ask Phil about it,' said Mills.

Nina sighed. 'Whatever.' Then she remembered her news. '*I* saw Dr Lang in Ingleton today.'

'He should have been sitting in on the student presentations,' moaned Nige.

Nina continued before he could start another outburst. 'He was talking to a young man called Chas. He's part of the caving club.'

'Not the same one as Fred,' said Mills, 'because he didn't know him… and Fred didn't know Lang either.'

'What about Ewa Prodanovic?'

Mills appeared to consider for a moment. 'No, he definitely didn't know her either. I asked him because she sent me a note at uni.'

Nina, feeling she should say no more since the force was her source of information, listened to Nige persuading Mills to ring Phil that evening and ask him directly if he had even heard of Lang when he was in Bosnia. She was gone a long time but eventually returned to report that Phil had been working at a place called Black Peak. However, he has a colleague who went out to Kamenica last year and he would ask her about Lang in the morning.

Mills had slept badly and woke early worrying about what to wear to dinner with Phil. To her surprise, Nina was already up and dressed.

'I thought Nige would be getting you breakfast in bed on Valentine's Day.'

'He wanted to, bless him, but I've got a check-up at the hospital at ten.'

'How are you getting there?' Mills was thinking that it could be handy to go shopping in Northallerton.

'Nige said he'd take me but he's got to get back for a lecture. He may have to leave me for a while.'

Mills offered to drive, admitting she wanted to find something to wear for the Valentine's dinner.

Nina looked excited. 'Great. It'll be fun… if you let me come shopping too!'

They set off in time to go straight to the hospital for Nina's appointment and were seated in the waiting area well before ten o'clock. Mills offered to find coffee for them and wandered along the corridor until she found a machine. She was concentrating so hard to avoid spilling the two cups that she almost bumped into a woman coming the other way.

'Hello!'

The woman was probably in her fifties, tweedy coat and wool hat, carrying a large plastic bag.

Mills studied the face without recognition.

'I'm sorry, love. Aren't you the archaeologist?'

'Yes.'

'I'm Mary Ryman. We met at Brian and Sheila's. The farm.'

'Of course. I'm sorry. How are you?' Mills asked automatically.

'Oh it's not me,' she laughed. 'It's Grandad. He's had an asthma attack and they're keeping him under observation. I've just brought him in some fresh pyjamas.' They stood smiling at each other. 'Oh well, I must get on.'

'I hope he's better soon,' Mills called after her, remembering the cheerful old man she had met at Long Witton Farm.

Nina was chatting to the girl next to her who looked about eight months pregnant. Mills drank her coffee while the two women exchanged notes about a range of symptoms.

'I've just seen Sheila's mother-in-law,' she said when there was a break in the conversation.

'Mary Ryman?'

'Yes, her grandfather-in-law is in here.'

'Yes, of course. His asthma.' Nina drained her coffee and looked at her watch. I think it'll be some time before they see me, Mills. Why don't you go off and start looking round the shops. I'll be fine here and I can ring you when I'm done.'

It had not occurred to Nina that old Mr Ryman would be in the hospital and it was too good an opportunity to miss. She had wanted to ask him about the neighbours that had helped on the farm. For example, would Mr Small's family have been around? It was a coincidence that the brother had also disappeared from the area, even though that was over twenty years later.

Eventually her name was called and she launched her wheelchair towards the cubicle. Frustratingly she had to be helped onto the bed and the nurse removed her clothing so the young assistant registrar could examine her. Each time she saw a new face she was asked about her disability and her notes would be studied at length. Normally she would be asking them about how the birth might be affected but today she had other things on her mind. As soon as the probing was over, she dressed with the help of a young nurse and wheeled herself to the information desk to enquire where to find Mr Ryman. The receptionist was not keen to give Nina any details until she explained she was a police officer. The wheelchair must have made the woman wary because she insisted on seeing identification before pointing her to Ainderby ward. She manoeuvred herself into the lift and along several corridors before finding him. He was propped up on several pillows looking frail, a plastic tube attached to his nostrils. To her relief there was no sign of his daughter-in-law so she found a nurse and asked if she could speak to the old man for a few minutes.

'Yes, all right, but he is tired, so please don't exhaust him.'

'Mr Ryman,' Nina called gently. The old man's eyelids fluttered and she could see his rheumy eyes. He looked worn out.

'I'm Nina. Do you remember me? I came to see you yesterday?'

He stared at her wearily and nodded slowly.

'How are you feeling, Mr Ryman?'

He gave her a look that said it all.

'I know you must be tired but I just wanted to ask you about your neighbours, the ones that helped on the farm.'

His breath was slow and rasping.

'Do you remember them?'

He shook his head.

'Small? Do you remember him?'

He nodded.

'Did he help your father on the farm?'

He shook his head again and closed his eyes. She sat for a few minutes watching him as he lay with his eyes shut, his chest rising and falling with the effort to breathe. She called his name and gradually he responded, staring at her without recognition. She asked him gently if she could talk to him about when he was a child at the farm. Did he have any brothers or sisters?

'George. George looked after us.'

'Us?'

'Me and Dorothy.'

'Was she your sister?'

'Yes. George looked after her. She was a young 'un, d'you see?'

'It's nice having a big brother.'

'Ay. He protected us.' He was trying to sit up but collapsed back exhausted. 'He always looked after us.'

'Who did he protect you from?'

He coughed several times and lay back on his pillow. She sat for a while until the ward sister came along and suggested he really wasn't coherent, it was the drugs. Nina thanked her and made her way down to the foyer to ring Mills.

'OK Nina, I'll come and get you now. I've seen a top but I'd value your opinion. It's quite expensive.'

It had been a while since Nina had been shopping for clothes and she enjoyed the opportunity to be pushed round the stores, advising her friend on what suited her. Eventually Mills decided on a tunic top that she could where over trousers, since she would be travelling to dinner on a motorbike. It was mid-day by the time Mills was placing her carrier bag on Nina's knees and pushing her along the street to Bettys Tea Rooms.

Nina reviewed the menu and chose a salad.

'You can't do that to me!' her friend protested.

'I can. I've put on so much weight with the baby and sitting in this all the time. I'm not using up enough calories.'

'Aren't you supposed to be exercising?'

'I have to practise standing with the frame.'

'So when do you do that?'

'Preferably when Nige is out; he makes such a fuss.'

'Well you can have something more substantial to eat now and do it when you get back!'

They had a glass of wine and chose high calorie puddings deliberately. Finally, over coffee, Nina leaned back and declared it was the best outing she'd had for a long time.

'I guess it's going to be hard when the baby comes, managing I mean, if you're still in the chair,' Mills looked serious.

Nina nodded assent but didn't reply.

'Did the doctors say how long it would be before you are on your feet again?'

'They can't be sure.'

'But it helps to stand?'

'Yes… and I should try putting weight on my legs. I just find it difficult because I don't have much strength in my arms.'

'You should start by exercising your arms then. I've got some weights; you can try them when we get back.'

'Gee thanks.'

Nina grimaced but was grateful her friend was showing an interest in her predicament. She insisted on paying for lunch then allowed Mills to push her back to the car park and help her into the car. There was a large parcel on the doorstep when they arrived home, addressed to Miss M. Sanderson, and an envelope lying on the door mat also for Mills. The box contained a bouquet of red roses in a glass vase; the message with the flowers said the same thing as the Valentine's card which was signed "all my love Phil". Mills went to take the vase up to her room but Nina insisted they should remain downstairs until Nige had seen them.

Mills ran upstairs anyway to fetch her hand weights and demonstrated to Nina how to strengthen her biceps. Despite feeling quite exhausted by her morning, she performed some bicep curls, laughing at her feeble efforts. Then Mills suggested fetching the frame and Nina showed her how she could stand briefly using her arms to take the weight of her body. The encouragement that her friend gave was immensely helpful, enabling Nina to remain upright for several minutes before collapsing back into the chair. After a short rest she tried again and after several sessions she began to feel confident enough to attempt a step forward. Mills was close by in case she needed her but unlike Nige she didn't interfere or panic. Her confidence increased so that by the end of the afternoon she had taken three steps.

'Don't tell Nige,' she asked Mills. 'I want to surprise him.'

'I think you've done fantastically,' Mills said. At this rate you'll be walking before the baby arrives.'

'I hope so. Otherwise I'll be so big I won't be able to get out of the chair!'

Mills excused herself to go and get ready for her date. Nige was home by four with a bunch of pink carnations but when he saw the roses he took his flowers through to the kitchen and left them there without comment. He kissed Nina, asking how her hospital visit had gone. She was touched by the fact he had come home early to find out but when he enquired what time Phil was due, Nina knew the true reason for his punctuality. When the doorbell rang he shot outside, saying he wanted to see the motorbike.

'Hi Phil! So this is it? Very nice.' He moved around the bike, asking about the horsepower and other technical details. 'So… did Mills ask you about Lang?'

'Yes. He wasn't in Bosnia when I was there.'

'Yes she told me that but your friend…'

'I spoke to her today and she knew the name. In fact she found a group photograph on her computer and gave me a copy. Lang was certainly there.'

When they went inside Nina could see that Nige was disappointed.

'Not good news?' she asked.

'He was in Bosnia. Phil's friend has a photograph.'

'I sent it to Mills,' Phil said.

'She's just getting ready,' Nina smiled at him and indicated for him to take a seat.

'I'll tell her you're here.' Nige was already climbing the stairs and Nina could hear him calling through to Mills about the photograph before he returned.

When Mills appeared, Nina noted privately how well the purple tunic went with her red hair and how, when Phil smiled at her, she glowed.

'I hope you've got a warm jacket, it's freezing out there,' Phil said.

'I'll get my coat,' she said. 'And here's the photo,' she added, handing it to Nige who snatched it and held it close to peer at the faces.

'Which one is he again?' asked Phil.

'This one at the end of the back row.'

'That's what I thought. Angela said in her message that he was next to her at the front. She must have got it wrong.'

Nina held out her hand and took the paper. Lang was definitely at the back, his head hardly visible behind the other cheerful faces. In fact he looked a bit lost, out on a limb.

'It would be good just to check with Angela,' she said. 'Ask her who this one on the end is if it's not Lang.'

It was just a feeling she had. Something was not quite right. But she couldn't share it with the others... not just yet.

Chapter 17

The CB Inn was warm and welcoming after the chilly journey across the hills on the back of Phil's motorbike. Mills could feel her cheeks glowing as she stood close to the fire sipping a glass of crisp dry white. The place was nearly full of couples although it was only seven-thirty, most of the women in fancy frocks. Mills told Phil she should have dressed up a bit.

'Rubbish, you look lovely. I think you're beautiful.'

No-one, but no-one had ever said that before. She looked up at him but he appeared to be serious so she sipped her wine, blushing. Phil appeared more embarrassed than she was and suggested they place their order and find their table. Soon they were settled opposite each other, holding hands. Mills had decided not to raise the issue of Dr Lang at dinner in case Phil felt it was inappropriate during their romantic dinner. But she needn't have worried. He was soon relating his conversation with the colleague who had worked with Lang at Kamenica.

'I asked her what Nina said about the guy next to her not being Lang but she was absolutely positive it was him.'

'Did you ask her who the man at the back was?'

'Yes, I wrote it down.' He produced a scrap of paper from his shirt pocket. 'That was funny because he comes from the same institution as Lang in the States. Some sort of technician who came out to join him. He did some of the routine stuff. He's called Hunter, Frank Hunter.'

'Can I keep the paper?' Mills took it and put it in her bag for Nina.

They were interrupted by the arrival of dinner and for the rest of the evening Mills exchanged reminiscences with Phil, learning as much as she could about his past until she felt she had known him for years. Only when they had finished eating did she excuse herself and while she was in the cloakroom she sent a text to Nina telling her about the mysterious Frank Hunter. Reluctantly they finished their coffee and ventured outside into the cold air. As planned, they drove to Phil's cottage where Earl greeted Mills as an old friend. She drank brandy, slumped in front of the fire while Phil coaxed the ashes back into life with a dry log. When the wood was crackling he sat beside her and stroked her hair.

'Happy?'

'Yes.'

'So am I. I don't know when I've felt so happy for a very long time.'

Her eyes were beginning to close as she relaxed in his arms.

'You go on up,' he said. 'I'll lock up first.'

Nina called Hazel early, catching her before she left for work. She told her she needed to visit Mrs Ryman in Ingleton again and could she clear it with Mitch? When Nige appeared downstairs she sat opposite him watching him eat his porridge.

'Nige, would you do me a favour without asking any questions?'

'Of course. What?'

'Would you ask Jake to find out what he can about that colleague of Dr Lang's?'

'Lang? Why do you want to know about his colleague?'

She sat looking at him with her head on one side. 'What did I ask you?'

'To make enquiries about Lang's colleague?'

'No, before that?'

'Did I want a cup of tea?'

'No, I asked if you would do something *without asking questions.*'

'Did you?'

'So would you ask Jake to make some enquiries about a man called Frank Hunter?'

'Frank Hunter?'

'Yes. It would be best if he could send a photograph.'

He looked puzzled and then he appeared to understand.

'I see.'

'No you don't. Please don't discuss it with Jake. I just want to see what he looks like and what his background is.'

'No problem. I'll be the height of discretion, I promise.'

'Well just don't discuss it with Jake, OK?'

He leapt up and grabbed his coat. 'I'd better be off then. Are you doing anything today?'

'I don't know. Probably not.'

As soon as he had gone she moved across the room and pulled the weights from the cupboard where she had hidden them. She practised her bicep curls until the phone interrupted her exercises. Hazel would pick her up in half an hour and take her over to Ingleton. By the time she arrived, Nina had pulled herself upright on the frame and stood for several minutes.

Then she had taken several steps forward, collapsing back in her chair, exhausted but happy.

'So why are we visiting Mrs Ryman?' Hazel asked as they approached Ingleton.

'The grandfather said something yesterday that suggested he might know about the body at the farm. He would only have been a kid but he got agitated when I asked him about it. I want to ask her about the old man's brother and sister.'

She peered across the road as Hazel parked her car outside the bungalow but there was no sign of the man called Chas who had been talking to Lang. Mary welcomed them and sat attentively while Nina explained why they had called.

'…so I wondered whether George and Dorothy were still alive?' she finished.

'No, love. Both gone years ago. Uncle George went to Australia in the fifties. Aunt Dorothy passed on before I married Bill.'

'Does she have any family?'

'No, she kept herself to herself by all accounts – a bit of a recluse. Never married. Grandad was devoted to her and he gets quite upset if anyone mentions her.'

'And his brother George?'

'He died a few years ago. Grandad wanted to go to the funeral but we said it were too far at his age.'

Nina had ensured she was seated with a view onto the street. 'Mrs Ryman, do you know the lad across the street with the ponytail?'

'Chas? Yes I know him.'

Hazel had stopped taking notes and Nina was aware that she was staring at her.

'Do you know where we might find him? Does he work locally?'

'I don't think he has a proper job. I believe he helps out in the pub.'

Nina thanked her and indicated to Hazel that they should leave. Outside she asked her to leave the car and push her along to the pub, in case Chas was there.

'So why do we want to see him?'

'Nothing particular.' Nina lied. 'He is part of the club that the caver belonged to, the one that was killed.'

'Murdered you mean, don't you?'

'Yes.'

As they entered the pub, Nina spotted the man with the pony tail working behind the bar.

'Would you get me a coke and ask if he'll come over? I'd appreciate a quiet word, on my own.'

Hazel shrugged, went over to speak to him and remained perched on a stool, sipping orange juice while he carried the coke over to Nina.

'You wanted to see me?'

'Yes, thank you. I saw you the other day. You were talking to a man called Lang.'

He looked puzzled. 'I don't recall. Can you give a clue?'

'I may have got it wrong. Possibly Hunter? He has a camper van.'

'Oh yes, I know Hunter. We cave dive together.' He sat down opposite her.

'Have you known him long?'

'Since we were kids. We were at school together in Sedbergh.'

'Has he always lived in the area?'

The man sighed and rubbed his chin. 'He was away for a year or two. In the States I think or maybe Canada.'

'When was this?'

'Quite recently. Look is this properly legal? I mean shouldn't we be at a police station or something?'

Nina smiled. 'No need. I just wanted to check my information.'

'Is this about Fred?' He looked concerned.

'No.'

'Ewa?'

'No. I just wanted to clarify a query. Could I have a contact name and number please?'

He wrote his number on her notepad.

'Thank you, Mr…'

'You can call me Chas,' he said with a smirk, rising to go back to the bar.

'What was that all about?' asked Hazel taking the seat recently vacated by the young man.

'It turned out to be nothing, as it happens.'

'So are we going to eat here?'

'If you like. Could you get me a sandwich? I just need to ring someone.'

She made a call on her mobile while Hazel returned to the bar.

'Are you in the cafeteria Nige? It's awfully noisy.' she asked.

'No, there's a lunch-time talk about to start. Another few minutes.'

'Have you heard from Jake yet?'

'Give us a chance. It's hardly breakfast time over there yet.'

'It's just that I've got confirmation about the name.'

'You mean Frank Hunter?'

'Yes. So please get back to me as soon as you can.'

The room went quiet as Nige switched off his mobile and the speaker was led up to the podium. The lecture was even better than Nige had anticipated. He knew it would cover his pet subject of ground penetrating radar because he had suggested the speaker's name to his head of department, but the talk included several new methods for finding bodies including laser techniques. He remained behind at the end to ask a number of questions until the visitor pointed out that he had to catch a train back to London. Nige wandered back to his office, enjoying the prospect of a quiet afternoon finishing his marking before the weekend. The door was wide open.

'Hi there!' Lang was seated in a chair close to Nige's computer, grinning. 'Enjoy the seminar?'

'Were you there?'

'Of course. I was sitting just behind you.'

Nige took the chair in front of his computer and waited to see what Lang would do. 'Do you want something?' he asked, trying hard to keep the irritation from his voice as he tapped the keyboard. His monitor immediately displayed his e-mails and he quickly closed the screen as he spotted a message from Jake entitled "Frank Hunter". Lang made some comments about the lecture and Nige muttered assent.

'I really came to ask your advice,' Lang said. 'I've been asked to look at a site by the National Park and I'll need to survey it. I know you're the expert on ground penetrating radar.'

'Yes?' Nige was puzzled by his colleague's unusually amiable behaviour.

'Yes. But it's quite urgent. Are you busy now?' He was polite but assertive.

'Not especially,' said Nige, assuming he wanted to sit and discuss his project.

'Good, I'll get my coat. I hope you don't mind driving; my van's off the road.'

'Where are we going?'

'Ribblehead.'

He jumped up and was out the door before Nige could respond. Curious, he decided to go along with him but sent a text to Nina quickly.

'OK?'

Lang was back at the door again in less than a minute, dressed in a quilted waterproof jacket. Nige pulled on his army coat as he followed him to the car park. Lang was excitable, talking non-stop as they set off. Nige put this down to the fact he had this new project, although he spoke little about it when asked, saying that he would explain it all when they got there. So to pass the time he asked Lang about Bosnia, convinced that he had never been there. Surprisingly his colleague seemed pleased to describe his work in detail until any doubts that Nige had had were completely eradicated.

When Mills woke she jumped out of bed and ran downstairs, expecting to find the cottage empty. But Phil was seated at the kitchen table reading a newspaper. Earl wagged his tail as he wandered over to greet her.

'You're awake,' he said, smiling. 'Come here and let me give you a kiss.'

'It's half past ten! I thought you'd gone to work.'

'And leave my beautiful girlfriend here alone? Certainly not. I took the day off.'

'What, just like that?'

'No, I booked it when I knew you'd be here.'

She watched him as he cooked her some bacon and he sat opposite her while she made a sandwich of it with her toast. Fat was dripping down her chin and she wiped it self-consciously but he just continued to observe her with a smile.

It was lunch-time before they emerged from the cottage to walk with Earl to the pub. The trees were white with frost and the road was icy when they went across to join the track by the river. Phil ordered soup while Mills settled by the fire with the dog and turned on her phone. Surprised to see a missed call from Nina, she rang her back immediately.

'Mills, I am so glad to hear from you! Are you all right?'

'Yes, of course. I'm sorry, I should have…'

Nina laughed. 'No, I'm not checking up on you, it's just that I am a bit concerned about Nige. It's difficult to explain over the phone. Where are you?'

'I'm in the pub with Phil.'

'In the Dales?'

'Yes.'

'Damn. I thought you might be back at the university. I wondered if you could have a look at Nige's e-mails for me.'

'I can open my e-mails from Phil's computer. I've done it before but it would be difficult to access Nige's without his password. Can you ask him?'

'No, his mobile's off. I know his password for the computer at home.'

'What is it?'

'Nimbus2000.'

'Harry Potter's broomstick?' Mills laughed.

'Yes, I'm afraid so.'

'Well, it's worth a try, Nina. Is there anything special he's looking for?'

'He asked Jake for some information on a man called Frank Hunter. If you can get in please look for a reply and let me know as soon as possible.'

'Frank Hunter? OK.'

'I wouldn't ask unless I thought it was important, Mills.'

'I know.'

Phil was happy to leave without eating but Mills insisted they waited for the soup since he'd already paid for it. The name Frank Hunter hadn't meant anything to Mills when Nina had said it but Phil reminded her that he was the second man in the photograph taken at Kamenica. As soon as they had eaten, they drained their glasses and walked to the cottage as fast as they could to switch on Phil's laptop.

Mills entered Nige's name into the university system for accessing e-mails remotely, using the same format as she would her own initial and surname: n.featherstone. That was fine but now it needed the password. She typed *NIMBUS2000* but it was rejected.

'Try lower case,' suggested Phil.

She did and it was rejected again.

'I've got one more try or we'll have to log out and in again,' she said. 'I'll try a capital N and the rest in lower case.'

She typed *Nimbus2000* and the screen changed. They were in. Nige had about a dozen new messages but none came from Jake. Mills searched the rest of the messages in the inbox and spotted one entitled "Frank Hunter". It had been read already. The message from Jake was brief: *Frank Hunter was a technician in the department but he went to Bosnia last year to help Dr Lang with his work. Frank*

Hunter sent a message to the administrator to say he was not coming back to the College. She thinks he got a job over there. Departmental photo attached.

She opened the attachment and grabbed Phil's hand as she continued to stare at the photograph.

'That's Terry Lang,' she said.

'No it's not. It's Frank Hunter, apparently. You'd better ring Nina in case it's important.'

Nina was finishing her pub lunch when the text from Nige arrived and she was able to make the call to Millie while Hazel went "to make herself comfortable" for the journey home. Now she had to play for time until her friend called her back because she would have no signal on her mobile once they had left Ingleton.

'You know, I'm still not happy about old man Ryman,' Nina said to Hazel when she returned. 'I wonder if we should pop back and speak to his daughter-in-law again?'

'Really?' said Hazel, pulling a face as she consulted her watch. 'I was hoping to get back early today. We're going out tonight. A belated Valentine treat.'

'It won't take long.' The problem was that she couldn't think what else to ask Mary Ryman.

'OK, but I want to leave by two thirty at the latest.'

Nina automatically checked the time, it was one thirty-five.

'Fine.'

As it happened, Nina need not have worried. Mrs Ryman seemed delighted to see them again and disappeared to make a cup of tea for them as soon as they were settled in the homely sitting room. She returned with a plate of her homemade ginger biscuits, insisting they sample them.

'I'm so glad you came back,' she began when she finally sat down opposite them. 'I had a look at the old family album after you went and I found some interesting photographs I thought you might like to look at. Shall I fetch them?' She waited for their response.

'Yes please, Mrs Ryman.' Nina smiled encouragingly.

'What?' Hazel asked Nina while they waited.

'They could be useful.' She knew she didn't sound convincing and her colleague grimaced, tapping her watch.

'Here we are!' Mary announced, returning with a handful of black and white photographs.

Nina wheeled herself over next to Mary's chair while Hazel remained motionless.

'This is Grandad with his Mum and Dad, and that's Uncle George.'

'He looks about five years older?'

'That's probably about right. And he was a couple of years older than Dorothy.'

The children appeared to be at the seaside. The parents were in their Sunday best but the children were dressed for the sun. The skinny girl with the high cheek-bones and straggly blond hair was in a floral sundress. The sturdy looking lads were in shirt-sleeves and shorts.'

'Grandad must be about ten or eleven in that one and this one.' Mary produced other photographs, this time on the farm. They were a series of several snaps taken of the men digging a ditch. Nina recognised the two boys from the previous picture.

'The older men, who are they?'

'That's Grandad's father, who owned the farm at the time.'

'And the other one?'

'I don't think it's a relation. It must be a helper. I'm sure they couldn't afford hired hands on a regular basis but they might get a neighbour or casual labourer in for a particular job.'

Nina studied the photograph. The man was perhaps in his forties or thirties. He looked very much like the farmer with nothing remarkable to identify his origins.

'Now let's see what else you've got there,' she said, hanging on to the group by the ditch.

Nina was playing for time now and she could sense that Hazel was becoming impatient. Very soon her colleague was standing up and putting on her coat.

'I'm sorry, Mrs Ryman, but I do have an appointment. We will have to be leaving.'

'May I keep this, Mrs Ryman?' Nina asked as they left, showing her the photograph that she had kept back. 'I can return it once I've made a copy.'

Hazel helped Nina into the car rather roughly and slammed the door on her.

'I thought we would never get away,' she complained as she settled into the driver's seat.

Nina was staring at her phone, silently urging Millie to call before they drove off. Finally, just as they turned onto the main road it began vibrating and she fumbled the buttons in her anxiety to answer it.

'Millie?'

'Yes. I did it. I've seen the message.'

'What did it say?'

'There was a photo of Frank Hunter. It's Lang. Lang is Frank Hunter.'

'Are you sure?'

'Yes.'

'Stop the car!' Nina pulled Hazel's arm, causing her to swerve into the kerb. 'Was there anything else?'

'Jake said that Frank Hunter worked at the College as a technician but went to Bosnia and has stayed working there, not going back to the States.'

Nina was trying to comprehend what the information meant. Hazel had stopped the engine and was listening intently.

'Nina? Nina?'

'Yes I'm here.' She paused. 'Listen. Nige has gone to Ribblehead with Lang… I mean Hunter. Why would he do that?'

'I don't know,' her friend replied.

'I think we'll go over there, just in case,' Nina continued. 'Thanks for your help Millie.' She closed the mobile and turned to Hazel.

'Don't tell me,' her colleague said. 'We're going to Ribblehead…'

'Thank you, Hazel.'

'…on condition you tell me what this all about.'

Lang had been curiously animated for the entire journey and Nige found himself giving a detailed explanation of how ground penetrating radar worked. Normally people became rather less interested when he explained the finer points of the patterns produced by objects buried beneath the soil, but Lang was fascinated and Nige was happy to impart his knowledge to such a receptive audience. The roads were clear despite the heavy frost that covered the hedgerows and fields and they made good progress, soon leaving Hawes behind, turning down towards Ribblesdale.

'So what exactly is the purpose of the work on this site?' Nige asked.

'Difficult to explain until we get there, mate. Now tell me how you came to be such an expert on GPR.'

So Nige continued until he indicated to pull up by the track that led to the viaduct and they sat for a minute looking at the snow covered hill.

'Right then, let's go across the road and I'll show you what I had in mind.' Lang jumped out of the car and Nige followed, locking the car and pulling his coat round him. There was an icy wind blowing that cut through him, making him wish he had brought gloves, scarf and hat. Lang, who led the way, was much better prepared.

'OK, so this is where all becomes clear,' announced Lang, turning to face Nige as they stopped under one of the massive arches. He fumbled in his pocket and, to Nige's amazement, produced a small gun.

'What's that for?' he asked.

'You'll see, mate.' Then he brought a handful of bullets from his other pocket and loaded the gun. Nige watched mesmerised. It was the first time he'd seen a real gun and it was pretty impressive.

'So, the plan is…' Lang was pointing the gun directly at him, '…to go up the track far enough to find somewhere discreet to leave you. I suspect there is sufficient wind chill factor hereabouts to be pretty terminal overnight.'

It was unreal, like in a film, 'What are you talking about?' he asked.

'Just get moving; I'll be right behind you.'

So he walked slowly up the track, his head in such a turmoil he couldn't think straight. It had all gone pear-shaped after he had contacted Jake about Frank

Hunter. He hadn't even had time to read the reply but was it possible that Lang had done so?

'I don't understand why you're doing this,' he called.

'Shut up, mate, and keep walking.' His voice lacked emotion.

'There's a signal box up here. Someone will see us.' He regretted it the moment he had said it. He should have kept quiet.

'You're right. We'll stop here.' He dragged Nige into an archway that ran under the railway line, ordering him to remove his coat and sit down. It was wet with snow and slush but he complied while Lang pulled his hands behind his back and tied wire round his wrists. Then he tied his ankles together.

'Now stand up.'

Nige tried to get up but fell back clumsily. Lang got hold of him roughly under his arms, dragging him further through the arch and along the edge of the embankment for about fifty metres, letting him drop to the cold, hard ground.

'Don't worry,' he said laughing, 'I'll come back tomorrow to undo the wire, although *you* may not notice.'

'Why are you doing this?' Nige asked again, his voice breaking as he tried to hide the emotion. 'Is it something to do with Frank Hunter?'

'Yes, you could say that. Let's say Frank doesn't like people nosing around in his business.'

'But I don't even know who Frank Hunter is!'

'Best keep it that way. That's why it was best you didn't read the e-mail you received this morning.'

'The one from Jake?'

'Is that who it was? Well don't worry, I sent him a reply. He thinks you've come out here all by yourself to watch the steam trains.'

'Don't be daft, there won't be any steam trains running today.'

'You see, Nige my old mate, just as I thought; you really are a train spotter. What a nerd!'

He walked away, flinging the army coat down as he went, leaving Nige lying helpless on the icy snow.

Chapter 18

The car was parked across the road from where the track to the viaduct started.

'No sign of Nige,' said Hazel unnecessarily.

Nina persuaded Hazel to help her into the familiar old Polo and stow the wheelchair in the boot before handing her the keys through the open window.

'Are you sure you'll be all right?' she asked. 'I feel really bad leaving you here.'

'Don't be silly, I'll be fine. He can't be long; it will be dark in an hour or so.'

She watched until her friend disappeared from sight, turning her gaze to the snow covered fell in front of her. There was no-one around, no other parked car, only the occasional vehicle making its way along the road. She counted the cars travelling towards Ingleton and noted that they outnumbered the ones going to Hawes. She turned the radio on for a while but, worried that it might run the battery down, quickly switched it off again. By three-thirty she was regretting having come. Anxiety for Nige's safety in Lang's company had been replaced by irritation. She followed the progress of a motorbike coming from Hawes, surprised when it slowed as it past her, then turned and stopped beside the car. It was only when the driver and passenger removed their helmets that she recognised Mills and Phil.

'We came to see if everything was OK,' said Mills, opening the driver's door and settling down next to her, while Phil climbed in the back.

'It's freezing in here, aren't you cold?'

'No, I'm fine but there's no sign of Nige and it will start to get dark soon.'

'D'you think he's all right? I mean after what we found out about Lang? It did seem a bit odd Nige coming down here with him after all he'd said about the guy.'

'I'm sure he's fine.' Nina knew she did not sound confident, she wasn't convincing herself.

'We'll go and see if we can spot him,' offered Mills and Phil agreed.

Nina sat helplessly in the car, watching the two figures become mere specks as they reached the viaduct and disappeared from view. Her legs felt cold to the touch and she knew her feet would be worse, as they always were. She stared across the road, willing there to be three figures returning down the track until eventually she could see her friends. Two figures in the distance... just the two. She bit her lip, trying to stay calm, arranging her demeanour so when the doors opened she was composed, ready to be positive.

'I'm sorry, Nina. We couldn't see them. They may be further up Whernside.' There was concern in her voice.

'Yes, of course.'

'It's nearly dusk,' said Phil. 'They'll be back soon.'

'Yes.' She forced a smile.

Mills took her arm. 'Why don't we go and sit in the pub? It'll be warmer.'

'No, I don't want to miss him. I'll be fine here. There's no need for you to stay.'

'I'm not leaving you here on your own!' she responded.

'You go and get warmed up. I'll send Nige over when he arrives.'

They spent several minutes trying to persuade her to join them, but finally Mills and Phil left the bike and walked to the pub, hand in hand. Another half hour of staring at the hillside as the light faded and they were coming back towards the car.

'It's getting dark,' announced Phil. 'We're calling the police.'

Nina had never felt more helpless in her life. She was a police officer and she could do nothing. Even the bloody mobile didn't work out here. Tears filled her eyes and she tried to wipe them away unseen. Mills stayed with her while Phil went to make the call. At least she was able to give him the number.

Eventually a car pulled up beside the Polo. It was a young police constable in uniform.

'How do, sergeant,' he greeted her. 'Any sign of the missing person yet?'

He took a few details, not that they had much information except that the car was here and so Nige must still be out there. It was dark now, his absence was becoming serious. Nodding in agreement, he returned to his car and sat talking into his transmitter. Mills and Phil kept her company until eventually the constable returned to inform them that the mountain and cave rescue had been alerted.

Nina had no idea how long they waited before a vehicle arrived across the road and figures with torches were disappearing in the direction of the viaduct. Mills suggested they went to help, so Nina was left alone again desperately unhappy that she was unable to join them. Time had slowed down so on each occasion she looked at the clock only a minute or two had passed. It was as though she was experiencing a peculiarly realistic nightmare, watching everything that was going on but unable to affect the outcome.

A blue light flashed in the distance. Torch lights swung across the moor. The car door opened and Mills was jumping in beside her, asking if she was all right. She explained that the rescue team had asked the RAF for help with the helicopter that had infrared on it to search for people. She noted that Mills had carefully avoided using the word 'bodies'. Had they not found anyone on the moor? No, apparently not. Nina assured her she was fine, even joked that Nige would be impressed by the use of infra-red, and insisted that Mills rejoin the others so she could report back if they had any news. Alone, she sat bolt upright while tears poured down her face unable to put into words the feeling of total powerlessness that she felt.

The sound of the helicopter was hardly discernible at first and it was the illumination of the viaduct that alerted Nina to its presence. She watched the beam of light flutter delicately across the hillside, onto the moor, then back again. Backwards and forwards for hours it seemed. Then suddenly it lifted and moved away, leaving the valley dark and depressing. The clock said that it was twenty minutes later when vehicle headlights began moving very slowly down the track. It started some distance beyond the viaduct and was moving very, very slowly. She noted the time, it was another ten minutes before the vehicle stopped on the track just below the viaduct and the police car moved to join it. She wanted to run over there, demand to know what had happened. Had they found him? Was he...?

The door swung open and Mills put her head in.

'They've found him.'

Nina let out a gasp, almost a scream.

'He's very cold. Not very well at all. They're waiting for the helicopter to take him to hospital.' She eased herself into the driver's seat and slammed the door closed.

Nina was too scared of the answers to ask Mills any questions. They sat side by side staring through the windscreen, waiting for the sound of the helicopter. But before that, an ambulance with siren screaming appeared from the direction of Ingleton.

'Please go and see what's happening,' Nina asked her friend but Mills refused to leave her. 'Maybe you could push me over there?'

'I think it would be difficult in the dark,' Mills said, 'and it's really cold.'

'Yes.' Nina knew she was right. She was trying to remain sensible because it would be a long night. She had to stay strong for Nige.

Mills was doing her best to put her at her ease, telling her what a brilliant job everyone had done and how quickly the support services had appeared. As if to demonstrate her point, they heard the sound of a helicopter overhead again. It hovered close to the road and then landed not far away. Nina had to remind herself that it was Nige on the stretcher as the drama was played out in front of them. This was no TV performance but her husband being carried off to hospital.

As the helicopter swerved up and away, Phil opened the rear door of the car.

'They're taking him to Northallerton. Can you drive Nina there, Mills?'

'What about you?'

'I'm going to Ingleton with the police, just in case Lang is in his usual haunt.'

They both looked at Nina but she said nothing. All she cared about was reaching Nige.

'The quickest way is back to Leyburn and through Bedale.'

'I know,' said Mills. 'I'll call you,' she added to Phil.

As they drove, Nina's curiosity about where they had found Nige and what he was doing got the better of her. Mills explained that she had been with the search party that gradually made its way across the moor and back, then up the track to the signal box and down again. At that stage there had been no sign of him and they contacted the police for help. Eventually the helicopter arrived with the heat sensitive camera and after a while they spotted something next to a small railway arch. The rescue team went up to investigate and Mills saw them carrying him on a stretcher back to the track. She and Phil walked down with the stretcher party and the rescue vehicle.

'So how was he?' Nina dared ask her.

'Unconscious but breathing they said.'

Phil arrived ahead of the police car and hesitated before walking into the pub. There were red heart-shaped balloons decorating the bar but he couldn't decide if it was a special night or they were left over from the day before. He ordered a half and looked around the room, spotting Lang at a large table in the corner with a group of friends. Phil planned to sit at the bar until the police constable arrived but Lang was walking straight to the bar carrying three empty pint glasses.

'Hello, Terry!' Phil said quietly standing up with his back to the bar. 'Fancy seeing you here.'

The other man stared at him warily.

'Phil Freedman,' he said. 'We met at the farm?'

'Ah, yes, of course.' Lang had placed the glasses on the bar and was looking round the room as if sizing it up.

'Is this your local?'

'No, no. Just visiting some friends.'

'Can I get you a drink?'

'No, it's OK. I've got to get these in.' Lang indicated the empty glasses on the bar in front of him. He was looking increasingly distracted as he tried to attract the attention of the barman. A member of his group came over with more glasses.

'Here you are, Hunter,' he said. 'Pint of best for Chas. Just a half for Sarah.'

'Is that what they call you?' asked Phil when the man had gone. 'Hunter?'

'Er, yes. It's a sort of nickname.'

'Would that be short for Frank Hunter, eh?'

He didn't reply but picked up the two pint glasses that had been filled and carried them back to his table. Phil watched him hesitate then return for the rest of the round, looking more self-assured. Phil was watching the uniformed constable arrive with his mate.

'I don't know what you want but, as you can see, I'm here with my friends, so clear off,' Lang said, picking up the full glasses.

'I think *my* friends would like a chat,' Phil muttered.

Lang slowly put the glasses down and stepped back along the bar.

'This is Mr Lang, officer.' Phil gestured to his companion.

'What's the matter? What do you want?'

'Just a question or two, Mr Lang, about an incident that happened this afternoon involving Mr Nigel Featherstone. I believe he is a work colleague of yours?'

'He is, officer.'

'I understand you went on a trip with Mr Featherstone today?'

'No, officer. There's been some mistake.'

'His wife received a text from him telling her that he was accompanying you today.'

'No, she's mistaken. I haven't been to Ribblehead today; in fact I was down here most of the afternoon. Ask my friends.'

'Who said anything about Ribblehead, sir?'

They took him away quietly but Phil was aware that the table in the corner had gone quiet. One of the group, a man with a beard and long black hair, came over to him.

'Trouble?'

'You could say that. Are you a friend of his?'

'Not a friend. We dive together sometimes.'

'Why do you call him Hunter?'

'Because that's his name. Who are you? Police?'

'No, just a friend of a guy who nearly died out on the moors tonight.'

'I heard the rescue team was out.'

'And the sea king helicopter.'

'Is he OK?'

'Don't know, it's touch and go.'

'So how come they've taken Hunter off?'

'He was supposed to be with the guy. He was left... well he was left helpless in the snow.'

'Shit. This is weird. First Steve, now Hunter. It's like there's some really bad karma round here.'

'Steve was in your group?'

'Yes. He was arrested for starting the caravan fire.'

Phil sipped his beer, thinking of the girl they had walked over Pen-y-ghent with. 'Did Hunter know Ewa?'

'They lived together before he went to the States.'

'You mean he's been here before?'

'He was brought up here. We were at school together.'

'So when did he leave?'

'About three years ago.'

Nina sat beside Nige in the intensive care unit watching the nurse as she adjusted the monitors above his bed. He was covered in wires and had a plastic tube in his mouth, to help him breathe they said. He looked pale against the sheets, almost transparent. The staff had been kind, helpful, sympathetic but they couldn't tell her what to expect. The next twenty-four hours were critical the doctor had said. Her husband was unconscious and they would continue to monitor his core temperature, letting her know of any change. They wouldn't know how well he was responding until his temperature had increased. Even then there could be other complications they said, like pneumonia or cardiac arrhythmia. She wheeled herself slowly back to the visitor's room where her friend was sitting alone. They looked at each other without speaking until Mills broke the silence.

'They say there is nothing we can do here.'

'I can't leave him.'

'They'll ring us if there is anything... You need to get some sleep so you're strong when he comes round.'

She had no resistance left. Mills pushed her to where they had abandoned the Polo earlier that night at the entrance to the car park. On the way home Mills told her that Phil had seen Lang being taken off by the police for questioning; although Nina could barely process the news. She let Mills prepare her a hot drink and tuck her up on the sofa in the cold, empty house and to her surprise she slept for several hours. It was still dark when she woke so she lay on her back running the events of the previous day in her head. Musing on why Lang would want to hurt Nige, she concluded that it could only be because they had discovered his true identity. She rang Mitch as soon as it was light.

Chas walked into Ingleton police station on Saturday morning and spent an hour with the sergeant. He was told when he left that he might be needed to give a further interview in due course. The sergeant sent her report across to Newby Wiske. Frank Hunter was being interviewed for the third time.

'You said you hardly knew the young lady, Ewa Prodanovic?' Mitch asked almost casually, flicking through his notes.

'Yes.'

'I've been told that you and she were cohabiting four years ago.'

'No comment.'

'Can you tell me where you lived then?'

'No comment.'

'Mr Hunter, you lived here in Yorkshire until you went to the USA three years ago, didn't you?'

There was no reply.

'And then you went to work in Bosnia with Dr Terry Lang.' He paused. 'We know all about Dr Lang now. He was quite an eminent scientist by all accounts. Found dead at the bottom of a cave.' He opened a file in front of him. 'It says here a tragic accident. Was it an accident Mr Hunter?'

'Yes, it was.'

'Were you there, Mr Hunter?'

'Yes I was!' His voice was filled with exasperation. 'He fell, I couldn't hold him. He smashed his head on the rocks. It was an accident!'

'Why didn't you report it? You kept very quiet. Was that so you could assume his identity? Pretty tricky thing to maintain I would think.'

'I just wanted to get a job back in England.' He emphasised each word. 'I didn't think it would do any harm to take up the position at the university.'

'It's an offence to impersonate someone else in this country. It's called identity theft. But that's not the real crime is it, Mr Hunter? The real crime was when they began to suspect who you really are.' He rifled through his files and pulled out a piece of paper. 'Ewa Prodanovic was killed in a fire set deliberately. Why was that Frank? She knew who you were, had she guessed that you were at the university or did you tell her?'

'She knew what I was doing, she didn't care.'

'So why did you kill her Frank?'

'I didn't.'

Mitch sat in silence, waiting.

'I wasn't even in Ingleton that night,' offered Hunter.

Mitch leaned forward, his elbows on the table.

'I think you were. I think she suspected you of another crime, one that had happened earlier and one that her boyfriend was later arrested for. Did you kill the lad who died in the cave? Was it Bosnia all over again was it?'

'I don't know what you're on about,' he sneered.

'I'm referring to the callous killing of a young man who was just starting out in a career in journalism. I'm talking about a young man who your ex-girlfriend was perhaps too friendly with.'

'You're talking nonsense.' Hunter turned his head dismissively.

Mitch paused. 'Did you know she was pregnant?'

Now he had the man's attention. He watched a series of emotions passing across his face. First bewilderment. Then annoyance. And finally distress.

'Was it your baby, Frank?'

He didn't answer but sat looking down, picking at a mark on the edge of the table with his fingernail.

'Why would you want to harm the mother of your child, Frank?'

'It wasn't mine. She would have said. And anyway we hadn't... we didn't... Not since she went to London.'

'Is that what made you kill her? Were you angry with her when you found out?'

'I told you. I didn't know she was pregnant.' He remained staring at the floor.

'Would it have made a difference, Frank? Would she be alive now if you had known?'

'No comment.'

Mitch stopped the interview. He was now convinced that Hunter was responsible for Ewa Prodanovic's death and therefore probably Fred Coulter's death also. But he needed evidence. He needed someone who saw Hunter in Ingleton the night Ewa was murdered.

Chapter 19

Nina had been sitting with Nige since eight in the morning, watching the nurses flitting like butterflies round his bed. They washed him and changed his gown, adjusted the drip and twiddled with the monitors. Throughout he remained unmoving and silent. She could not remember a time when she had seen him so still; even when he was asleep he would be moving constantly, often muttering under his breath. She talked to the nursing staff in an attempt to discover the truth about his condition but they were careful to say nothing that might sound either optimistic or pessimistic, telling her that the consultant would be round in due course. When he did eventually arrive, he was accompanied by two young doctors. He described Nige's 'accident' and his condition, saying that he was stable but we would have to be patient. It was early days. Nina remained silent throughout their visit.

At lunch-time she wheeled herself along the corridor to the snack bar and bought a sandwich. After two mouthfuls she placed it back in the cardboard wrapper, sipping her tea slowly while she decided what to do next. She had told Mills not to come for her until later in the afternoon but if she was honest with herself it was too stressful to sit all day watching her husband lying unconscious. And then she saw a familiar figure. Mrs Ryman from Ingleton was at the counter chatting to the woman who was serving her. They obviously knew each other or perhaps had got to know each other well. Was this how it would be for her after weeks of spending every day watching Nige? She searched for a handkerchief, dried her eyes and turned away as Mary Ryman made her way past her table, relieved that she hadn't noticed her. Her thoughts turned to old Mr Ryman who was clearly still up on the ward. She needed something to do to take her mind off her husband's body lying inert along the corridor. She would take the opportunity to have another chat with him while his daughter-in-law was around. That way no-one could suggest she was taking advantage of a sick old man.

The smell of lunch hung on the air as she approached Ainderby ward but the dishes had been cleared and there was tranquillity about the place; the space between meal time and visiting when the elderly patients would probably be dozing. One or two patients had curtains round them but she could see Mary Ryman seated beside her father-in-law's bed chatting to him.

'Why, hello!' The woman greeted her with a smile. 'Grandad said you'd been in to see him.'

'I was just passing,' she lied. 'How are you, Mr Ryman?'

'He's not so good,' the woman said in a low voice. 'He's got very weak.' She looked knowingly at Nina.

'I'm sorry to hear that,' she said. 'Actually I wondered if he would mind me asking him about the time he was a boy again.'

The older woman laughed. 'Oh he won't mind that. It's all he talks about now, isn't it Grandad? I said it's all you talk about now, the old days.'

'What's that?' The old man was propped up on a pile of pillows, his gnarled hands lying limply on the bedcovers, the rest of his body covered in gaudily striped pyjamas. He still had an oxygen supply clipped to his nostrils.

'I wanted to ask about when you were children; you and your brother George and your sister...'

'Dorothy,' his daughter-in-law interrupted. 'He was so fond of her. He was heart-broken when she died. He's been talking about her more since he's been ill.'

Has he? thought Nina, that's interesting. 'Mr Ryman, could you tell me about your sister? Dorothy, it's a pretty name.'

'Ay, we always called her Dorothy, not Dotty or Dot. They called her Dotty at school but at home she was always Dorothy.'

'Your daughter-in-law showed me a photograph of you all. She was a very pretty little girl.'

'Ay.' He looked away into the distance and then shut his eyes.

'There's been something worrying him,' Mary said, turning to Nina. 'I couldn't make it out.' She looked at him and then back to Nina, running her tongue along her bottom lip. 'He was probably a bit delirious when he said it...'

'Said what?'

'That something had been on his mind and he wanted to put it right before, you know... I said I would get the vicar to pop in and see him but he just went on muttering about needing to make things right.'

'Do you think he might talk to me?'

'Maybe.' She looked sceptical.

'Mr Ryman,' Nina called. He opened his eyes again. 'Is there something you'd like to tell me? Something that happened a long time ago?'

'You can talk to her, Grandad, if you want to. I can leave you alone if you want.'

'No, lass. Stay here. She wants to know what happened to the Traveller.'

Mary went to speak but Nina indicated for her to keep silent.

'Go on, Mr Ryman,' she said. 'Take your time. The Traveller was helping on the farm?'

'Ay. He'd been before, on the way to the fair.'

'The horse fair in Appleby?'

'Ay.'

Nina felt in control, she could see he wanted to tell her and so she led him gently. His daughter-in-law was staring at them both, sitting rigid in her chair.

'So he was working on the farm that day?'

'Ay, up on the ditch.' He paused to catch his breath. 'We went up to shoot rabbits.'

'You and George?'

'Ay.'

'You had a gun?'

'George did. I wasn't allowed to shoot.'

'So you went up to the ditch and what did you see?'

He didn't answer for a while. He seemed to be struggling to find the words. 'He was lying on top of her... I thought they were playing... that she was laughing... wriggling about... on top of her.'

'But she wasn't laughing?'

'No, she was screaming. Screaming.' He stopped again and lay back, eyes closed, struggling for breath. Nina thought Mary would ask her to stop but the woman was sitting transfixed.

The old man's eyes opened in a stare. He sat forward in a terrible effort. 'He'd pulled her little dress off... she was screaming for him to get off her.'

'So what did you do?'

The old man was lying back on the pillows, breathless and pale.

'What did George do?'

He was suddenly calm and clear. 'He walked up to him. He didn't even notice us. He put the gun to his head and...'

There was a gasp from Mary Ryman.

'Did George shoot him?'

'Ay.' He glared at Nina defiantly.

Nina glanced across at Mary, who was sitting with one hand across her mouth the other clutching the bedcover.

'It's OK, Mary. Don't worry. Everything's all right.' She wanted the woman to stay calm while she got Mr Ryman to finish his story.

'Was he dead?'

His voice was stronger now and clear. He spoke slowly. 'Ay he was and good job. Poor Dorothy, she never laughed again, not her whole life.'

'Did you help George bury the Traveller?'

'Ay.' He relaxed back and closed his eyes. His breathing was easier.

Mary looked expectantly at Nina.

'It's all right, Mary. Leave him. He must be exhausted. Why don't we find a cup of tea while he has a rest?'

The two women sat together in the cafeteria, while they each absorbed what they had just witnessed.

Finally Mary asked, 'What will happen to him now?'

Nina slowly set her cup down on the table without looking up. 'Don't worry. I'm sure it will be fine.'

'But they'll want talk to him. Ask lots of questions. I don't think he would be able to cope.'

Nina didn't answer.

'They said his heart isn't good. That's why he's so tired. They said they weren't optimistic. That's what they said.'

'I understand, Mary. Don't worry. I've got to go now but I'll let you know if there is anything else, you know...'

'But what shall I tell Bill? Brian and Sheila? And there's Kate. Surely she's not to find out?'

'I suggest you discuss it with no-one at present, Mrs Ryman. It would be best for the time being.' She picked up her handbag, glancing across at the woman's expressionless face. She continued with an air of authority. 'Now I must be going. I've got to get back to my husband.' She backed the wheelchair away from the table, turning to move along the corridor back to the intensive care unit where Mills would be waiting.

'Are you all right? We wondered where you were,' said Mills jumping up from her seat in the visitors' room. Phil smiled benignly.

'I was just having lunch,' lied Nina. 'Have *you* eaten?'

'No we haven't,' said Phil. 'Would you like some time while we grab a sandwich?'

'That would be good. I'd like a few minutes before we go.'

Nige looked the same as when she had left. What had she expected? The nurse seated at the foot of his bed smiled and resumed writing up her notes. Nina got as close to him as she could in the chair and stroked his hand. There was no response, not even a slightest movement. She wanted to shake him, like she used to when he was in a deep sleep and she needed him to get up.

*

'...so how will Nina manage when you go back to Manchester, Mills?'

They were sharing a cheese and tomato baguette in the busy snack bar.

'I'm not going yet. She says she can cope but I can't leave her. I'll stay as long as necessary... until Nige is better.'

They exchanged glances and Mills could see that Phil was as concerned as she was about Nige's recovery.

'I'm glad you're staying because I was thinking that if you needed something, to tide you over...'

'It's OK, I think the department will need a hand with Lang, I mean Hunter, gone and Nige...'

'Oh, right. Good. So you'll stay here until...'

'Yes, until everything is sorted out. If Nige isn't better by the time the baby comes...'

'So you could be here some time?' He took her hand. 'That's great. But you need someone to look after you as well, and I'm here for you, you know that don't you?'

Mitch threw the crusts of his sandwich in the wastepaper basket and brushed the crumbs off his jeans. His coffee was cold but he gulped it down, returning to the open folder on the desk in front of him. Frank Hunter admitted that he had been impersonating the lecturer Dr Lang after his death. The man was clearly without any sense of guilt regarding the accident, if it was one. If he had killed Lang in order to take his place, then he was also capable of murdering the young journalist. Mitch picked up another file and searched for the name; Trevor "Fred" Coulter. He spent some time reading the details and when the phone rang he picked it up without taking his eyes from the report. When he recognised the voice of the sergeant at Ingleton he gave her his full attention.

'So this young friend of his definitely remembers seeing him on the night the caravan was torched?'

'He was in the pub that night although the lad's recollection is not good. He can't give us a time.'

'Go and have a chat with the landlord, he might remember something.'

'I can do better than that, sir. We advised them to install CCTV after they'd had a couple of nasty fights on a weekend. I'm on my way to collect them now.'

'Well done, sergeant. Let me know what you find as soon as poss.'

Opening the file marked Ewa Prodanovic he was confronted by the photograph of the young blonde woman. It was a professional portrait and the girl was dressed in a posh frock, her hair swept up in a fancy style. She was good-looking, she was popular and she was the only person who knew that Hunter was leading a double life: still Hunter to his old friends but an eminent archaeologist at the university. Was she threatening to expose him? Or did she know something about the death of young Fred Coulter? Considering the close involvement that Hunter had with the cavers, it was strange coincidence that he wasn't on the trip when Fred was killed and wasn't in Ingleton the night Ewa died. He made some notes, staring at them without inspiration until the phone disturbed him again.

'So the baby was definitely Bellamy's?' He scribbled a note and put it in the file. 'Good, send a confirmation as soon as poss.'

So Hunter was right; the child wasn't his. Was that a strong enough motive to kill her? Maybe not but

Mitch knew it was enough to rattle him. Grabbing his jacket he made his way back to the interview room.

Hunter looked tired and drawn when he was brought in by the custody sergeant. He sat slumped in the chair, staring at the floor until the duty solicitor arrived back. Mitch unwrapped a new tape, inserting it into the machine and went through the formalities. This time he felt more confident, certain that he had Hunter on the run.

'I'd like to go back to the night that Ewa Prodanovic was burnt alive in the caravan, together with her unborn child.'

Hunter was looking about him like a nervous animal.

'Can you tell me again where you were that night?'

'At home.'

'Not in Ingleton?'

'No.'

'You were seen drinking with your friends in Ingleton.'

'Who by?'

Mitch ignored the question and moved on.

'Were you worried she would blow your cover, Frank? Had it all got a bit out of hand? Was she going to tell someone at the university?'

There was no answer but Mitch didn't care because he could see a connection now.

'OK, Frank. Let's explore your act at the university. You were worried that your cover had been blown, weren't you? That's why you tried to kill Nigel Featherstone. Oh yes we know that.' He paused, allowing Hunter to stew for a bit longer. 'I think you were concerned about your other colleague, Mills Sanderson, isn't that right? After all, she was a friend of Fred Coulter's wasn't she? Were you worried they might put two and two together and discover that her friend Lang and his friend Hunter were the same person, like Jekyll and Hyde?' His voice was getting louder, too loud.

Mitch took a long drink of water and then continued calmly. 'I've been studying the file and it seems to me that there are a number of similarities between Lang's 'accident' and young Coulter's death.' He counted to five. 'You killed him didn't you?'

Hunter sat motionless.

'Didn't you, Mr Hunter?'

No response.

'For the benefit of the tape, Mr Hunter is offering no response...' There was a knock at the door, '...and Detective Constable Quinn is entering the room.'

DC Quinn handed Mitch a fax neatly typed up and signed by the sergeant from Ingleton. It was a report of the CCTV in the pub on the night the girl died. He scanned it quickly for the information he needed.

...showing Frank Hunter drinking with his friends until 20.42 when he was joined by Ewa Prodanovic. She seemed agitated and they left together at 21.05. He returned at 22.15 alone and stayed drinking until the pub closed at 23.00.

'We have CCTV evidence that you were in Ingleton on the night Ewa Prodanovic died, and that you were with her that evening. You knew she was staying in the caravan, didn't you? Didn't you?' Mitch was standing across the desk, shouting at Hunter, who stared defiantly and then seemed to crumple.

'She wanted somewhere to stay.'

'Did she ask to stay with you?'

'Yes but she couldn't could she? In the end she suggested the caravan. I helped her get in.'

'Why did you say you weren't there?'

He shrugged.

'I believe you went back when the pub closed and threw diesel over the caravan, setting light to it and murdering Ewa and her unborn baby.'

Hunter's shoulders were shaking but Mitch couldn't see his expression, his head was hanging down so low.

'We can do forensic tests on the diesel used to start the fire. We'll be able to match it if there's a can in your vehicle. It would be better to admit to it now than let us find out the hard way.' Mitch was speaking softly now.

The room was silent except for the whirring of the fan heater in the corner. Mitch kept deliberately silent and motioned for his DC to stay put. The solicitor looked impatient but seemed reticent to break the spell. Mitch, sensing that Hunter was about to open his mouth, kept the room suspended in silence for at least a minute.

'I want to make a statement now,' said Hunter, raising his head and looking straight at Mitch. 'There's no point in dragging this on any longer. Let's get it over with.'

When Nina received the call from Mitch she knew she would not be allowed in the interview room with Hunter while Nige was still lying unconscious in intensive care. But she knew that the man who left her husband for dead was only a few yards away in the interview room next door. Mitch wanted her to hear Hunter go over his statement and so she was seated in front of a monitor which allowed her to watch the proceedings unobserved. While they waited for Hunter to arrive, Hazel chattered on about what had been happening during her absence.

Mitch put his head round the door to say they were about to start and Hazel switched up the sound. While the first few minutes were devoted to formalities, Nina stared at the tiny figure on the monitor. The picture was distorted, and she would not have recognised Hunter as the man she had seen on a few occasions when he was known as Dr Lang. She thought she would feel strong emotions but he was just a weak, arrogant man who thought he could literally get away with murder. She was so deep in her own thoughts of Nige lying inert on the white linen of the bed in intensive care that she missed the start of the interview but she heard the name Millicent Sanderson and began to listen.

'... knew that Mr Coulter was a friend of hers?'

'Yes.' He looked relaxed.

'And that's why you killed him?'

'It was a problem. He knew me as Frank Hunter. I was Terry Lang to her. You see the dilemma.' He waved his hands to accentuate his point.

'But to kill him...?'

'It was the only answer.' He was nodding. 'Don't you see? It was the only way to solve the problem.'

'The man's a nutter,' Hazel whispered to her.

'You say you followed Mr Coulter into the cave that morning?' Mitch asked.

'Yes. I didn't go with the group, so no-one knew I was there. Didn't want to be seen, you see?'

'So you planned it carefully.'

'Oh, yes, every detail. No-one saw me go in or out. One swift blow is all that's needed.'

'Is that how you killed Terry Lang?'

Nina could see Hunter was smiling. 'Oh you don't catch me that easily, inspector. I have never said I killed Terry, did I?'

'No?'

Hunter leaned forward and wagged his finger at Mitch. 'I'll never admit to that one.'

'We think he did kill Lang,' whispered Hazel, 'but it will be very difficult to get any evidence now.'

'Will he be charged with attempting to kill Nige?' Nina asked.

Hazel looked away. 'Yes, attempted murder.'

Nina knew that she would have added "at this stage" if it had not been Nige. She had been in the force long enough to know that they would be waiting to see whether the victim recovered. Otherwise it would be murder. She turned back to the monitor.

'...went off to London. I asked her to stay but she decided she didn't want to continue our relationship.'

'But she lived with Steve Bellamy.'

Hunter laughed. 'That was because we couldn't be together. It would have blown my cover. But she and I we were an item all right.'

'The baby was Steve's.'

'No, I don't think so.'

Mitch ignored his denial. 'So you decided to get rid of her?'

'It wasn't as simple as that, inspector. She rang me late one night and said she'd got nowhere to stay. Well, I told her we couldn't be seen together so I helped her get into the caravan she knew about. I thought that was the end of it.'

'But it wasn't, was it?'

'No. She rang me again when I was back in the pub and said she'd worked out that I'd killed Fred. She was frantic. Said the police thought it was Steve and she would never let him be punished for it. So what could I do? I had no option.'

'Cold-blooded or what?' Hazel said. 'The man's a psychopath.'

They watched the man on the screen describe in detail how he had obtained the diesel and gone back to the site in the early hours. He appeared proud of the care he had taken to cover his tracks, expressing irritation that the CCTV had caught him out as a liar.

'And finally, Mr Hunter, you tried to silence Dr Featherstone...'

'Old Nige, bless him! He was a bit of a boffin but he knew his stuff.'

'Was he becoming a nuisance as well?'

'He was practically investigating me. When I saw the e-mail I knew he was getting to be a serious problem.'

'Another of your problem-solving exercises?' Mitch was beginning to sound irritated.

'I thought that would be the end of it. That Mills was going back to her own university and things would settle down. I just needed to finish off.'

'He is lying, seriously ill in hospital. He could die...'

Nina sensed Hazel turning to look at her; she remained facing the screen.

'... his wife is expecting a baby. Don't you feel any regret at what you've done?'

'It would have stopped there. It was all sorted.'

'I very much doubt that it would have stopped there, Mr Hunter. I very much doubt it.'

*

When the interview was over Mitch came in to see them. He gave Nina a hug, asked if she was OK and quickly changed the subject.

'Anyway, Nina, I think you wanted to update me on your conversation with old Mr Ryman about the body at the farm?' Mitch smiled enquiringly.

'Oh, it was nothing really, sir.' She thought of the frail figure in the hospital and his daughter-in-law's anxious face. 'He started to tell me something about the Traveller but he wasn't really *compos mentis*. I don't think we'll be able to get any further. It was a long time ago and everyone involved must be very old or dead by now.'

She was glad to finally get back out into the sunshine, looking round the car park anxiously for the Polo as she said a hasty goodbye to Hazel.

'By the way,' Hazel said, as she turned to go back inside, 'That old boy we interviewed in Ingleton...'

'Mr Ryman?'

'That's right, Mr Ryman. He died last night. I thought you'd want to know.'

Mills pulled up in the car almost immediately.

'OK?'

'Yes, I'm fine, thank you.'

There was silence when they set off. Nina was digesting what Hunter had said, wondering whether Nige would turn out to be his final victim.

Eventually she turned to Mills, 'Hunter followed Fred into the cave and hit him on the head with a rock. I'm sorry but I thought you'd want to know. He left him lying in a pool of water. That was how he was found.'

Her friend continued to stare straight ahead. 'So it wasn't Steve?'

'No.'

'But why Fred? It makes no sense.'

Nina hesitated. How could she tell her friend that she was, in a way, responsible.

'Hunter was worried that Fred might cotton on to the fact that he was impersonating Dr Lang.' She continued before Mills could interrupt. 'And he killed Ewa for the same reason. She knew what he was doing all along.'

'So Steve wasn't involved?'

'No.'

'Poor guy. I suppose he's been released?'

'Yes. He's planning to take her body back to her family in Serbia when it's released.'

'You said she was pregnant.'

'Yes. The baby was his.'

Would Mills ask her about Nige? Nina waited.

'What about the real Dr Lang? Was he murdered as well?'

Nina relaxed. 'Hunter insists it was an accident. We may never know.'

'So Nige was right all along. Dr Lang, or Hunter as he is, was not a very clever archaeologist.'

'That's why he let you do all the work I suppose.'

'What will happen about the body at the farm now?'

'I think that will remain a mystery, Mills. There is no-one who knows who the man was and old Mr Ryman has died. I think the truth will be buried with him.'

'That's the end of it then.' Mills sounded disappointed.

Nina made an effort to lighten her voice. 'You'll be able to go back to Manchester and finish your PhD now then, Mills.'

'Oh, didn't I tell you? I've had an offer from the university to help with the lecturing until they sort out a more permanent arrangement. I'm going to be around for a while, if that's all right with you?'

'All right with me?'

'Yes. I'll need somewhere to stay, won't I?'

'Of course, yes that would be great.' Her mind was working overtime.

'I thought you might like some help, at least until we know... I mean... until Nige is better... with the baby and everything.'

Nina sighed and then smiled at her friend. 'Yes, I know what you mean.'